Miles from Memphis

BY

MICHAEL DILLON

ISBN: 978-0-9860577-1-7 (paperback)

Published in the United States by Oosik Publishing.

Also by Michael Dillon:

Changing Cadence, a travel memoir.

On a TWA to the promised land
Every woman, child and man
Gets a Cadillac and a diamond ring.
Don't you know we're riding with the king?

—John Hiatt, *Riding with the King*

For Emily

Much of this story is true.

One

The drone of the cicadas rose steadily with the heat. At first it was just subtle background noise, almost unnoticeable like the thrum of highway traffic. After several hours its intensity increased, as if the insects were demanding their presence be acknowledged, until by afternoon, they had created a veil of sound in the woods surrounding me.

Something I had read earlier in the week in a column in a local newspaper explained how these insects, as part of their life cycle, were emerging to molt and mate. The article described how cicadas burrow beneath the dirt, disappearing underground for as much as a decade before exploding to the surface for a few weeks of frenzied cicada lovemaking. I'm sure this was followed by a bit of post-coital nuzzling; perhaps, even the exchange of the pheromone equivalent of cell numbers before they returned below ground to begin the cycle anew. Given the sounds around me, these bugs were definitely gettin' busy. It was as if the woods had suddenly turned into an arthropodal version of the Playboy mansion circa 1972. I imagined a scientist analyzing a recording of the insects and discovering that the sound they were emitting was a high frequency version of Marvin Gaye's *Let's Get It On.*

At least this is where my mind wandered as I sat on the side of the road and contemplated the magic of dusk in the Mississippi hill country on a warm June night in 2010. There's really nothing quite like it. The last rays of daylight filter through the loblolly pines as the sun rolls off the horizon; dogwood leaves rotate silently on dark, dank pools; tendrils of steamy mist begin to fill the spaces between the trees and reach out for the asphalt roadway. And the cicadas noisily enjoy their sexy time.

As a musician, I'd witnessed the transcendent beauty of these Southern summer evenings many times while traveling with bands on what we referred to as our "Waffle House" tours. Ubiquitous, always open, and cheap, these restaurants are a fixture in the South for farmers, ranchers, and starving musicians alike. While driving from gig to gig, I'd look out the window of our van or—if it was a successful tour—our bus, and watch as night would close in and the landscape would take on an aura of mystery.

The view today had been different. I'd spent much of it sitting on my worn canvas duffle bag swatting flies and staring down the road into the distance, no sign of movement other than a line of turkey vultures taking purchase on a sagging section of ancient wooden fence.

Since leaving Austin earlier in the week, I'd been lucky with rides. It seemed I'd just throw out my thumb and before too long someone would stop. Traveling with a guitar and portable amp might have been part of it. These aren't generally considered weapons of choice for serial killers.

My lucky streak ended when my last ride dumped me here earlier in the morning. Jimmy, the ham-headed driver of a logging truck, had picked me up outside a small Mississippi town named Wiggins. He was in his early thirties, wearing jeans, a frayed denim shirt with the sleeves ripped off at the shoulders, and a camo-colored baseball cap pulled down low over his greasy, shoulder-length hair. We drove for a bit, exchanging the normal small talk— the weather, places we'd traveled, the type of truck he was driving. I've found that you can always get a long-haul driver talking when you ask him which rig is best, a Peterbilt, Kenworth or a Euro model, like the Volvo. I've done enough hitchhiking to have heard every side of the debate, so it's a bit boring to me, but it's a good way to make nice when someone's giving you a ride.

When Jimmy nodded toward my guitar case the conversation turned to music. "You play that thing?" he asked.

"Yeah, a bit."

"Looks like it's 'lectric."

"It is. The amp has a battery, but you can also plug it in."

"Are you in a band or somethin'?"

"Yeah, I play with one in Austin."

"What kinda music?" he asked with growing excitement.

"Mainly blues and some folk stuff."

"That's it?" he asked disappointedly. "No rock?"

"I've played in some rock bands before, but not now."

"Do you like Slayer?"

"Not really."

"How can you not like Slayer? Here, check this out man," he exclaimed as he punched a track on his CD player and spun the volume knob.

Instantly, the cab of the truck exploded with the eardrum ripping sounds of Slayer's *Black Magic* as Jimmy began shaking his head so violently to the screeching guitars that his cap slid to the side of his head. Then his body began to convulse as if he was having some sort of grand mal seizure, causing the truck to weave back and forth in the lane. I looked nervously at the road ahead and reached up and turned off the music.

"What the hell d'ya' do that for? Ain't that a great song?"

"Sorry, but it's not really my kind of music."

"What about Anthrax?"

"Not really."

"Trivium?"

"Nope."

"Megadeath?" he asked confidently. "Surely you must like them, you bein' a musician and all."

I shook my head slowly. "There's an old saying among guitar players that if you can't play well—play loud and with distortion. That's what they do. Same with most of those other bands."

Jimmy glared at me with equal measures of shock and contempt. I watched as his cheeks grew flush and the muscles in his tightened jaw pulsated. It was at that moment that I realized that our conversation had reached its end—as had my ride. Jerking the rig over to the side of a remote dirt-logging road, he yelled angrily, "You don't know shit about music, boy. Megadeath rules! Now, get the hell outta my truck."

I held up my palms in quiet apology and then tossed my bag to the dirt, grabbed my guitar and amp, and jumped out of the cab just as Jimmy released the air brakes and pulled away, coating me in a blanket of dust. I could hear him heatedly gnashing through the gears as he drove far into the distance.

Some people are just *soooo* sensitive about their music.

Brushing myself off, I pulled my gear to the side of the road, confident another ride would come along soon. After all, I'd already managed one ride that morning. But the moments turned into minutes, and then hours. Skipping stones off the roadway and munching a bag of stale pretzels and some other snacks I had buried in my bag kept me occupied for the remainder of the morning. Occasionally, I'd spot a family of white-tailed deer crossing the road without the least bit of concern for traffic. That should have been a sign that I wasn't going anywhere soon.

As the sun drew high overhead, I moved to the edge of the woods and pulled out a well-worn pulp detective novel that someone had left at a gas station. Using my duffle bag for a pillow, I alternated between reading and napping in the shade of a pine, keeping an ear open for the sound of a car or truck. But there were none. In the afternoon, still with no ride, I sat on my bag and pulled out my guitar to work on some songs. Mostly though, I just gazed down the road into the distant stillness.

It was at times like these that even an itinerant, emotionally repressed musician like me can get a bit introspective. "How the hell did I get here?" was a question I asked myself repeatedly, as I idly plucked at the strings. Was I somehow predestined for a life of emotional and physical transience? Why was life so damn complicated when all I wanted from it was something simple like playing the guitar.

Here's the thing. I've never had a problem attracting women. It you want a visual, I think you can describe me as a guy who looks like he could be Ryan Gosling's brother. Okay, if I'm going to be honest, maybe not his brother, but at least his cousin. Fine. His second or third cousin. My point is: finding a girlfriend has never been an issue. My problem has been staying with them.

It was at the request of an ex that I first saw a shrink. Something about dating for two years with no sign of nuptials on the horizon made her eager to introduce me to a member of the psychiatric profession. Of course, that was after making me endure every episode of *Gilmore Girls* and a constant stream of movies like *500 Days of Summer* and *P.S. I Love You.* I don't need to pay a hundred bucks an hour for some guy who endlessly repeats the phrase "How did that make you feel?" to know I have commitment issues. (And for damn sure, I don't need to watch *The Notebook*—three times. That should be reserved for breaking hardened criminals.)

It's probably no surprise that for most of my life I've been like one of those pinballs in the old-time arcade machines, always in motion, bouncing from town to town, never staying in one place for too long—a life filled with nothing but music, beer and transitory relationships. That was the state of my life as I reached my 27th year. I had no real home, no car, no health insurance, no 401k plan, and few possessions that I couldn't walk from without thought or regret. At that place in my life, the commitment involved in even purchasing a bookshelf at Ikea filled me with paroxysms of anxiety.

That all began to change after I met my girlfriend, Mo. Cautiously, I found myself setting down roots with her in Austin and discovering that the idea of permanence was…well, not as bad as I had feared. In fact, I was beginning to get comfortable with it. But now even that phase of my life was possibly over. And as I sat there on the side of the road in that isolated stretch of who-the-hell-knows-where Mississippi, banging out blues riffs on my guitar, I gradually began to realize how much I missed it.

Like Robert Johnson, I was at my own crossroads.

Two

With day quickly giving way to night, I tucked into a pine-needle-covered depression on the side of the road, lay my head on my duffle bag, and stared up at the first stars of the evening. Given my growing concern about finding a ride, I knew it would be a interminably long night. We've all had them. The kind where it feels like morning will never arrive. For hours I tossed, flipping from one side to the other, trying to quiet my mind seeking the refuge of sleep. Eventually, the warm humidity and the sound of the cicadas enveloped me in a blanket of thick air and white noise, and I drifted off.

It was in the early morning—I'm not sure exactly when—that I was awakened by a sound that didn't fit, something that wasn't natural. Faint at first, it slowly grew in volume until it was distinct from the sound of insects. I held perfectly still, straining to identify it for minutes without success. What was I hearing? An engine of some type? Was it a plane? Heavy equipment? A chainsaw? I stood up and squinted down the highway in both directions.

Nothing.

The sound continued to gradually grow louder. Then, far off in the distance, in the woods across the road from where I was standing, I noticed what appeared to be a faint pinpoint of light bouncing in the darkness. I'm not too embarrassed to admit that I've seen things like this in the past, but usually only after an evening with a bit too much Cuervo. Not the case tonight. Even through sober eyes, I had no idea what the hell I was seeing.

As the light drew closer, it began to divide into two. I blinked several times to focus my vision, but the lights continued to move erratically in my direction, growing ever larger. Adrenaline flooded my body as my mind began to replay some of those Sci-Fi movies from my youth. Didn't the extraterrestrials always land in a remote forest in the South? It was definitely time for me to get the hell out of here.

I jammed my gear into my duffle bag, secured the clip of the bag and slung it and my guitar over my shoulder while grabbing my amp. Taking a quick look behind me, I prepared to sprint deep into the forest on the opposite side of the road. By now the lights had grown much closer and I realized that they were headlights of a car that was weaving between the pine trees along some ancient ruts running into the forest. As the sound of the car grew more prominent and distinct, I noticed that it had a loud, creaking suspension and an engine with a concussive misfiring cylinder.

Like an apparition, the vehicle suddenly appeared before me, oscillating over the roots of a large pine tree and onto the asphalt. I jumped onto the road and began waving my arms as the headlights caught me in their glare and the car slid to a stop, enveloping us in a cloud of dirt and leaves. I coughed, brushed off my shirt and walked to the driver's side of the car where I saw an elbow in a ragged sleeve resting out of the open window.

"Man, am I glad to see you! Thanks for stopping. I've been waiting here all day. Can you give me a lift?"

It was quiet for a few moments. Then from the darkened front seat, a deep, baritone voice asked, "Where ya' headed?"

"Anywhere you're going. You're the first person I've seen all day, so I'm not picky."

"Anywhere I'm goin', huh?" he asked quizzically. "I guess I can take you there. Hop in."

"Thanks," I replied, as I ran back around to the passenger side. It was then that I first focused on the car—it was a filthy, and I mean *filthy*, mid-1970s convertible Cadillac Coup de Ville—and the interior was even worse. When I opened the back door to put my gear on the seat, an overpowering smell of ammonia assaulted me causing me to involuntarily retch. The rear seat was filled with feathers, bits of straw, and a layer of chicken shit.

I hesitated and looked down the road in both directions, praying for the appearance of another ride. But none were in sight. Reluctantly, I tossed in my guitar, amp, and duffle bag, climbed into the passenger seat and slammed the door shut.

As the car rumbled out onto the road, I took stock of the driver. By the light of the dashboard he appeared to be in his mid-to-late seventies, muscular, with a solid build, as if he had led a physical life. He was wearing tattered overalls, ancient work boots, and a denim shirt, faded with age. It was his hair, however, that was most striking. The driver had a thick, full, gray mane and a beard of ZZ-Top proportions.

I reached out my hand. "Thanks again for the lift. The name's A. J., A. J. Shanks."

There was an uncomfortably long pause before he took a hand from the steering wheel, reached over and shook mine. Then he tentatively replied, "Mine's Aaron."

Noticing me wrinkling my nose, he said, "Sorry about the car. I haven't driven it for a while and it seems my chickens decided to use it for a high-class coop. You might want to roll down your window."

I did as he suggested, and the car was instantly filled with a blinding whirlwind of dirt and chicken plumage causing Aaron to slam the brakes and swerve to a stop. He looked at us both covered in feathers and gave a short chuckle before pushing a button on the dashboard and lowering the convertible top.

"Maybe we drive with the top down for a bit."

With the top secured, Aaron hit the gas and we headed off under a warm, star-filled Mississippi night, leaving a trail of feathers flowing behind. As we motored down the road, I looked furtively at my traveling companion. Several times I tried to raise a conversation, but it was clear from his clipped responses that he was not interested in talking. Leaning back in my seat, I concentrated on the beams of the headlight bouncing off the dirt road and the rhythm of the car's misfiring V-8, becoming lost in thoughts of my own. Most of them were of Mo and what I'd walked away from in Austin.

But while I thought I knew what I was leaving behind, I had little vision for what lay ahead. After this guy dropped me off—what then? Where was I going to go? What was I going to do? How was I going to live? I didn't realize it at the time, but this was a ride that would answer my questions—and change my life.

Three

I awoke to the sound of muffled voices. How long had I been asleep? As I looked out through heavy-lidded eyes, I saw that we were parked in a run-down service station named Flack's Amoco. Through the crack in the open hood I saw a mechanic and the driver who gave me a lift hovering over the engine. What the hell was the guy's name?

"Hey there," he said, walking over to my window. "You really sacked out last night."

I yawned and sat up, stretching my arms. "Sorry about that. I meant to offer to drive…and I'm embarrassed to say that I forgot your name."

He waved his hand dismissively. "It's Aaron and I think you said you're A. J., right?" I nodded. "Well, A. J., it looked like you could use the sleep and I like drivin'. It's been a long time since I've had a chance." He paused and looked around the shop before continuing, "But we do have a bit of a problem. Seems like that noise in the engine was worse than I expected. I was barely able to nurse the car in here this morning. The mechanic says he needs to get into the engine to find out what's wrong and that we should check back at the end of the day."

"Where are we?" I asked, stifling another yawn.

"Town called Potts Camp. Don't really know much more. Listen, I've got to do a bit of shoppin'. Tell ya' what, if you still want a ride, be here at five. Otherwise, I'll assume you caught one with someone else."

"Ok, thanks," I said, reaching out my hand.

As he shook it he nodded his head toward my guitar in the backseat, "You play that thing for real?"

"Yeah, I've been in a few bands. Local mainly, around Austin."

He looked at me for what felt like minutes. Then he gave me a strange smile, dropped my hand, turned, and walked down the street.

* * *

It had been nearly a day since I had enjoyed a real meal, so I decided to explore Potts Camp and find something to eat. Given the size of the town, this took all of about ten minutes. With my guitar case strapped on my back and my duffle bag and amp in hand, I entered a barbeque joint situated next to an appropriately named "This N' That" shop. You find these kinds of stores in almost every small town in the South. They're a throwback to the general stores of the past, trying to satisfy everyone with a bit of everything, from barbed wire to Barbie Dolls to glassware and guns.

The restaurant was just opening and the smoker—a big black barrel-shaped grill out front—was not yet fired up. So, I took a seat by the window and ordered a bowl of soup, a chocolate shake, and a piece of pie. I looked out as I ate, considering my options. I could kill the rest of the day in Potts Camp and catch a lift with that old man—what was his name? Aaron? But what the hell would I do until then? Other than the gas station, a motel, a couple of restaurants and a few other declining businesses, there didn't seem to be much to see here. It would make for another long day. Or, I could try to catch another ride. I made up my mind as I finished the last of my pie. It was time to get moving.

Opening my wallet, I realized how little money I had. I had left Austin in such a hurry that I'd forgotten to get any cash—not that I had much in my account. I was going to need to be a frugal traveler until I figured out how to replenish my funds. I tossed a few bills on the counter, left the restaurant and walked a few blocks to the intersection of Highway 178. Someday I'm going to need to look up the definition of "highway." To me the word suggests a busy roadway, something with regular vehicular traffic. This was anything but that. I dropped my gear on the side of the road and waited. After an hour, a tractor drove by, the driver giving me a friendly wave. An hour later, a delivery truck passed without stopping despite my outstretched thumb. A few hours after that, a semi-loaded with bales of straw passed, likely for a local farm. That was it for five hours.

In the early afternoon I walked back to the restaurant and ate a pulled pork sandwich before returning to my lonely vigil alongside the highway. Nothing had changed and only a handful of vehicles passed, including the same tractor heading in the opposite direction, with the driver again giving me a wave. With darkness approaching, I decided I'd better cut my losses and see if I could still catch a ride with Aaron, if he was still around, or find a place in town to crash for the night.

Retracing my steps in the fading light, I listened to the rising sound of the cicadas and found myself thinking of Mo, and feeling strangely lonesome. What the hell was I doing? I was a few years short of thirty with a only a few bucks in my wallet, all my possessions on my back, walking alone through a community that was so small that it made the word "town" seem pretentious. All because I was a coward.

Lost in a cloud of self-pity and emotional self-flagellation, I eventually found my way to the Amoco station, which was by now closed for the night and with no sign of Aaron. I stood next to the gas pumps in the deserted station and looked down the road in both directions. It was like an abandoned movie set. All was silent in the town except the sound of the wind herding dust and trash down the asphalt roadway. It was the sound of a closing car door that drew my attention across the street to a couple walking into a family-style restaurant and bar. With the thought of food, my stomach was churning again.

An old shed stood on the side of the station. It had a rusted metal door, but with a few tugs it scraped open enough for me to wedge in my stuff next to a pile of old rags and some dented oil barrels. I figured it would be safe there. Then I walked across the road to grab dinner and come up with a plan for how to get the hell out of Potts Camp. Another day in this place and I'd die of boredom.

The restaurant was one of those eateries that are typical in rural parts of America—the kind of establishment that, like the local store, tried to be all things to all people in order to survive. Greeting me as I entered was a large bulletin board covered with advertisements for used farm equipment, trucks, and double-wide trailers, as well as notices for "VFW Meeting – 7 p.m. Tuesday" and "Singles Swing Dancing Nite – August 17th, 6:30 p.m.!!" A group of chairs and tables filled the floor next to a row of worn, red vinyl booths. On top of each table was a greasy metal box of condiments and a well-thumbed paper menu. Nearby, a large chalkboard listed the daily special with what I think we can all agree is the world's most enigmatically named meal: "Chicken Fried Steak."

Lines of faded plastic pennants crisscrossed the smoke-stained ceiling above the large stage at the far end of the room. On the walls surrounding the stage was a dusty tribute to testosterone and beer-fueled hunters of the past—dozens of stuffed coyote, deer, jackrabbits, and birds that quietly surveyed the patrons below. At that time of the early evening this consisted of only a handful of people.

These joints always give me a sense of déjà vu, perhaps because I've spent so much time in them while on the road. They're each different, yet somehow the same. That sameness isn't the physical location, but rather the sense of nostalgia they evoke. They're like portals to the past. That's what I was thinking as I surveyed the place and noticed someone who looked like…Aaron, eating alone at the bar.

As I approached, I noticed how different he appeared. He had had a haircut and a shave, which made him appear years younger. His overalls and worn t-shirt had been replaced with a garish floral-patterned nylon shirt, bell-bottom jeans, and a wide white macramé belt. A pair of matching white leatherette slip-on loafers completed the ensemble. All looked like they were from a second-hand clothing store—or a Halloween costume shop.

"Hey, A. J.," he said with surprise when he saw me, "wondered what happened to you. No luck with the ride?"

"Afraid not," I said staring at his outfit as I sat down on the creaky bar stool next to him.

Aaron smiled, noticing my gaze.

"Got it at a bow-teak store down the street. The owner said he doesn't meet many men with such good taste in clothes anymore. Kinda cool, ain't they!" he said proudly. Then his face grew more serious. "Kid, I'm happy to give you a ride, but we've got a problem."

"What's that?" I asked.

"Well, that sound we heard last night was a blown head gasket. The mechanic said he doesn't have any in stock, but he can have another one here tomorrow and can repair it first thing in the morning. 'Course, that means we're stuck here for the night."

"Okay," I replied tentatively.

"And there's another thing. The repair is going to cost two hundred and fifty bucks. As you can see," he said, gesturing to his clothes, "I did a bit of shopping today, and I've only got about a hu'red left."

"How about a credit card?" I suggested.

"Don't have one. You?"

This was weird, I thought. I was used to catching rides with strangers, but now I had this guy, who I had known for less than a day, asking me to contribute money to his car repair. I began to smell a con. Yet there was something about Aaron—I didn't know if it was his personality or his smile—that made this request feel normal, like we were long-time friends, or even family.

"I do, but it's tapped," I replied. "And I've only got a bit more than you in cash. Even if we sleep in the car, we don't have enough for repairs."

"Well, if we can get to Memphis, I think I can get some more money. The question is how to get enough until then..." His voice trailed off. "Well, we'll figure somethin' out," he added, before returning to his hamburger and fries.

I flagged down the bartender and ordered a plate of nachos and a Budweiser and sat quietly watching Aaron devour his food. Each time I took a sip of beer I could feel my forearms stick to the dull wooden counter top, which was permeated with the remnants of beer from ages past.

"So, what's your story, kid?" Aaron asked between bites.

This kind of open-ended question from a stranger always launched me into a bit of emotional gymnastics. You would think given all my wanderings that by then I would have developed a rote response. But I hadn't, and the question threw me. What *was* my story?

"What do you want to know?" I asked hesitantly.

"Well, why don't you start with something easy like your name—what's A. J. stand for?"

I sighed deeply, before responding, "My full name's Armitage James Shanks. I know, it sounds like I should be an actor on *Masterpiece Theatre*, rather than a musician."

"Masterpiece what?"

"It used to be a British T.V. show. Never mind."

"Family name?"

"No, but it tells you something about them and, especially, my dad. The story is that he was in England on a temporary training assignment with the Navy while my mom was pregnant with me. He came home the week before she gave birth and presented the name to her like it had come to him in some sort of mystical vision. His son would be named 'Armitage'." I pronounced the name with a dramatic flourish. "On reflection, I think he liked the name because he thought it was a way to class up the Shanks family. Or perhaps he was just being a prick."

"What'ya' mean?"

"During the summer after my freshman year of college, I was bumming through England and stopped to take a leak in a bus station. I unzipped and looked down—emblazed in cursive across the urinal, I saw the name of one of Europe's largest manufacturers of commercial grade bathroom products."

"Armitage Shanks?" Aaron inquired with a grin.

"Yep. You guessed it." I paused to take a swig of my beer.

"Well at least he had a good sense of humor. Are you close to him?"

"God, no. The word asshole is a better noun than father when referring to him.

"Sounds like you two didn't get along too well."

"Yeah, you could say that. Dad was career Navy. *Anchors Aweigh* and all that shit. He had dreamed of being a fighter pilot, but his family couldn't afford for him to go to college. Instead, after he finished high school he enlisted in Naval Flight Support."

"What's that?"

"Fancy way of saying that he became a mechanic. His job was to fix jets at bases around the country, and he dragged Mom and me behind him on each new deployment."

I took a deep gulp of my beer as I began to relive some long buried memories.

"So you moved around a bit?"

"More than a bit. You know that song *I've Been Everywhere?*"

"The Hank Snow number?"

"Yeah, but I think most people know the Johnny Cash version. Anyway, that was my life growing up. If it had a naval air station, we were there. Life was just a parade of green and yellow Mayflower moving vans. To this day, the smell of cardboard and masking tape sends me to a very lonely place."

"What about your Mama?" Aaron asked as he signaled to the bartender and ordered another Pepsi and a beer for me.

"She passed away a few years ago."

"Sorry to hear that."

I nodded and took another swallow of beer. "Mom was an only child like me. Her dad was a Presbyterian minister. I think they thought that when she graduated, Mom would continue the work of the Lord. Instead, she got knocked up by Dad right after she graduated high school—yours truly would be the result—and they had to get married."

"But you were close to your Mama, weren't ya'?" Aaron asked softly.

I thought about that for a minute before answering.

"Yeah, I guess I was, but Mom was different."

"What d'ya' mean *different*?"

"Well for starters, she chose a different religion than her parents—the god she worshiped was Elvis Pres—"

My words were interrupted when the glass slipped from Aaron's hand and crashed to the floor. For a moment, I thought that the old man had had a stroke. I reached out and put a hand on his shoulder as a waitress appeared with a rag and quickly began to clean up the mess under his stool.

"Are you okay?" I asked with concern.

As if awakening from a dream, Aaron slowly nodded. "Sorry about that. Gettin' a bit clumsy in my old age, I guess."

The waitress finished wiping the floor and sweeping up the broken pieces. Then she walked back behind the bar where she poured another Pepsi for Aaron. He thanked her, turned to me and with a strange air of nonchalance asked, "You were sayin' somethin' about Elvis Presley?"

"Yeah," I continued, "for Mom, Elvis was everything. She was twelve years old when her friend took her to her first Elvis concert. He was at the end of his career then, but at that moment he became the love of her life. In fact, I always wondered if Dad was jealous of him."

"Well, a lotta ladies liked him."

"No, I don't think you understand. Mom was *obsessed* with Elvis. I was raised by one of the foremost Elvis freaks on the planet. While my friends went to the Catholic Church or the Methodist Church or the Mormon Church, I was schooled at the Church of Elvis. And my mother was the pastor. Everything in her life was Elvis. Our house was covered in Elvis crap—framed album covers and photos, embroidered pillows, you name it. It seemed that every night we watched an Elvis movie, and his music was always playing when I was a kid."

"She sounds like a big fan."

"Way more than that. Mom would do weird stuff like sing *Return to Sender* when I brought home a bad report card or put bacon in my PB&J because 'that's how Elvis liked it.'"

I took a long pull of my beer and began peeling off the label, staring at the tears of condensation running down the glass.

"The other thing about Mom was that she was a drunk. Big time. Toward the end, I think Mr. Seagram may have been her only friend. She really pounded that stuff. And it only got worse after she and my dad split up."

"Sorry to hear that, kid."

"Probably shouldn't have been a surprise; my parents were always more like roommates than people in love. I don't ever remember them giving each other a hug or kiss—but at least they had been civil. I was in high school in Pensacola when they really began fighting. It was like my parents had worked to bury their anger all those years and they just didn't have the energy to lift another shovel. You know, I had a shrink who once told me, 'If you don't deal with your demons, they go down to the basement and lift weights.' Given the fighting in our house, I think my folks' demons had been pumping serious iron for years."

As I spoke, I ran my fingers over my right cheek feeling a residual flash of pain and humiliation. I was ten years old and had come home from school to find my parents in another argument. I entered the room and saw my father looming angrily over my mother, waving his burly arms and delivering a torrent of profanity-laden insults.

"You bitch! I was never good enough for you or your Bible-banger parents!" He growled.

The back of his broad neck was scarlet and flush with sweat. In front of him, my mom cowered, seeking refuge in a corner next to our old refrigerator. She flinched each time he moved his meaty hands.

"You aren't good enough for *anyone*. All you care about is yourself! You spend all your time goin' out drinking with the boys, instead of home with your wife and son."

"Shut up or I'll slap you!"

"Go ahead. It wouldn't be the first time," she taunted.

Without thinking, I grabbed my father's left arm, yelling for them to stop. Roaring with spite, he turned so quickly that I never saw his fist crash into my cheek. Then everything went black. I awoke to Mom cradling my head in her arms, her tears dropping on to my face and mixing with mine.

I turned to Aaron and reburied the memory, wanting it to finally be forgotten. "Anyhow you know the story—Dad went out for a pack of smokes…" I offered him a pained smile, flagged the waitress for another beer and dug into my nachos as I watched a waiter bring a microphone stand up on to the stage.

Four

How strange, I thought. I had had a succession of relationships over the years where girlfriends pleaded with me to "share more of myself" or "talk about my feelings." As an aside—I've developed this strange tic that manifests itself in the form of an involuntary eye roll whenever I hear those phrases. Almost all of those relationships came to an abrupt end because of my inability to open up and trust. At least that's what one of my ex-girlfriends told me. Yet, somehow, here I was, in this little bump-in-the-road of a town, telling this goofy old man all the gory details of my life. Maybe he was just an outlet for all the emotion I had built up around Mo, but Aaron had this unique capacity to draw things out of me. He had this way of listening that was casual, yet made you feel that there was nothing more important in the world. Having said this, there were some places I didn't want to go.

"How old were you when your Dad left?"

"Almost sixteen," I replied curtly, hoping he would get the message that our therapy session was getting into dangerous waters.

"Must have been rough, kid. When's the last you saw him?"

"Jesus, take a hint, old man," I snapped.

Chagrined, Aaron looked down at his Pepsi in silence.

I sighed, realizing that I was overreacting, Aaron didn't know the dysfunction that constituted the Shanks' household of my youth.

"It was probably a year or two after that," I finally answered, feeling my throat swell. "I remember because I was always asking him to teach me to drive. 'Sure, kid, sure', he'd say. But he never did. Then he moved out of the house to live back on the base. For a while I thought he'd left because

I was pestering him to show me how to drive. He'd drop by every once in a while, mainly when he knew Mom wasn't around, but sometime later he was transferred to the base in Virginia Beach, and we didn't go with him. I haven't seen him since."

"I'm sorry to hear that. A child shouldn't have to grow up without his daddy."

"I've done okay."

"So, how'd you get into music?" Aaron asked.

"I think that's one of the only things I can thank my dad for, although it wasn't like he wanted me to become a musician. You know that old Fender I had in your car?"

Aaron nodded.

"I bought it at a local pawnshop when I was thirteen. I don't know what drew me to it, but when I held it in my hands it was like holding lightning. I knew I had to have it. After a long summer of mowing lawns and returning empty bottles, that guitar was mine. It was the only thing that kept me sane when I was young."

"I'm not sure I understand. What did your dad have to do with it if he didn't buy it for ya'?"

"A lot of kids start out wanting to play the guitar, but most of them give up because they don't want to put in the hours to learn. I wasn't one of 'em. I practiced as often as I could. I'd play before breakfast, when I got home from school and before I went to bed. I'd play for hours on the weekends. And my main motivation was that it bugged the living shit out of my old man. He couldn't stand listening to me play."

"Did you take lessons or teach yourself?"

"Please! I learned on my own. My dad wasn't about to shell out for lessons, and besides, I was a gawky, insecure high school kid, and I figured that practicing guitar would make me cool to my peers—like I was some kind of budding rocker, instead of a geek. In reality, they probably didn't even notice I was around."

"Geek?"

"You know, a nerd, a loner, an outcast."

Aaron nodded his head, and I sensed that he understood.

"With practice, my playing improved. And, if you're performing for an audience of one that is my mom, well, you're playing Elvis, especially after Dad left. It seemed the only time I ever saw her smile was when I sat beside her bed at night, surrounded by all her Elvis stuff and strummed *Are You Lonesome Tonight.*"

"What did ya' do after high school? Is that when you joined a band?" Aaron asked this abruptly, almost as if he was uneasy.

"After graduation I headed off to college. My test scores got me a scholarship at the University of Oregon, which was a surprise to everyone because I was a shitty student. I think what did it for me was reading. I loved books like *To Kill a Mockingbird, Look Homeward Angel* and *The Prince of Tide.* Have you read any of those?"

"Can't say that I have, but I saw the *Mockingbird* movie years ago."

"Well, back then if I didn't have a pick in my fingers, I was reading a book."

"What kind of degree did you get?" Aaron asked.

I polished off my beer and signaled the waitress for another before responding with a touch of embarrassment. "Actually, I never graduated. I'd try a class until I got a feel for it and then I'd quit it and move to another. Some semesters I'd drop more classes than I finished. I became a master at just getting by—doing only what I needed to maintain my scholarship, but nothing more. Instead, most of my time was spent playing with pick-up bands at Rennie's Landing—that was the local watering hole for the frat boys. I didn't make much money, but the girls and free beer made up for it."

Aaron grinned. "And after that?"

"Well, halfway through my junior year, I quit and decided to try to make a living with my guitar. My parents were long divorced by then and Dad was completely out of the picture. I feel bad about it now, but I seldom spoke with Mom. When I did, the conversations all ended the same way, with her on a drunken rant about Dad. I remember I called her to let her know I was dropping out of school, but I don't think it really even registered. The only thing I heard was ice clinking against glass and her saying, 'That's okay, son. You know, Elvis never went to college.'"

It was subtle, but I swear that Aaron tensed when I said this. It wasn't anything he said or did, just a feeling I had. Then he seemed to again shift the direction of our conversation asking, "Tell me about your music. What d'ya' play?"

"I've played about everything, but what I like the best are some of the really old gospel and country tunes from the forties and fifties, stuff by folks like Roy Acuff and Jim Reeves—not sure if you've heard of them."

Aaron's smile indicated that he had.

"A friend turned me on to that music. Unfortunately, there isn't a big audience for it in Austin these days with all the indie bands popping up."

"Indian bands?"

I laughed. "No, no, 'indie,' as in 'independent.' Meaning artists who write their own stuff and who don't have the support of a major recording label or producers."

"Oh," he responded. "When I was young, Memphis was the place to be for music. That's where you went to make your name. There or maybe New York or Chicago. You make it sound like the music's moved to Austin."

"Hell yes!" I exclaimed. "There's nothing new in New York since the Strokes, or maybe Lady Gaga. Memphis and Nashville are only producing that pop country crap. Nothing's happened in San Francisco since ska, and Seattle died with grunge."

"Gaga? Ska? Grunge? What's that? I'm talkin' about music."

"That is music! Where have you been? You mean you've never heard of Lady Gaga?"

Aaron looked down at his Pepsi and was somber for a moment. "Guess I'm just a bit out of touch. What you're describin' sounds different than any music I'm used to."

* * *

From there the night was a bit of a blur as I continued to work my way through a succession of beers and ploughed through my food. My conversation with Aaron had definitely caused me to cast off my emotional moorings and my mind kept drifting to Austin…and Mo. What would she be doing right now? Would she be home thinking of me? Maybe, she was staying with friends. I knew she must be frightened as hell… but so was I.

A stream of people slowly began to fill the restaurant as the sky darkened to night.

"Wonder what's goin' on?" Aaron asked.

"I think it's a karaoke contest, there was a sign advertising it on the front door. They're offering some decent prizes considering the size of this town. I think the grand prize is something like a hundred and fifty bucks."

"Kid, what's that mean, "Kar-ee-okay? Is that how you pronounce it"?

"You don't know what karaoke is? How is that possible?" I asked incredulously. "It's where people get on stage and sing to a kind of jukebox that plays instrumental versions of popular songs. You don't have to know the words because it shows them on a TV screen."

"You don't need to memorize lyrics? Guess that makes it a whole lot easier to be an entertainer these days!" Aaron let out a laugh and slapped me on the shoulder.

From our bar-side vantage, Aaron and I nursed our drinks and listened as the restaurant owner, who served as MC, introduced a succession of townspeople vying to win the karaoke prizes. The evening's contest consisted of two songs; one selected randomly by the karaoke machine and the other the choice of the performer.

First on the stage was a tall young woman in tight Wrangler jeans and a peasant blouse singing an impassioned version of *You Belong to Me*. Sadly, she did not sound even remotely like Taylor Swift. She followed this with *Rolling in the Deep*. Unfortunately, she sounded even less like Adele. Up next was an overweight, middle-aged guy who made a valiant, but unsuccessful attempt when the karaoke machine selected Miley Cyrus's *Party in the U.S.A* for his first number. He recovered, however, by next delivering a heartfelt but very rough version of the C&W classic *Please Help Me I'm Fallin,* to his proud, but self-conscious wife who was fidgeting in her chair as he sang on bended knee. From there, the songs flowed with the drinks far into the night as the patrons of this restaurant let loose while Aaron and I watched from our barstools.

Karaoke requires liquid courage. That's why you only see it done in bars. Although I can carry a tune, I've found from past experience that there's never been enough alcohol to get me to sing in public—even on stage. I've tried, but it's so frightening that even the idea of contributing to a harmony fills me with dread. I'm a guitar player, not a singer. In fact, just watching these people made me want to reach for the comfort of my Fender.

Toward the end of the evening, as an obviously intoxicated young farmer slurred a boisterous rendition of Journey's *Don't Stop Believing*, I ordered another beer and realized that I had been doing all the talking; I still knew nothing about Aaron. While you may think that I was just being a self-absorbed millennial, the truth was that Aaron was as effective as my shrink in pulling things out of me, so much so that I hadn't even thought of asking him any questions. As the song drew to a close, I started to ask why he had been driving through the woods when we met, but before I could open my mouth, he turned to me and said, "I've got an idea." Then he took a long gulp of his drink, stood, and raised his hand, indicating that he wanted to sing next.

Five

As Aaron walked up on stage, the MC, barely audible over the noise of the crowd, asked, "Well, old timer, what's your name?"

"Aaron, Aaron Smith."

"Where are you from, Mr. Smith?"

Aaron paused for a moment as if stumped by the question before replying, "Kinda all over, I guess."

The MC looked at Aaron as if considering whether to ask a follow up question. Thinking better of it, he bellowed over the noise of the crowd, "Okay, up next, Mr. Smith from 'kinda all over.' Let's see what the machine picks for you to sing tonight!"

With that, he hit a button on the screen and we watched as the karaoke machine flashed titles randomly like a roulette wheel before coming to rest on a single song.

"It's *Call Me Maybe* by Carly Rae Jepsen!" shouted the MC excitedly. "Are you ready to go?"

Aaron looked perplexed. "Can't say that I've heard of that song. Can we pick another?"

"No, I'm afraid that's not how the contest works. But don't worry. You'll be fine. Just sing the words on the screen." With that he handed the microphone to Aaron and hit the play button.

As Aaron brought the microphone to his lips, I had a vision of impending catastrophe—like the explosion of the Hindenburg, the failure of the Ninth Ward levees or the return of the mullet as an accepted hairstyle—this was going to be an epic disaster.

Aaron looked at the screen and haltingly began singing a few lines. He seemed lost, stumbling over each lyric as it rolled past, moving stiffly to the beat.

"This is harder than it looks. I'm sorry folks," he said as he squinted at the screen.

"Here, try mine, Mr. Smith," volunteered the MC, pulling a pair of reading glasses out of his shirt pocket and handing them to Aaron.

Aaron put on the glasses and gave a quick smile as he sang. The bar's patrons, accustomed to the perky, energetic musical styling of Ms. Jepson, did not appreciate Aaron's almost spoken word rendition of the song as he tried to fit the words to the recorded music. He looked clumsy and out of place as he bent over and stared at the screen with his reading glasses, singing the words through the microphone and snapping his fingers a few seconds out of time with the music. Damn, it was painful to watch. I know most of the people around me felt the same. Some were bored and ignored the old man, but many were laughing and pointing at Aaron as if he was a comedy act. From parts of the bar I even heard an occasional jeer or insult hurled at him. It was a brutal three minutes and thirteen seconds.

Mercifully, the song at last ended. I was embarrassed for Aaron and stood up to get him so that we could bolt, certain that the MC would put an end to this humiliation and quickly usher him off the stage.

"Well, Mr. Smith, you gave it a good try. How about a big hand for him, folks," encouraged the MC as he took back the microphone.

Aaron and the MC had clearly lost the attention of the crowd. Most people had returned to their drinks and conversations and didn't hear Aaron quietly ask, "I thought I got to pick a song?"

"Well, sure you do," stammered the MC awkwardly. "Are you sure you're up for another?"

"Yes, sir. I am."

The MC looked out at the crowd and realizing that most were not paying attention, shrugged his shoulders and said, "Okay, you're the last performer tonight. What are you going to sing for us to close tonight's contest?"

Aaron leaned into the microphone. "It's an old song from my generation, I don't think many of the youngsters here will know it. A gentleman named Junior Parker wrote this one. It's called *Mystery Train*."

"Okay, let me see if we've got it in the system," said the MC as he paged through the screen of the karaoke machine. "Well, lucky for you, it looks like we do. Everyone, Aaron Smith singing *Mystery Train.*"

The MC punched the play button and handed him the microphone. As he did, Aaron passed him back his reading glasses.

"Won't need 'em for this number," he said confidently.

Slowly, I buried my head in my hands and tried to shrink from sight in complete embarrassment. I looked at Aaron in his Bee Gees-era jeans and dorky shirt, standing somewhat uneasily on stage under the spotlight in the middle of this boisterous bar. Mentally, I willed him to return to his seat. *Please, you old geezer, get off the stage!*

What followed will remain one of the most astounding moments of my life. To think of it now, many years later, still causes my hair to rise on the back of my neck.

The music began with a few syncopated drumbeats. Aaron stood under the spotlight, motionless except for a slight tapping of his right foot He looked out at the crowd, his face expressionless, and after a moment of hesitation, began to sing.

It was Aaron's voice that most surprised me. There was a richness to it as unexpected as his phrasing. It was like he was caressing the lyrics as they left his mouth. It was also his confidence. Where with the previous song he had seemed like a doddering old codger, the man now on the stage before us had presence. And the song—where had I heard it before? It was familiar, yet distant, like an old memory that you can't quite retrieve from an ocean of remembrances.

As Aaron began the second verse, it was as if he had lost himself in the song, like he was in a different place or time. I noticed the noise of the crowd began to die down and watched people elbow each other and gesture toward him. Even the bartender stopped pouring drinks and looked toward the stage.

By the third verse, the bar was transfixed, as if we were witnessing a perfect game being pitched in the World Series. The crowd looked up in disbelief at the elderly man singing and moving around as if he was fifty years younger. I'm not sure where it came from, but Aaron was suddenly swinging, spinning and dancing like he was channeling Prince or James Brown at the Apollo Theater.

By the fourth verse, Aaron was strutting like a man possessed. It was as if he were leading a Baptist revival, and his barroom congregation responded with clapping and cheering. Some patrons jumped to their feet and began gyrating, while others hammered on tables to keep rhythm. Even the waitresses started dancing while holding their trays overhead.

Then as suddenly as it had begun, the song was over. The crowd in the bar rose almost in unison clapping and hollering for more. In response, Aaron dropped his head in a short bow, placed the microphone back in its stand and began to step off the stage before he was intercepted by the MC. The man grabbed Aaron's arm and shouted into the microphone, "Ladies and gentlemen! I think we know who's tonight's winner! It's Aaron Smith! Congratulations, Aaron. Here's your one hundred and fifty dollars!" Aaron waved to the applauding crowd with a sheepish smile as the MC counted the bills into his hand. Then Aaron made his way back to the bar through his well-wishers—men shaking his hand or patting him on the back, young women giving him a hug or a kiss on the cheek. He leaned toward me as he passed and whispered, "Let's boogie."

I threw a few bucks on the bar for a tip and followed Aaron out the front door.

"Holy shit!" I cried once we were outside. "Where in the hell did you learn to sing like that?"

Aaron ignored my question. Instead, he pointed across the street at the town's only motel and said, "Kid, it's late and I'm tired. What if we see if we can get some rooms for the night?"

There are points in our lives when we later reflect on what would have happened had we taken a different path, chosen a different course. Like in high school when I gave up New Kids on the Block for Clapton, I would look back at this as one of those moments. Given my history, the normal thing for me to do in this situation would've been to split. I'd thank Aaron for the lift, shake his hand and then grab my stuff from the gas station and... and what? What was I going to do for the evening in Potts Camp, Mississippi? Where was I going to sleep? More importantly, what had just happened tonight and *who* was this guy? First, he has me confiding things like he's Dr. Phil, and next he's singing and moving around the bar stage like he's a senior citizen Mick Jagger. And the thing was, there was something about being with him that felt right, like it was karma or destiny. I considered this for a moment before replying "Okay," and retrieving my gear from the gas station.

The motel wasn't much, just a single-story, U-shaped structure with about ten rooms and a flickering neon sign out front that advertised AC and cable TV. It was one of those places built in the early 1960s as part of economic euphoria of small towns as they became interconnected by asphalt. But the promise of tourism and business travelers never really came through. Places like this one remained unchanged as their owners just tried to get by. The motel was familiar to me, despite the yellowed sheets, musty curtains, moldy showers, and tattered towels, because for musicians pursuing their first big break, these places are called home.

I unlocked the door to our room—there were no singles available—and leaned my guitar and amp against a wall. "Do you want the bed by the window or the door?" I asked.

There was no response. I looked back to the doorway to see if I had lost Aaron, but there he was standing right behind me, his eyes surveying the room.

"Which bed do you want?" I asked again.

Aaron remained silent until I put a hand on his shoulder and gave him a nudge. "Which bed do you want?"

Aaron snapped out of wherever he had been moments before. "Sorry, it's been a while since I've stayed in a place like this." Then he lowered himself to the bed closest to the window.

"I know it's pretty low rent, but that's how things are in these small towns. Plus, we need to save money, right?"

Aaron nodded.

"Hey, man, that was really something back there. Seriously, do you have any idea how well you sing?"

"Well, I used to sing a bit when I was younger."

"That was more than just singing 'a bit when you were younger'!"

"I don't reckon I know what you mean."

"Aaron, I've played with dozens of bands. Many of them had a great lead singer. But, none of them—and I mean *none* of them—sang like you just did. You could do this for a living."

He looked at me for a few moments, then with a wistful smile said, "Kid, I used to sing years ago, a long time before you were even born. I'm not an entertainer now; I'm just an old man—a tired old man. Good night, A. J." And with that, he stripped off his clothes, crawled into his bed, and was instantly asleep.

I'd like to say I did the same; however, sleep eluded me until long after I turned off the light. I was exhausted, but I kept replaying the evening in my mind. To be honest, the ceiling was spinning from those last few beers, but I was also kind of freaked out by what I had witnessed. I had this feeling that something big was right in front of me. I could sense it, yet I couldn't see what it was. I thought about Aaron's voice, his gestures as he held the microphone, the way he owned the crowd.

It all felt hauntingly familiar.

Six

The sunlight streaming through the crack in the curtains pierced my sleep like a laser. Slowly, I swam to consciousness, lifted my head, and gazed around the room. Where the hell was I? My mouth was parched, like I had been chewing cotton balls, and my head felt as if Dave Grohl was using it as a drum kit. Groggily, I reached over to the nightstand to check the time on my phone. I held it to my face and saw that there was a text from Mo.

> Honey, it will be okay. You can do this. WE can do this. Call me! I'm worried. I love you.

Slammed back to reality, I responded the only way I knew. Crushing the pillow over my face, I willed myself back to sleep.

An hour later I awoke again. It was painfully apparent that Mr. Grohl was still playing what I now realized would be an extended day-long drum solo. I shuffled into the shower and hung my head under the hot water, trying to pull myself together. God, I felt like shit. I toweled off, looked around the room and, for the first time, noticed that all traces of Aaron were gone. Quickly I threw on some clothes grabbed my gear and walked over to the garage thinking I would find him there, but the mechanic said I missed Aaron by about fifteen minutes. Damn. He had vanished. It was if he had never existed.

It was odd that Aaron had left so abruptly. Last night I sensed that there was a connection between us. Now he was gone. I almost felt that I had been jilted. Had he mentioned that he needed to leave early for some reason? Had I said something that had offended him? Nothing made sense and now, I was alone in Potts Camp with little cash, a hangover, a big bag of guilt, and a call I couldn't bring myself to make.

I walked out to the highway, dropped my belongings, and turned to stick out my thumb, anticipating a long wait. As I did, however, a car pulled alongside. I glanced up, my head in pain from turning too quickly, and there was Aaron leaning out of the passenger window of his old Caddy offering me a Styrofoam cup of coffee.

"Hey, stranger! I picked up the car and stopped for a cup of coffee. Figured you'd need it after last night." He let out a chuckle as he pushed the coffee toward me.

For a moment, I was paralyzed. That grin. I'd seen it before. Who was this guy? It was weird, but I couldn't shake the feeling that I somehow knew him. Aaron broke my concentration as he gestured with his free hand and implored, "Come on, kid, get in. We've got to get goin'."

I threw my guitar and gear in the back seat, closed the door and took a long draw of coffee. "Thanks," I said, as Aaron accelerated down the road.

We rode for miles in silence. Occasionally Aaron would look over at me with a warm but enigmatic smile. I gazed at my coffee and the blur of the countryside, trying to focus on what it was that was nagging at me. My brain was dancing around an answer, but it wouldn't lock in.

Years ago, I had a girlfriend who was one of those kooky chicks who was into things like yoga, Hinduism, and being a vegetarian. And, because she was hot and I was horny, I became interested in things…well, like yoga, Hinduism and being a vegetarian—at least until my passion for bacon resurfaced and ended our relationship. I recall her explaining that many religions, like Hinduism, have belief systems that include the idea of reincarnation; that we have all lived past lives. Being with Aaron made me almost believe that this could be true. Could we have met in a previous life? Peering at him out of the corner of my eye, I felt he was someone I knew, yet how was that possible?

"Where are we?" I asked.

"Near a town called Holly Springs. We should reach Memphis in a few hours." In a faint voice, he added, "Almost home."

We drove on for another fifteen minutes before Aaron announced, "There's a fillin' station up ahead. We should probably stop and get some gas." He steered the big Cadillac onto the highway exit ramp and pulled alongside a pump at a Sinclair gas station. When he turned the car off, I jumped out.

"I'll gas it up. I want to stretch a bit and I'll pay."

"Good," he replied. "I spent the last of money on the repairs. I need to use the john. Be back in a minute."

I placed the pump into the tank and watched as Aaron walked into the bathroom on the side of the station. My brain continued to churn. Who the hell was this guy? It was really starting to creep me out, making me feel almost anxious. Aimlessly, I started the pump and walked behind the car. I'm not sure what I was looking for, but my eyes came to rest on the license plate. It was covered with mud and chicken shit, but it was a Tennessee plate with a tag dated 1975. I squatted down to take a closer look and wiped my fingers across the letters on the plate. There were only three: "TCB."

My body tensed as the thought bolted to the surface of my consciousness. It wasn't possible—it couldn't be—he was *dead*. With a trembling hand I removed the pump from the car. Almost mechanically, I screwed the cap on the tank, walked into the gas station, and handed the cashier a $20 bill.

Maybe Aaron was some kind of down-on-his-luck entertainer? That could be it. But that voice, the way he had paced the stage with an almost sexual energy, the way he worked the crowd, his movements, his smile…it had to be him. After all, he said he was heading to Memphis.

"Sir? Sir?"

The attendant's voice pulled me from my daze. "Sorry, what?"

"Here's your change, sir," she said, holding out her hand.

I thanked her and headed back out to the Caddy. Opening the door, I sank into the seat, trying to clear my head of the obvious conclusion. There had to be some other explanation. There *had* to be. I felt bewildered, almost dazed by what was racing through my head. My thoughts were interrupted when the passenger door creaked opened and Aaron pulled himself behind the wheel.

"Ready to roll?"

"Yeah," I replied as I focused on his face, searching for any resemblance.

We drove for a few miles, before Aaron, perhaps, sensing my confusion, asked, "A. J., is everythin' alright?"

The question unleashed the thought which I had been using logic to avoid. I couldn't contain it any longer. "How can it be?" I exclaimed. "You're supposed to be dead!"

"What are you talkin' about, kid?"

"I know who you are, but it just isn't possible. It can't be."

"A. J., you're not making sense. What are you saying?"

"You're Elvis. Elvis fucking Presley!"

My accusation startled Aaron, causing him to jerk the wheel toward oncoming traffic. Quickly, he wrestled the car back into our lane and took a long, deep breath to calm himself before replying with a forced laugh, "Kid, that is the craziest thing I've ever heard. That makes no sense, no sense at all."

"It doesn't. But it's you. I know it."

"Elvis died before you were born. How can I be Elvis? Are you doin' drugs? Were you smokin' marijuana back there?"

"That song you sang last night—*Mystery Train*. You recorded it for Sun Records in 1955. Your best-selling 45 had *Hound Dog* on the A-side and *Don't Be Cruel* on the B-side. You made thirty-one movies. The first was *Love Me Tender* in 1959. The last was *Change of Habit* in 1969."

"How—how do you know all that?" Aaron responded in a bewildered voice.

"Remember what I told you about my mom? She knew everything about Elvis! And she made sure her son did as well."

I expected Aaron to continue to press his denials, but he was silent for a few moments before quietly asking, "You didn't say much about your Mama. Tell me more about her."

"Who? My mom?"

"Yeah."

"I told you all you need to know. She was a drunk. She died a few years after I moved to Austin," I snapped.

Aaron looked at me and gently replied, "No matter what, she was still your Mama. She is part of you and always will be. I know 'cause I lost my Mama when I was young as well. I still miss her."

"Don't change the subject. I know you lost your Mama. I know! Her name was Gladys Love Smith. She died in August 1958. How do I know this? Because *my* mother told me! She felt Elvis loved his mother the way a son should, and she never let me forget it!"

I hung my head in my hands. It felt as if any moment it would explode. I was so fucking confused. "I just don't understand how the hell this can be…" I murmured.

Aaron glanced over at me with concern and said, "This is a conversation we probably shouldn't have while we're drivin'. I think you maybe need to walk around, get some fresh air, and calm down a bit." With this, he put on the blinker and we exited the highway and pulled into an empty roadside rest stop.

Seven

I trailed closely behind Aaron as he got out of the car and walked toward a graffiti-covered concrete picnic table where he sat down. I couldn't seem to catch my breath. I almost felt sick. Was I hyperventilating? Pacing back and forth, my mind swirling, I tried to make sense of the history I knew and the man I saw before me. Finally, I sat down opposite him at the table and looked into his eyes while trying to settle my nerves.

"Sing *That's All Right*," I commanded.

"What?"

"Sing *That's All Right*!"

"You're joking, kid. I ain't no juke box."

"Sing it," I said forcefully.

Aaron looked at me, sighed and then, closing his eyes, began to sing.

"Holy shit!" I interrupted. "Now, *Blue Suede Shoes*!"

"What? No." Then, seeing the committed look on my face, Aaron opened his mouth and sang the famous first stanza to one of Presley's biggest hits before I interrupted him again.

"Holy shit! Holy shit! Now sing *In the Ghetto*!'"

"Stop it, kid. Everyone my age knows those songs. So what?"

"So what? So what? People may know those songs, but no one sings them with that voice. You're him. I mean, you. I mean Elvis! Shit! How can that possibly be?"

"It's not. You've made a mistake, kid. Elvis is long dead. My name's Aaron."

"Aaron, was Elvis's middle name."

"A lot of people are named Aaron."

He held my gaze as I looked into his eyes for a long moment. I'm sure he was hoping that I could be convinced it was all just a crazy idea.

"Your car is the same make and model that Elvis used to drive."

"It was a popular car, thousands of people had 'em," he responded calmly.

"It has a license plate with the initials 'TCB,'" I said, my eyes boring into his. "'TCB' stands for 'Taking Care of Business.' That was Elvis's personal motto. He used to give his band and crew medallions and jewelry with those letters." I paused, feeling light-headed, like I would lose consciousness at any moment. "And the way you sang last night at the bar....Damn. It's really you."

"Take it easy, kid. Calm down, calm down. Take a breath."

"How can I calm down? You're the most famous person in rock n' roll history. You're a legend—more than a legend—you're practically a musical god! Damn it, tell the truth, it's you, isn't it? Isn't it?" I pleaded.

Aaron went silent, looking off toward the horizon as if weighing a decision of immense consequence. I watched him, willing myself to remain still, not wanting to frighten him from the revelation I so anxiously wanted to hear. After what felt like hours, Aaron took a breath so deep that it seemed to reach into history and turned toward me.

"It was so long ago," he began. "When I think about it now it seems as if it's a different person. I've been Aaron for more of my life than I was the King of Rock n' Roll. So, I wasn't lying when I said Elvis is long dead."

"Holy shit! You're admitting it? That you really *are* Elvis?"

Aaron held up a hand, patiently indicating for me to hold my questions before resuming his story. "I was a shy high school kid from a poor family with only a few friends. You don't know what it was like back then, havin' nothin'. I'd go through the school hallways unnoticed and unrecognized by almost everyone. I was like a shadow, a kid from the wrong side of the tracks. Then one day, I walk into Sun Records and meet Sam Philips. After that my life was never the same—or my own. Within a year, I'm on the road playing shows across the South and hearin' my voice comin' out from the radio. A couple of years after that, I'm one of the most famous people on earth. I'm in Hollywood; I'm in Hawaii; I'm hangin' out with Sinatra, Sophia Loren, and folks like that. Back then more people knew me than the President. My life was a blur of music, movies, money and women," he said with a wistful smile.

"Wait a second," I interrupted, "why are you telling me all this?"

Aaron regarded me with a look of slight bemusement.

"Kid, I've been gone a long time. After the last couple of days, I can already see that things are much different than I remember. I've got somethin' I want to do and I'm thinkin' I might need a bit of help. I've gotta feelin' about you… somethin' that makes me think I can trust ya'. Besides," he said with a mischievous smile, "even if someone else remembers me, I don't think they'll believe your story."

Hesitantly, I asked, "What is it you need my help with?"

"How 'bout I finish my story first?"

I can't fuckin' believe this, I thought, nodding my head as Aaron resumed.

"When you come from nothin' and suddenly have almost endless money, well, you go a bit crazy. I bought just about anything I wanted— houses, horses, planes, jewelry, cars, it didn't matter. Anything that made me happy. The thing is, money and fame can take away your soul too. You forget who you are and where you came from. That's what happened to me. And I started to get into some bad things. At first it was just food. I'd eat damn near anythin' I wanted—even had a full-time cook who would make me my favorite fried chicken day or night. After a while, all those years of eatin' caught up with me and I put on almost seventy pounds. I didn't even recognize myself in the mirror.

"It was also the women. They'd damn near throw themselves at me. Even when I was just gettin' started, I'd be walkin' somewhere and girls would just be all over. I go from bein' this guy who was too shy to talk to 'em to one who didn't have to 'cause they were comin' at me. What warm-blooded man would try to fight that? I didn't."

"There are worse problems," I said, my voice quavering.

"Yeah, I guess so. But at some point, I thought the time was right for me to settle down. I ended up marryin' the most beautiful woman on God's Earth. I met Priscilla when I was in the Army and she was just a teenager. We waited seven years before we got married. There was never a woman like her…" Aaron shook his head and looked off in the distance for a moment.

"You'd think that life with her would be enough for me, but it wasn't. It didn't take long before I was back to my old ways. There were actresses, stewardesses, secretaries—whenever I was touring or on a movie set, my room was filled with women. Of course, Priscilla always found out. I'd apologize and buy her sumthin' nice—jewelry, a horse or maybe a car, and promise to change, but there was just too much temptation. When people call you 'the King' all the time, you start to act like one. That's what happened to me."

Aaron paused for a moment and stared at his rough, calloused hands before continuing. "By the time Priscilla left we had grown so far apart that it didn't matter. I could deal with her leavin', but she took my little girl, Lisa Marie, with her." He looked away as he wiped his eyes. "I acted like I didn't care, but it hollowed me out. She was the only thing in my life that was real. I sure wasn't much of a daddy back then, but I truly loved that little girl."

More than how he spoke about Priscilla, the way Aaron uttered his daughter's name moved me. I could hear the longing and regret in his voice.

He paused to look at a car passing by on the highway before turning back toward me and beginning again. "I also got into drugs. Over time, that's what did me in. I can admit it now—I was addicted. You know, it's kind of funny, I'd always supported law enforcement fightin' what back then they called the War on Drugs. I'd work with police departments, shake hands at events, show up at fundraisers and donate money. Heck, I was made an honorary policeman by about every department in the country. Had a whole collection of police badges. But back then I didn't realize I was addicted myself. It just seemed different 'cause I got my drugs from doctors. I'd tell 'em I was tired and needed something to keep playin' and they'd pull out their little pad and scribble a prescription because I was famous.

"That was later in my career, but even when I was just startin' out the drugs were all around me. All of us musicians used 'em. We'd take bennies 'cause they gave us energy for those long days and weeks on the road. Honestly, back then I thought they were some kind of vitamin. You gotta remember that in those days most of our touring was by car or bus. We were always tired. It really wore ya' down. We'd play a gig until late in the night and then drive all day and play another. Day after day it was like that. The pills were what kept us going.

"Pretty soon me and the band, and my Memphis boys were poppin' 'em all the time. I was takin' so many that I had to take other drugs to help me wind down. Within a few years, I was takin' all of 'em—Demerol, barbiturates, amphetamines, Morphine, Valium—whatever it took to keep me workin'. I used drugs to wake up. Drugs to perform. Drugs to help me crap. Drugs to sleep. It got so bad that even when I was hospitalized for what my manager, Colonel Parker, told the newspapers was 'over exertion,' my boys would sneak me whatever I needed."

I felt like I was having an out of body experience as I listened to Aaron's story. One part of my brain was critically weighing the evidence, but another was responding as if I believed him completely. It was as if I was a character in some movie about time travel. Almost as a reflex, I heard myself asking, "Wasn't that the way it was in the sixties and seventies? Drugs were everywhere—weren't they? Didn't a lot of musicians die of overdoses back then?"

"It wasn't just them, it was everyone in the business—session players, backup singers, roadies. Yep," he said, shaking his head, "I lost plenty of good friends back then. 'Course I was so drugged up myself, I couldn't think clearly about it. To make things worse, the music was passin' me by. First it was the Beatles. Then it was bands like The Who and The Rolling Stones. I mean what kinda band names are those? Then it was singers like Bob Dylan." Shaking his head, he continued, "How could a guy with a voice like his sell more records than me? It just wasn't right. By the middle of the seventies, I was washed up. I tried going back to my roots, singin' blues and gospel, but it was too late. Kids wanted to listen to the new music. Even guys like Dylan," he said with a sigh.

I was having difficulty accepting what I was hearing. It was all so preposterous. I'd grown up hearing all the "Elvis lives…" stories from my mother: Elvis is alive and living in Argentina; Elvis appeared as a walk-on in the movie *Home Alone* to signal fans that he was still alive; Elvis is living in a small town in Arkansas where he works as a signing preacher. I always considered these proof that there are a lot of conspiracy nuts out there. Yet, everything Aaron was telling me matched what I knew about Elvis and, as he shared it, his story was chipping away at my reservoir of doubt. Could this be the one "Elvis lives" story that turned out to be true? Gradually, my doubts began to give way to the belief that I could have a first row seat to the biggest story in the history of rock and roll.

"So…this must've been toward the end of your career?" I calmly asked, as I tried to mask my growing excitement.

"Yeah, it was. Back then I knew I was headin' for something bad, but there was no one who could help me. You would think my boys—folks called 'em the 'Memphis Mafia'—would try to turn me around, but they weren't really my friends. They were just parasites looking for a handout. None of 'em would've been with me if I didn't write 'em a check. The same with the Colonel, all he cared about was making money or, I should say, *takin'* my money. He worked my ass off and hawked me like the carnival barker he was when he began his career. Bastard took half of what I earned. I've always suspected he stole even more."

"But didn't any of your family try to help you?" I asked.

"My daddy and some of my girlfriends could see what was happening. They were the only ones who tried to get me straight, but by then I'd lost all control. I was no longer a person, I was just a show pony, turned loose to entertain the crowd and then fed, groomed, drugged, and put back in my stall at Graceland until the next performance.

"By 1977, it seemed that everything was breakin' down. I had high blood pressure, glaucoma and problems with my colon. My weight was really balloonin' as well. I think I was up close to somethin' like 260 pounds. Can ya' believe that? Sometimes I'd get on stage and feel like a buffoon—all fat and puffy and forgettin' the words to songs. The fans didn't seem to care, but I did. I may have been the King, but I was a lonely and depressed king and I knew that soon I was gonna be buried with my Mama, even though I was still a young man."

Aaron took a long pause and looked off in the distance. "I had a concert in Rapid City, I think it was. My memory of it is kind of hazy, but I recall that when I returned to Memphis, I felt run down and really sick, man. As soon as I got home to Graceland, I went right to bed and fell into a fitful sleep. In the middle of the night, I got up and took a sleepin' pill, but it didn't help. I spent the night thrashin' and sweatin' in my bed until early in the mornin'. That's when mama visited me."

Instantly, my innate skepticism reasserted itself. "Wait…I thought your mother died much earlier in your life?"

"She did. She had passed away more than twenty years before, but there she was. At first, I smelled the perfume that she used to wear. It always reminded me of lilacs. Then I felt her fingers brushin' my hair and when I opened my eyes, she was standin' on the side of the bed. I know it may be hard to believe, but, God's truth, she was there just like you're sittin' across from me now. It filled me with such love. I felt so happy havin' her back even though it was only for a few seconds."

Aaron wiped his eyes and cleared his throat, "Mama told me that she missed me, but that she didn't want me to join her yet. It was too soon. She said that I had to get healthy and away from all the bad things in my life. She was so real; so close. I could feel the warmth of her breath and see her smile. I reached out to hold her hand, but as I did she faded away, leavin' me alone, sobbin' in my own private prison called Graceland."

Eight

Imagine meeting a stranger who tells you one of those strange stories that
you've always known was bullshit, but yet that some small part of you
wanted to be true: That there was a second gunman on the grassy knoll in
Dallas; that NASA scientists captured a UFO near Area 51; that Rob Pilatus
and Fab Morvan of Milli Vanilli really had great singing voices. That's how
I felt listening to Aaron. Everything he said sounded plausible, almost true.
And it wasn't just what he was saying, it was his voice, the way he spoke,
the words he used. My mind was churning as I listened to his story while
making sense of it all.

Aaron's voice interrupted my thoughts. "Sorry, kid, I'm rambling."

"No, no. Please keep going. I really want to hear everything."

He held my gaze for a moment as if considering what to say next. Then
he ran his hand through his hair, briefly nodded, and continued, "Well, over
the next few days I thought about what Mama had told me. I just couldn't
get it out of my head. I didn't want to die before my time. I needed to find
a way to get my life back—to be the person I started out to be before I was
the King. But how would I find him?

"Back in those days, people thought I was just some uneducated hick
who'd struck it rich. May've been some truth to that, but I was always curious about things. I don't know, maybe it was because I was insecure about
not goin' to college, but as I grew older I became a bit of a sponge tryin'
to learn different things. To give ya' an example, in one of my movies they
taught me to ride a horse. Never done it before, but it turned out that
I liked it—liked it so much that when I got back to Graceland I began
learnin' everything I could about horses. Then I started buyin' and sellin'

'em. Soon I had so many horses that we had to get a ranch in Mississippi. Same thing with martial arts. I learned about karate when I was in the Army in Germany. When I got home, I spent years trainin' under special masters across the country until I got my black belt. Later, I became fascinated with Indian mysticism. I read everythin' I could about it. Then I started meeting with spiritual masters and learnin' from them until I was an expert. I was like that with everything that caught my interest. I'd just find something and absorb it all.

"It was the same thing with genealogy. I think it was because Daddy and Mama didn't talk much about their families that I wanted to know more about where our people had come from. It seemed like reporters were always trackin' down folks who claimed to be long-lost relatives. I was flooded with letters from people who said they were blood. My boys read 'em for me, but most all the people just wanted money. When I was in Germany, I even heard a reporter say that I might have relatives living there!" Aaron shook his head in disbelief.

"I wasn't makin' much progress on my own so I hired this genealogy expert and asked him to figure out who my kin were and where they were from. I paid him some money, gave him all the information and papers I had about Daddy and Mama and then he disappeared for over a year. I'd actually forgotten about him until one day when he showed up at Graceland with all these documents and charts of my family. Turns out that Mama had relatives on the Mansell side of the family who were livin' in a remote town in the hills of Mississippi. I had never heard of 'em. Nobody—not Daddy or Mama or any reporters—had ever mentioned these kin."

"Sorry to interrupt, but I'm confused. What does this stuff about your family genealogy have to do with anything?" I asked.

Aaron stopped talking. Then he looked at me with knowing eyes and calmly said, "Kid, you're just like I was at your age, always after the answer before ya' even know the question. Why don't you just listen for a bit?"

Feeling chastised, I sat silently and waited for Aaron to continue.

"After that expert fella' left, I put away all that genealogy stuff and didn't think much more about it until I had that visit from Mama. That's when I got the idea."

"What id…?"

Aaron's irritated glare stopped me cold.

"Sorry," I said sheepishly.

Aaron paused, waiting long enough to let me know that his patience was coming to an end. "Dr. Nick had been my doctor for a long, long time and we were friends. He was always trying to get me clean, but in the end, he would always give me what I needed to get through a show. Now I had a plan that would get me healthy and finally give my life back to me, but I needed help. I shared my plan with him knowing that as my friend and doctor, he would keep it secret.

"You see, a few weeks earlier, I had been speakin' with one of my Yogi masters. He was helping me with my breathin' and explained that when he was in a full meditative state his heartbeat dropped to just a few beats per minute. He mentioned that the only way to get your heartbeat lower was a drug made from somethin' called a puffer fish. Funny name, ain't it? Anyway, I told this to Dr. Nick and after some research he confirmed that what the Yogi had said was true. With the right dose, this drug could make a person's heart rate drop so low that it would look like he was dead. Dr. Nick didn't want to give it to me because it was so dangerous. 'Elvis, you can't do this,' he said. 'It's too risky. There's not much research on this. I would have to estimate the dosage, and if I get it wrong it could kill you.'

"'Doc,' I told him. 'If I don't do this, I'm a dead man. This is the only way.' I could tell by the look in his eyes that he knew I was right, but he didn't say a word. He just disappeared for a few days and came back with a small, unmarked envelope with some powder in it. I remember he said, 'I strongly wish you'd reconsider. I read all the research I could find on this, but there isn't much. I'm really not certain about the dosage.'

"'Doc, we talked about this before,' I told him. 'You know I've got no choice.'

"He hesitated, then handed me the envelope, 'Mix it in a glass of water and drink it quickly,' he said.

"'Thanks, Doc,' I told him as I gave him a hug. 'Now, let's talk about what happens after that.'"

Aaron looked away suddenly without saying a word. When he turned back, I realized he was holding back tears. He let out a long sigh and finally continued, his voice cracking with emotion, "On August 16th, 1977, I was scheduled to head out on a tour starting in Portland, Maine. But with Dr. Nick's help, that was the day I was reborn.

"Early that morning, before I went to bed, I told my girlfriend, Ginger, that I was goin' to the bathroom." Aaron let out a wry laugh. "That's how crazy my life was back then. Instead of waking up in the morning, that's when I'd be headin' to sleep. Truth is that back then I slept whenever I wanted. I was the King, I didn't have to pay attention to things like night and day.

"My plan was to take the drug Dr. Nick had given me and get back into bed before it did its work. I'd fall asleep and then Ginger, or one of my boys—maybe Joe, Billy or Ricky—would discover me and think I'd died."

"Wait a second. Are you really telling me that you faked your death by taking some kind of neurotoxin made from a fish?"

"Kid…"

"I know, I know. I'll shut up."

Hesitantly, Aaron began again, "I remember as I got out of bed I heard Ginger tell me not to fall asleep in the bathroom. Little did she know. After closin' the bathroom door, I pulled the envelope out of a book where it was hidden and mixed the powder with a glass of water before tossin' the envelope in the trash with some discarded fan mail. You'd think that I'd have reservations; that I'd think about it for a bit before takin' the drug. But I knew what I had to do. Quickly, I put the glass to my lips, tilted it back and swallowed. The problem was that I had no idea how fast it would work. I'd never thought to ask Dr. Nick for that little bit of information. In hindsight, I wish I had. Instead of headin' back to bed, I decided to take a crap. That was my big mistake. I remember puttin' my butt on the toilet seat and then gettin' dizzy and fallin' over. My last thought as I hit the floor was, 'How embarassin'. Now everyone is going to think the King of Rock 'n Roll died while takin' a shit.' Then everythin' went black.

"I heard somewhere later that Ginger was the one who found me. Poor thing. She was a nice young gal. She yelled for Joe who tried to resuscitate me. Luckily, the drug worked, and I didn't feel a thing, but I guess I left quite a mess.

"Someone called for an ambulance and Dr. Nick arrived 'bout the same time as it did, just as we had planned. He got out of his car and helped the medics load me into the ambulance. Then he jumped in the back with my body and slammed the doors shut. Dr. Nick had arranged for them to take us to a secluded turn-out on the edge of some woods about ten miles away from Graceland.

"After they parked the ambulance, Dr. Nick gave me some kind of shot to bring me back to consciousness. It took me a few minutes to wake up and I was groggy as hell once I did, but for the first time in years I felt something, something other than loneliness. I felt my life comin' back to me.

"Once Dr. Nick was able to help me get to my feet, the ambulance drivers took the stretcher I was lyin' on and ran back into the woods. A few minutes later they returned with a body covered by a sheet and loaded it into the back of the ambulance. Then Dr. Nick turned to me, gave me a big hug and said, 'the King is dead. Good luck my friend.' A moment later, they were gone.

"Well, as ya' may have guessed, the body in the ambulance was a fake. It was a model of me made by a retired sculptor who had worked in London for this famous wax museum kind of place. I had secretly commissioned him to make it based on my measurements and some photographs I mailed him. To make it more realistic, I even asked him to include autopsy scars in the same places where a...what do ya' call that kind of doctor?"

"A pathologist?"

"Yeah. In the same places where a pathologist makes the cuts. After the model was completed, I had it shipped to Dr. Nick who staged it in the woods."

"How can this be true?" I asked incredulously. "Dr. Nick and the drivers kept this a secret all these years? What about the doctors at the hospital? The ones who were supposed to actually do your autopsy? Didn't the cops investigate? And no one's ever said a word all this time? How is it possible that all these people would keep it a secret?"

Aaron raised his eyes to mine. "I don't think the police investigated anythin'. They probably relied on the doctors. As to them, the answer is money, kid. Lots and lots of money. Although Dr. Nick was the closest thing I had to a friend, I paid him a fortune to recruit doctors and ambulance drivers who he could trust to keep our secret. I pretty much emptied out one of my bank accounts to pay them, but the way I spent money back then, I knew nobody would notice. I wasn't really sure if everyone would keep their end of the bargain and stay quiet forever, but all I needed was time to get away with the rest of my plan. That part I didn't share with anyone, not even Dr. Nick.

"After the ambulance pulled away, I walked through the woods along the road for 'bout a half mile to a deserted parking lot. Days earlier, I had a couple of the boys park one of my cars there—the car we've been driving in the last couple of days. I used to ask 'em to do crazy stuff all the time so I figured they wouldn't think nothin' of it, especially with all the commotion around my death. Opening up the trunk, I pulled off my filthy clothes, cleaned up, and changed into some jeans, an old work shirt, and some boots that I had stashed earlier. Then I put on a baseball cap, climbed into the front seat, and drove."

Nine

Aaron paused and looked at me as if expecting questions. But my brain was frozen trying to process what I had just heard. I was too stunned to say a word. Could it truly be possible that I was speaking with the real Elvis Presley? That he had managed to fake his death and live unnoticed for these last more than thirty years? My mind was swirling.

Sensing I wasn't going to ask anything, he continued, "I drove for two days on remote country roads, hiding out and trying to avoid any town or city as I made my way from Memphis and through Mississippi. I slept in the car at night. When I stopped for gas or food I wore my baseball cap pulled down low over my eyes and threw on a pair of sunglasses that I kept in the glove box. I had a few close calls. At one gas station there were a couple of women standing in front of me waitin' to pay at the cashier. The attendant asked if they'd heard the news that Elvis Presley had died. They didn't believe him at first; then they started cryin' and wailin' as if they were in terrible pain. I've gotta tell ya' kid, it really unnerved me. I walked around them, threw a twenty on the counter and tried to disguise my voice as I told the attendant to keep the change. Then I got outta there quick as I could, hopin' no one would notice me.

"For many miles, I followed a map that the genealogy fella' had drawn for me, but it was easy to get lost once I got into the Mississippi hill country. Many of the roads were marked with landmarks, not street signs. The map would say things like, 'turn left onto the dirt road marked by an old sign for fresh coon meat,' or 'take a left on the dirt road by the abandoned Dodge flatbed.' Things like that. Eventually, I ended up right about where I found you yesterday. Of course, thirty years ago it was even more remote, and

I had to get out of the car and search on foot for a bit before I found the road into the woods. Once I turned down it, I wasn't sure it even was a road, but I kept drivin'. I really didn't have any choice. I was so damn tired. What my Daddy used to call 'bone tired.' Tired of the crowds and travel. Tired of the drugs and women. Tired of the fame. Just plain tired of bein' the King. It seemed like I drove through those woods forever. I drove for so long that I began to get worried that I would run out of gas. I drove across dry creek beds and through an endless maze of pines. At times the road disappeared, and I had to guess on the direction, but I kept goin'.

"Finally, near dusk, after hours in the woods, I saw a valley ahead in the distance, covered in a cloud of low-hanging wood smoke. Through the trees, lanterns and an occasional outdoor wood fire came into view. As I drove closer, I began to see a few dozen scattered buildings looking like something from a hun'red years ago. I crossed an ancient wooden bridge to the entrance of what looked like a little village. It was real small. Then I stopped, turned on the light in the car and looked at my map before slowly creepin' forward. It was so damn quiet, like somethin' out of one of those old horror shows. As I drove I remember feelin' like I was bein' watched. I'm tellin' ya' it was spooky, man.

"After I passed a group of old wooden buildings, I turned left and drove slowly toward a house that was set up against the hillside. It was like the rest of 'em, but this one was a bit bigger and had a porch covered with broken wooden furniture. I came to a stop in front of it, parked and turned off the engine. Everything was still. It kinda felt like that Hitchcock movie, ya' know, the one with the Bates Motel. Quiet and creepy-like.

"I got out of the car, shut the door, and walked softly up the steps to the front door and knocked. From inside a dog barked angrily until I heard someone shush it. Then, I listened to the sound of squeakin' floorboards as someone came to the door to answer. There was a bit of fumblin' of the doorknob before the door opened a crack and I saw an old lady with long grey hair in a tattered dress. She was holding an ancient .22 caliber rifle and pointing it right at my nose.

"'Who are ya'? Wadda' ya' want?' she yelled.

"I threw up my hands and said, 'Aunt Rholetta? I'm your sister Gladys's son.'"

"Wait a second," I interrupted, "you mean to tell me that for more than thirty years you've been living in some remote hick town in Mississippi? You've got to be kidding me."

"Kid, you keep interruptin'. Ya' want to hear the story or not?"

I sighed, impatient for answers, and nodded.

"That little village was so small it didn't have a name. After I lived there awhile, I realized it didn't need one because folks almost never left. Most of 'em didn't know any other place, so why did they need a name for it? The place had been founded as a coal supply depot before the Civil War. When General Sherman marched through the South, the Union Army ripped up the tracks and the town was forgotten by the outside world. That was all right by the townsfolk. They had plenty of streams for fishin', game for huntin', and room for plantin'. Over the years the town grew more isolated while the rest of the world moved on. They never had modern inventions like electricity, television, or radio. 'Course every once in a while someone would go into town to get things they needed, but it wasn't very often 'cause it was a long trip."

"A bit different than living at Graceland, I'm guessing."

Aaron didn't notice my sarcasm. "Yeah, a bit. It took me some time to convince Aunt Rholetta who I was. Up til that point she never even knew I existed because she hadn't seen my Mama since they were little girls. It wasn't til I told her that my grandma was 'Doll' Smith that she began to believe me. Grandma's real name was Octavia Lavenia Smith, but everyone in the family called her 'Doll' 'cause she was so beautiful." He paused, before adding, "Guess that's where my Mama got her looks from as well."

I couldn't contain my impatience. "So what happened? Did you live with her? Who else lived there? Didn't anybody recognize you? For God's sake, you were the most famous person in the world! How could they not know you?"

"Hang on kid, hang on. Let me tell the story." He hesitated for a few moments before pulling back the curtains of memories long past.

"It took a bit of persuading, but finally Aunt Rholetta agreed I could stay for a while. I think she could see what bad shape I was in. I hadn't taken any of my drugs since I left Graceland, and I was on the edge of a breakdown. I could feel it happenin'. I'd had 'em before when I tried to get clean and each time I ended up in the hospital. So I knew what was comin'. When it hit me, it hit hard. I was laid up on an ancient, wooden framed bed in Rholetta's house. For weeks, life was a blur of me crappin' my sheets, pukin', sweatin', and wishin' I would die. Yet, whenever I had a moment of consciousness, I'd look over and see Rholetta sitting on a cane chair watchin' over me, putting a cold cloth on my head or bringing me soup she had made from a chicken she just slaughtered. You know, that was the first time I truly understood that I was a drug addict. Until that point, whenever I tried to kick it, if the withdrawal got bad enough and I asked for medication, there would be someone who would give me somethin'—a doctor, one of my boys, or maybe a girlfriend. But now there were no medications to make things better. I had to get dried out whether it killed me or not.

"As it turns out, it didn't—although it sure felt like it was killin' me at times. Slowly, I got better. Those first weeks were the worst, but it took months before I was able to get my strength back. I started easy by walkin' around Rholetta's place. She had a full garden out back as well as an orchard of apple and pear trees. Sweetest fruit I ever tasted. The creek behind her place was filled with trout, and she had chickens runnin' all over the place."

He pointed to the Cadillac parked across from us and grinned. "As you saw, over the years a few of them decided to use my car as a coop when I parked it in her barn."

"Yeah, I did notice that," I said, brushing some feathers off my jacket. "So why did you stay? Did you plan to live there forever? Were you really going to give up everything?"

"Well, ya' know, I thought about leavin' many times. I was only planning on hidin' out for a bit and gettin' straight. Just long enough for people to forget me. Then I was goin' to disappear and live somewhere else, maybe Mexico or Canada. But somethin' happened, and over the years I came to really love that little valley. To the people 'round there, I wasn't a celebrity. I was just kin of Rholetta's who came to live with her. I'm not sure that any of them had even heard of Elvis."

"Did Rholetta ever understand who you were?"

"She was always quiet, what you would call reserved, but on occasion she would ask about her sister. I would tell her about Daddy and Mama and our life in Tupelo and Memphis, but Rholetta hadn't seen Mama since they were young, so it must have been like hearing about a stranger. She never really got a chance to know Mama." Aaron looked down for a moment as his eyes began to mist.

"But did she ever ask about *your* life?"

"You mean as Elvis, the celebrity?" he smiled.

"Yeah."

"It was kind of strange, but Rholetta never asked about my history. I don't think she cared why I was there, she just liked having someone around. Once I was feelin' better, she'd take me out every day to help with the chores. In the spring, we'd plant beans, tomatoes, corn, turnips, okra, and squash. In the summer, we'd go huntin' for deer and boar. When fall come around, we'd harvest and preserve what we'd picked. Then there was always cuttin' firewood, fishin', repairin' the house, and a bunch of other things. Seemed like we were always busy. Most of our talkin' back then was Rholetta teachin' me things. I could care for the horses, 'cause I had 'em at Graceland, but everythin' else I had to learn. I snagged my pants one time and wore 'em ripped for a week 'cause I didn't know how to sew. Rholetta had to teach me how to do that.

"Anyhow, the closest we ever got to talkin' about my past was one afternoon when Rholetta asked me to get a couple of chickens for dinner. I went out back of the house to the fenced area where we kept 'em and spotted a chicken peckin' at some grass. Slowly, I walked toward it until I was only a few feet away. With my arms outstretched, I made a dive for it, but came up with nothin' but dirt. The same thing happened when I cornered it by the side of the barn. This went on for twenty minutes, before Rholetta's voice interrupted me. She'd been watchin' me from the back porch.

"'Elvis, what are you doin'?'

"'I'm gettin' a chicken like you asked,' I said.

"'Boy, I'm not seeing a lot of gettin', just a bunch of missin'!'

"With that, she walked down the steps toward the chicken. She reached into her apron pulled out a handful of corn, and dropped it at her feet. Several chickens quickly ran toward her. When they were inches away, Rholetta slowly bent over them and as fast as a strikin' rattlesnake snatched a chicken in each hand. For an old gal, that woman could really move!

"'Here,' she said as she handed me a chicken, 'you take care of this one.' With a single motion, she grabbed her bird by the neck and gave it a quick turn. It made an awful sound. As you might imagine, this was also somethin' I never had to do at Graceland," Aaron said light-heartedly.

"I guess I stood there looking kinda stunned, because Rholetta reached over with her other hand, grabbed my chicken by the neck and flicked it like a whip until I heard its neck snap too. She took them over to an old stump by the pen where we kept a couple of hogs and with a hand axe she chopped off the chickens' heads and began to gut them while the hogs ate all the innards she threw in their slop box.

"It was one of the most disgustin' things I'd ever seen and all of the sudden I found myself feelin' very sick. Rholetta must have noticed 'cause I heard her say, 'Boy, you alright? You don't look too good.' That was all it took, next thing I was sprinting to the outhouse.

"After I had cleaned up and felt a little better, I went back to the porch where Rholetta was dipping the chickens in a pot of boiling water. She looked at me to see if I was feeling better, then pulled one of the chickens out of the water and handed it to me to pluck. Problem was that I really didn't know what to do and Rholetta clearly got irritated waiting for me to get started.

"'Elvis, you don't know nothin' about planting or hunting or even pre-parin' a chicken. Didn't my sister teach you anything when you was growin' up?' she asked.

"'We lived in the city, Rholetta. We bought all our food at a store.'

"'Well, what about when you became a man, how come you didn't learn it then?'

"'I didn't have to,' I said feeling somewhat embarrassed. 'I had people who would make my food for me.'

Rholetta stopped pluckin' and looked at me for what seemed like for-ever. Then she grabbed one of my hands and opened it, running her fingers across my palm.

"'Damn, boy. These are the softest hands I've ever felt. What did you say you did back at home?'

"'I was an entertainer, Rholetta, a singer.'

"She continued to rub her fingers across my palm, searching for a callus. Then she let go and muttered, 'Must'a been a good one.' That was the only conversation we had about what I did."

"You mean in all that time you lived with Rholetta, she never understood how famous you were?"

"Nope. You gotta understand, kid, it didn't matter to her or anyone else there. It was like we were all off in our own little world. And in that world, it was much more important to understand whether the frost was over so you could plant than to understand who just signed a big recordin' contract."

Aaron paused for a moment and stared up the road.

"Rholetta taught me all about that world—how to live, how to feed myself. She also shared stories of her life in the valley and the folks 'round those parts. She reminded me so much of Mama—it was almost like she had never died. At first, Rholetta took care of me, but as she grew older I ended up taking care of her, and along the way I found I couldn't leave her. I owed her that much because she saved my life," he said, looking away as tears rolled down his cheeks.

"So you stayed for her?" I asked.

Aaron sniffled, wiping his nose with his sleeve, "Of course. But there was also the music. That was another reason I stayed."

"What music?"

"One night after I had been livin' at Rholetta's place for many months I heard instruments playing off down the holler. It reminded me of how much I missed my music. I'd been playing and performin' for more than twenty-five years, but when I found Rholetta, I stopped. At first, it was no big deal. I was more focused on gettin' healthy. But over time, I realized how much I needed the music. When I heard those notes cascading across the valley, I knew I had to follow 'em.

"It was the first time I had been away from Rholetta's and I was kinda worried about the reaction I would get from people as I walked through the village—I wasn't sure if they would recognize me, or treat me like an outsider. But folks were real friendly. I think they had gotten the word that I was related to Rholetta and 'cause of that they made me to feel at home.

"That music really drew me in. I wove between the trees and cabins as I headed toward it. It was music I hadn't heard since I was a little boy. Music of the hills. Music of the pines. Music of the soil. I wandered for about a mile before I saw an old wooden home with a large porch. Sitting on it were a group of men, one playing a fiddle, a couple on guitars, and one keeping rhythm on an old tin wash basin. As I walked toward them, they noticed me, and the music came to a stop.

"'Who are yew?' one of the guitar players asked.

"'I'm Rholetta's kin', I said. 'Liked what you're playin'.

"'You play?' the fiddle player asked.

"'A bit of guitar, but mainly I sing.'

"'Well, come on. You know *Lonesome Blues*?' asked the other guitar player. When I nodded they started playin' again and I stepped up onto the porch and began singin'. As I did, I saw the drummer and fiddle player smile at each other. 'Course I knew my voice would win 'em over. It always has. Ever since that day, I've been playing with Virgil, Wes, Dean, and Del. Sometimes we played once a week, sometimes we played every night. We were the only real entertainment in that little village, so we ended up getting a lot of gigs—weddings, birthdays, harvest celebrations, you name it," he said, laughing.

"What I liked most was that we played the songs that always meant the most to me. The songs of my parents and the Mississippi hill people. The songs that I wanted to sing before I became famous."

"Okay, you've told me about Rholetta and the music, but there must have been something else that made you stick around?"

Aaron looked at me, clearly puzzled.

"For God's sake! You were one of the biggest sex symbols in the world…"

"Oh," he said with surprise, "you're askin' about the ladies?"

I nodded.

"Well, I know this may be hard to believe, but I kind of left that part of my life behind as well. I'm not sayin' there wasn't a little foolin' around over the years, but the truth is, I was always busy. When you have to work to live, you don't have much spare time. Seems like I was always exhausted at the end of each day. Plus, it was a small place, so there weren't many gals around…and there were no secrets. It was bad enough when I was filmin' in Hollywood and I would go to dinner with Ann Margret or have a date with

Ursula Andress. It seemed that before I got back to my hotel there would be a picture in the paper. But it was even worse in that little village. It seemed that everyone knew everything 'bout everybody."

"You really expect me to believe that—that you had a thirty year dry spell? Seriously?"

"Kid, I'm just tellin' ya' how it was."

"Okay, okay, so why did you decide to leave?"

"Well, over the years, I thought about leaving many times. I'll admit it; sometimes I began to miss the fame. Can't say that it was easy goin' from the most popular person on Earth to workin' on a farm. And I'd wonder what was happening in the outside world. Were we at war with the Russians? How was the economy? Who was the most popular entertainer? Who was president? Mostly though, I thought about my little girl, Lisa Marie, and how much I missed her. I'd think about what her life was like without her daddy around. How lonely she must be. Can't say I was ever much of a daddy, and I don't expect a young fella' like you to understand, but there's just something special about a father and his little girl. There's a bond that's always there—doesn't matter the time or the distance. She was my constant source of wonder as the years went by. Sometimes, I was so curious about what was happenin' with her that I thought about goin' into town to see if I could find out anything. But I couldn't bring myself to leave. Call it selfishness…or fear. That little place was where I needed to be. I knew that if I went back too soon, I'd just get sucked back into the way I used to live, especially all the bad things. The only way to keep that from happenin' was to let some time pass until I was forgotten. Plus, I had somethin' there that had been missin' from my life. You know what I'm saying? And I couldn't leave Rholetta. Each year I could see her slowin' down more and more. It was a tough place to live when you're an old woman. She needed someone to care for her. So, I took care of her just like I would've taken care of my Mama."

Aaron's voice crackled with emotion as he said, "Truth is, if I hadn't found Rholetta, I wouldn't be here now. Kid, without her I'd be dead."

Ten

We sat quietly, the stillness enveloping us, our thoughts disturbed only by the sound of an occasional car passing on the highway. In the silence, I waited for Aaron to regain his composure and considered what I'd just heard. My excitement in learning Aaron's true identity was tempered by the obvious sorrow he'd felt over what he missed in his battle with the seductions of fame. It was a common story with other entertainers, politicians, and athletes. Yet, seeing it through his eyes and hearing the sacrifice he had made to avoid the temptation made the pain more immediate and palpable.

Aaron inhaled deeply and began again. "It was about six months ago, that Rholetta took ill and died. Most everyone came up to our house; they brought food and helped me put her to rest underneath a large oak that sat atop the hill behind her place. But after everyone left, I felt alone again, just like when Mama died. It churned up a lot of black feelings in my soul. After we buried Rholetta, I continued to keep up things like I had before, but I was just goin' through the motions. I fed the chickens, cut the wood, made repairs on the house, but it wasn't the same. I even stopped goin' over to Virgil's to play music with the boys. It wasn't 'till a few weeks ago that I snapped outta my fog and realized that it was time. Time to go back. Time to find something I've been missing."

In a karmic bit of timing, my phone, which I had placed beside me on the picnic table when we sat down, began to vibrate.

"What's that?" asked Aaron, noticing it for the first time.

"What, my phone?"

"That's a telephone?"

"Yeah, of course," I said, as I picked it up.

"I used to have one of those in my car," he said proudly. "Course it was a whole lot bigger."

It was only then that I realized Aaron had missed the advent of the Smartphone while he was up in the hills of Mississippi. I held it up to him. "Everyone has them now. You can call anywhere in the world, even send a text." He looked at me with a dumbfounded expression. "It vibrated to let me know I just got a message from someone."

I looked at the screen. It said:

A. J., I'm getting worried. Please let me know you're all right. I love you.

"What's it say?" he asked.

"Nothing. Never mind," I replied and stuffed the phone back in my jacket pocket.

"In that case, how 'bout we get goin' so I can get us some more money."

With that, Aaron rose from the concrete bench and headed toward the car. As I watched him walk away I felt bewildered, almost disoriented, but I couldn't tell if it was from the tale he had just told or the message from Mo. My head began to throb again as I stood up and followed him back to the car.

"Where exactly are we heading now?" I asked as I slid in and shut the door.

"Well, we need money, right? I figured we go to Memphis. Hopefully, my old place is still around. If it is, there was a secret place where I stashed some money just in case of an emergency."

"Old place? Do you mean Graceland? How do you think you're gonna get in?"

"My plan is to knock on the door and explain that I lived there when I was younger, and I want to show the place to my grandson—that'll be you," he said pointing in my direction. "Once we're in, you'll distract them, and I'll say that I've got to use the bathroom. Then I'll go and get the money."

It was only then that I began to understand how convinced Aaron was that he had escaped his life of stardom; that he was some forgotten entertainer of the past and that Graceland was just a piece of Memphis residential property that had had multiple owners over the years. How was I going to explain things to him?

"Aaron," I asked, "did you ever receive any news at all from the outside when you were living with your Aunt Rholetta?"

"Not often, and it's been a long while since I did. We only had a few people who left the village—mainly young people, and they rarely returned. Most of the time the news would come from the Stickley brothers who would get their old truck started and go into town for supplies every year or two. They would load their truck with produce we'd grown and sell it on the side of the road. They'd use the cash to buy a few things that we needed—like seed, flour or sugar—in the closest town, Hickory Flat. It was about a four-hour drive. That's how I got the Caddy goin' again—when the Stickleys went to town after Rholetta passed, I had 'em buy a new battery and five gallons of gas. Put 'em in and she started right up.

"Anyway, Hickory Flat's a little town, really not much of a place at all. It does have a bar though. We knew that because the Stickley boys would always return drunk as hell with crazy stories."

"Stories about what?"

"Some of 'em I expect were true like the Berlin Wall comin' down and the U.S. at war in some of the A-rab countries. But some things were just plain silly. Like when they came back from town last year and claimed that a colored man had been elected President of the United States! That's when we knew they'd been drinkin' all our money. When they returned from that trip, we all swore we'd never let 'em go again without one of us keeping 'em company," he said with a soft chuckle.

My God, I thought, he doesn't know anything that has happened in more than thirty years. I thought back to my history classes in school. Jimmy Carter was the last president he remembers. He's never heard of the Internet, the Challenger explosion, Chernobyl, or the AIDS epidemic. It was stunning to imagine. Of course, on a positive note, at least he'd missed out on Members Only jackets, Jerry Springer, and the cinematic greatness of Adam Sandler. I was going to have to find some way to let Aaron know all that he missed.

We got into the Cadillac, closed the doors, and Aaron fired up the engine and pulled slowly onto the asphalt.

"So, you really haven't had much news of the outside world?"

"Not much. I'm sure there have been changes and other things that have happened, but I haven't really missed it. Like I said, I was busy in the valley with Rholetta."

It was then I should have said something. Something about how Graceland was the second most visited home in the country next to the White House, or that millions of copies of Elvis songs were still being sold around the world each year, or how grocery store rags like the *National Enquirer* constantly carried bogus headlines like: "Elvis is Alive!" That said, given my situation, maybe I should have reevaluated my feelings about the *National Enquirer*'s journalistic standards.

Instead, I chickened out. I said nothing. I just leaned back trying to sort things out in my head as we drove through Northeastern Mississippi, toward the Tennessee border.

Sweet Jesus, what was I getting myself into?

* * *

Perhaps it was the warm summer sun on my face or the exhausting process of trying to make sense of Aaron's story, but I drifted into a sleep filled with visions of Elvis. It was like a highlight reel from the past, as if my brain was subconsciously testing for pattern recognition. I'm not sure how long I was asleep when I felt something pulling me back to consciousness.

"Kid. Kid. Your phone thing is shaking again," Aaron said as he pointed to my phone vibrating on the dashboard. I picked it up and drowsily looked at the text. It was from Mo again.

A. J., you okay? Answer me, you little shit!

I stared at the message for a few minutes before letting out a long, audible sigh. Then I started typing:

I'm fine. Really sorry. Just having a hard time handling this. Need some time…

I turned off the phone and put it away in the pocket of my shirt.

"Everything okay?" Aaron asked as he steered along Highway 78.

"Some problems at home, but nothing to talk about."

"Fair enough. Fair enough," he replied, looking out the windshield at the road ahead and a highway sign that read "MEMPHIS – 37."

Eleven

As we drew upon the outskirts of Memphis an hour later, I sensed something different in Aaron. It wasn't anything he said, it was just something I became conscious of as I watched him. He was driving slowly looking out the driver's window as if searching for something. Was it anxiousness? Anticipation? Worry? With a single sentence, I realized it was confusion.

"Where is everything?"

"What's the matter?" I asked.

"It's all different. It's so crowded—where'd all these people come from? I don't recognize anything. Where do I go?" he asked, with growing agitation.

"Hang on. No problem. I'll use my phone," I said, as I pulled it out of my pocket and turned it on.

"Who you gonna call? Do you have folks in Memphis?"

"No, no. I'm not going to call anyone. I'm going to use the map."

"Of course that thing has a map," he responded with undisguised sarcasm as he rolled his eyes. "The next thing you'll tell me is that it plays music too!"

I ignored him and said, "Take a left."

I continued to give Aaron directions as we traveled through a mixture of run-down houses, fast food restaurants, and auto repair shops. Then I said, "Take a right onto Elvis Presley Boulevard."

"That's more like it!" he responded with pride. "I remember when they renamed it. Think I was the first one to get my own street in Memphis. We should be getting close now, but are you sure this is the right way?"

"It should be. That's what the map says."

"Well, everythin' is really different. Graceland used to be on the edge of town, kind of in the country. Everythin' around here looks wrong. It's all shops, apartments, and food joints. It just don't feel right."

Looking a few blocks ahead, there was a large group of people milling about across the street from a souvenir shop. It had to be the place; it had to be Graceland. I couldn't wait any longer.

"Aaron, there's something I've got to tell you."

"What's that?"

"I'm not sure how to break this to you. I know you think that after thirty years that you—I mean, Elvis—has been long forgotten by people. But the truth is, Elvis is still hugely popular."

"What d'ya' mean?" he asked as his eyes latched onto the enormous queue of people standing across the street in front of Graceland. "What the hell…?"

"Take a left here and find a place to park the car. We've got to talk."

Aaron turned and proceeded for a few blocks before finding a space in a parking lot next to a barbecue restaurant.

He turned off the engine and looked at me.

"Okay, what's goin' on?"

"I've been trying to tell you. Elvis is more famous today than ever. People from all over the world come to pay tribute to you—I mean, him. His records still sell millions of copies. Graceland has become almost like a religious site for fans. Every day the Elvis faithful gather to tour the mansion and pay their respects at his grave."

"You mean…?" His voice trailed off.

"Yes. All those people are here for you."

Aaron looked stunned as he tried to comprehend what I had told him. His fingers continued to grip the steering wheel and his eyes stared off vacantly over the hood of the Caddy. We sat motionless for minutes. Finally, I broke the silence, asking, "Do you still want to go to Graceland? We don't need to worry about breaking in. We can just buy a ticket and stand in line with everyone else."

Aaron turned his head slowly toward me and nodded, and we stepped out of the car and walked down the street to join the crowd waiting to purchase Graceland tickets. As we stood in line, I could see that Aaron was trying to make sense of what he saw around us. It had been twenty minutes since we had parked, and he still had not uttered a word. Surrounding us in line to buy tickets were people from every country and walk of life. By the sound of their voices, I could identify tourists from Britain, France, Germany, Japan, Korea, and Australia. Although most were in their sixties or seventies, many were college-aged, and there were even a few clusters of teenagers.

The emotions of those waiting in line varied as much as their age and nationality. A group of Japanese men wearing matching white sequined jumpsuits and pompadours sang *Hound Dog* complete with hip gyrations and exaggerated sneers. A bald, pot-bellied American man belted out an a cappella rendition of *Always Love You* to his blushing wife. Two teachers fought a losing battle trying to keep their class standing patiently in line as they explained the rules for a school field trip. Many people were mopping their brows and fanning themselves in the early afternoon heat and humidity. Others clung solemnly to a photograph, well-thumbed concert ticket, or other personal remembrance of Elvis as if it were a religious relic.

At least a few people were openly distraught, like the attractive middle-aged woman standing alone behind us. As we slowly moved forward in line, we heard her quietly weeping and in need of comfort. Finally, Aaron turned to her and broke his silence, asking in a low voice, "Ma'am, are you alright?" She nodded, pressing the tissue to her nose and eyes, but continued to cry. A few minutes later, Aaron turned again and placed his hands on her shoulders. Looking deep into her eyes, he said, "Ma'am, I know we don't know each other, but you look like you need a shoulder to lean on." With that, he drew her in a deep embrace. Instantly, the woman broke down and began sobbing pressing her face against Aaron's chest.

It took a few minutes before her crying subsided, all the while Aaron patiently patted her on the back before finally asking, "What's the matter, darlin'?"

"I thought I could do this. I really thought I could for Beth..." Her voice trailed off momentarily before she cleared her throat and began again. "She was my sister and my best friend. I miss her so much..."

"Ya' sound so sad. Can ya' tell me about her?" Aaron offered.

The woman blew her nose on the tissue and nodded.

"We were twins, but we were so different. Beth always wore skirts; I wore bell-bottoms. I ran with some of the wilder kids at school; Beth was a band geek. But the biggest difference was that I was a Beatles fan and for Beth, there was no one but Elvis. After years of listening to her go on about him, she wore me down and I agreed to go see him in concert."

She paused for a moment, looking down at an old black-and-white photograph. Then she held it out to us. It showed two teenage girls with long blonde hair, arms around each other; one dressed in jeans and a peasant blouse; the other in a summer dress.

"That's us at that show." She hesitated before saying, "You know what? Beth was right. Elvis *was* amazing. He more than lived up to the hype. It didn't matter whether he was singing a ballad, telling a story or rockin' out, everyone in the crowd that night was spellbound. But the best part of the concert was seeing the happiness on my sister's face. God, she loved Elvis."

Her voice wavered, and she began crying again, "I can't believe I'm telling you all this. I don't even know you."

Aaron squeezed her shoulder and said, "Some things, ma'am, are easier tellin' to a stranger."

She looked deep into his eyes for a moment as if searching for a reason to trust him. Then she began again.

"A week after that show, Beth was hit by a car. She never regained consciousness and died two days later." She was silent for a few minutes as she dabbed her eyes with a tissue. "The next years were rough for me. I didn't know how to go through life without my sister. I got into drinking and drugs and a few unhealthy relationships. My life spun out of control for a long time. Then, a few years later, when I was in college, I heard Elvis would be playing a concert nearby. This was back in the mid-70s. He was well past his prime then, but I decided to go, to honor Beth. I got lucky and was able to get a ticket in the front row. That would have made my sister so happy."

She looked ahead as the crowd moved slowly toward the ticket booth. "Elvis looked awful that evening. He was bloated, forgot the words to songs and stumbled around the stage. I felt embarrassed for him. From personal experience, I could tell he was stoned. But here's the thing, in the middle of the song *I'll Remember You*, he walked toward me, leaned over the edge of the stage, and reached out for my hand. He looked into my eyes as he sang the chorus. Do you know it?" she asked, and began softly singing.

"I know this sounds silly, but at that moment it wasn't Elvis who was singing those words to me—it was Beth. I was certain of it. I could feel her presence, feel her there with me, and it changed my life. I've been an entirely different person since. I kicked drugs, earned my degree, had a great career and traveled the world. I've never married, but I have plenty of friends. Elvis gave that to me," she paused. "I only wish he were still alive, so I could tell him." At this, she broke into tears and began softly sobbing again.

Instinctively, Aaron pulled her toward him and patted her back. As he did, I heard him say, "Don't worry honey, he's here. He's here," as he flashed me just a trace of a smile.

* * *

Despite the attire of some of the people around us, the ensemble Aaron had purchased at Potts Camp was getting him some odd looks. His outfit looked like it had been created by a rogue Parisian fashion designer with a fetish for the 1970s. I could tell the attention—and the polyester—were making Aaron uncomfortable, so I excused myself, walked across the street, and bought a cheap t-shirt from a guy hawking them out of the trunk of his car. I returned and tossed the shirt to Aaron. "You'll be cooler in this. Why don't you go to the car and change? I'll save our place in line."

A few minutes later, Aaron returned sporting a gray t-shirt with the words "Elvis Lives!" emblazoned in large letters on the front and back. I stifled a laugh as he leaned over and whispered, "Ya' don't think ya' could've found anything a bit more subtle?"

As the line drew closer to the ticket booth, Aaron grew quieter, more solemn. It was as if he was being emotionally whipsawed, trying to piece together memories with the reality surrounding him. After nearly an hour in silence, we reached the booth, and with most of our remaining money I purchased two tickets for the Graceland Platinum Tour. From there, we were loaded onto a shuttle bus and driven across the street and through those iconic iron gates adorned with musical notes. Although I'm not religious, for me it was an almost spiritual moment. So much of the music I played, that we all played, flowed from what was behind those gates. Graceland was the headwater.

We unloaded from the bus at the mansion entrance and I showed Aaron how to use his tour audio player. It was one of those devices that you wear on a cord hanging from your neck with earphones. It was difficult to get him to pay attention to my instructions because he was distracted and kept looking over at the mansion. When the front door opened to begin the tour, I stepped forward with the crowd, but felt Aaron's hand on my shoulder holding me back. "Let's let everyone else go first," he whispered. Then a few moments later, he took a deep breath and stepped through the doorway.

Twelve

I don't know if you have ever taken the tour of Graceland, but it's much smaller than what you might imagine. I had always envisioned it as this grand antebellum estate—like something you would see in *Gone with the Wind*. In reality, it's more of a large suburban house, one frozen in the style of an owner who enjoyed the tasteless extravagance of the 1970s. But as a symbol of rock music, there's nothing bigger.

We stepped into the foyer and I turned and looked into an almost blindingly white living room, which contained a fifteen-foot long white couch and two white sitting chairs. Adjacent was a music room with a baby grand piano, framed perfectly by a pair of stained glass windows, depicting two large peacocks. It wasn't hard to imagine the excitement of musicians who accompanied Elvis while he played that piano. For many of an earlier generation, this was a musical Mecca where rock 'n roll adherents visited to pay tribute to the King. Late one night while on tour as a young musician, Bruce Springsteen even jumped the gate, hoping for the chance to meet Elvis. Unfortunately, he was on tour elsewhere. But in the 1970s, I suspect this would have been a common occurrence.

I turned to ask Aaron about the celebrities, performers, and politicians who had been entertained in the room, certain that he would have some story to tell, but when I looked over, Aaron was gone. Looking down the hallway, I caught a glimpse of him stepping over a gold velvet sash that blocked the stairs to the second floor. Then, he disappeared.

The second floor contained Elvis's bedroom and the bathroom where he had died. Was that where Aaron was talking about hiding his stash? Our audio player had said that at the request of the Presley family it had always been closed to the public. Did that floor have guards or an alarm system? What if Aaron was caught? He was going to get us both thrown in jail. I just knew it.

Feeling my anxiety rising, I took a deep breath to calm myself and walked back to the living room. I pretended to be listening to my audio player and mingled with the crowd for a few minutes, until the last of them drifted down the hallway. It was then that I heard a security guard yell, "Hey you! Get down from there. No one is permitted on the second floor!"

Rushing toward the staircase, I arrived just as Aaron was stepping back over the sash, facing a very irritated guard, who quickly patted Aaron down to make sure he hadn't stolen anything. With little thought, I blurted out the first thing that came to mind, "Grandpa, where have you been? You've got to stay with me. You know you can't be wandering away by yourself." I turned to the guard and whispered, "I'm sorry, it's the Alzheimer's. My fault for not watching him more closely." Grabbing Aaron's arm, I ushered him quickly down the hallway, while looking over my shoulder at the guard who eyed us suspiciously. We caught up with the rest of our tour group as we passed through the kitchen. When we did, Aaron leaned over to me, his voice seething with rage. "Damn Colonel. He cleaned me out."

"What do you mean?"

"My safe. It was hidden behind a mirror in the bathroom. I always kept about $50,000 cash in there just for emergencies. Everything in the room is just like I left it, includin' the safe. But, when I opened it, it was empty. There was only one other person who knew about it and had the combination—Colonel Parker. That bastard took my money."

"Well, there's no chance of doing anything about it now. I heard Colonel Parker died about ten or fifteen years ago."

"Good riddance! He can't steal from me anymore," he said in an angry whisper.

I gave Aaron a gentle push and we continued to move away from the guard and toward the famous Jungle Room, or as I like to think of it— Ground Zero for Rock 'n Roll debauchery. Keith Moon driving his car into a swimming pool, Hendrix setting fire to his guitar, Led Zeppelin's Boeing 707, Ozzy Osbourne peeing on the Alamo, MTV *Cribs*—it all began here. Elvis was the first musician with the money to indulge his every desire, and the legendary Jungle Room was where he started. Entering the room, we were surrounded by dark burl tables, a zebra-skin-covered couch, and matching ottoman, as well as Polynesian furniture—all framed by green shag carpeting on both the floor *and* the ceiling. There was even a waterfall running down one of the walls. Not my taste, mind you, but you had to give Elvis credit for his commitment to excess. Perhaps sensing what I was thinking, Aaron leaned over to me and murmured, "It was the times, kid. It was the times."

After exiting the Jungle Room, Aaron and I moved with the crowd through the Pool Room and into the TV Room, complete with its three large color console televisions embedded in a row across the wall. From there we entered what our audio player indicated was formerly Elvis's racquetball court. Now, it housed rows of glass display cases containing his bejeweled concert jumpsuits, guitars, awards, and other memorabilia. There were so many gold records on the walls that at first glance I thought they were wallpaper.

Aaron noticed me looking at them and leaned over and poked his elbow into my ribs. "Bet none of your Indian bands have done anythin' like that," he said proudly.

"It's 'indie,'" I protested before noticing Aaron's smirk and realizing that he was teasing.

After a few minutes, the ushers gestured to us to move along and we exited the room and joined the stream of fans waiting to visit the Meditation Garden. Unlike in the mansion, the mood here was silent, almost reverential. People slowly shuffled forward fingering their Elvis artifacts—a photograph, a scarf, or an album cover—as if they were the rosary beads of the faithful entering St. Peter's Basilica. After more than an hour, we finally arrived at the inner courtyard, the final resting place for members of the Presley family. Flowers, photographs, ribbons, votives and other offerings from the faithful covered the gravesites.

When we passed the final resting place of Gladys Presley, Aaron gripped the low iron railing in front of the grave as if experiencing sudden pain. "Oh, Mama," he moaned in a low mournful voice, his emotions laid bare. A man next to me looked strangely at Aaron and commented to his companion, "He said 'Mama'?" Aaron didn't take notice, and I could see him mumble a few words before he moved forward and stood solemnly in front of Vernon's grave. After a few minutes, he turned and walked quickly past Elvis's gravesite and toward the exit without more than a glance at it or the surrounding crowd.

Once we left the grounds and headed back to the shuttle, I turned to Aaron, "Are you okay, man? That must have been tough. I can't imagine how you must feel visiting your parents' graves after all this time. I'm sorry."

"Brings back a lot of memories. No one had a Mama or a Daddy like mine," he said wiping a tear from his eye. He handed me his audio player and took a seat in the back of the empty shuttle bus. Gesturing to the area to the side of the mansion, he said, "Over there's where I taught Lisa Marie to drive a little dune buggy. She was just a child, only about eight or nine years old, but the girl could drive. The boys and I used to race go-karts around this driveway during the summer when we weren't on tour. Out back is where we had some of our horses. Priscilla and I would ride there together on warm evenings when we were first married." Aaron inhaled deeply and continued, "When being a celebrity got to be too much, I could always come here and get away from things. Yeah, we had us some good times here."

The vibration of my phone distracted me. Pulling it out of my pocket, I read the text:

A. J., we need to talk. You owe me that.

Suddenly, I was slammed back to real life. I let out an involuntary exhale, causing Aaron to turn and stare at me as I hurriedly typed my reply:

I just need time to clear my head. I'm sorry.

This wasn't a conversation I wanted to have nor the place to have it.

When the bus reached the plaza, I tapped Aaron's shoulder and told him I'd meet him in the car after I returned our audio players. He gave me a distracted nod before exclaiming, "Wait, wait. I almost forgot!" With that, Aaron bolted off toward two jet planes parked behind the plaza.

"Aaron, what's going on?" I yelled as I chased after him.

He pointed ahead. "Those were my planes. The small one is a Lockheed Jetstar. I named it *Hound Dog II*. I bought it when I was renovatin' the bigger plane. That one's a Corvair. Named it after Lisa Marie. Really decked that one out. It had everything—color televisions, bedroom, conference room, kitchen...everything. Think I was the first celebrity to have his own jet," he said with a touch of pride.

"That's great, but why are we going to see them?"

Aaron leaned toward me as we walked and said, in a whispered voice, "I had another hiding place for my cash. This one was on the *Lisa Marie*. It's a little lock box with a combination hidden behind the telephone. I always kept about $20,000 in there in case of emergencies. Once, we had to gas up the plane, but my boys had left my checkbook at Graceland. The airport filled up the plane anyway 'cause they knew who I was and that I was good for it, but after that I had that lock box installed just in case. With luck that money will still be there."

We arrived just in time to tag onto a small group of tourists being led by a guide up the ramp to the rear entrance of the *Lisa Marie*. We walked into the galley and then past the bathroom. But what a bathroom! All of the fixtures were gold, even the toilet. I stood there gawking, until Aaron leaned over and whispered, "A king needs his throne," and then walked past, laughing.

From there, I followed Aaron through a teak-paneled bedroom with a queen-sized bed covered in a pale blue velvet bedspread. He nodded his head toward the bed with a salacious wink, but continued walking through to the conference room area where six plush leather chairs surrounded an oval glass table.

By now we had fallen well behind the rest of the tour, which was nearing the cockpit of the plane. It was then that I heard Aaron say in a loud voice, "A. J., I don't feel well. Don't feel well at all. I'm really dizzy. Think I'm gonna faint." With that he landed with a thud in one of the chairs at the end of the table.

Before I had the chance to react, the guide leading the tour appeared next to me and took Aaron's hand feeling for a pulse.

"Are you okay sir? Sir?" Turning to me, he reached for his cell phone. "Hang on. Stay calm. I'll call for help."

I glanced at Aaron. He was motionless, his eyes closed. Was he still alive? I cupped my hand near his nose and was relived to detect a trace of a breath.

"Shit!" exclaimed the guide. "My phone's dead. I forgot to charge it last night. Please stay with your friend. I'm going to go get help!"

I watched as the guide motioned the rest of the tourists off the plane and scurried to find a medical attendant. I felt my pulse accelerating as perspiration coated my body. What the hell was I going to do now? What would I tell them about Aaron when they returned? What if he had had a heart attack? How would I explain things to the authorities? Did Aaron even have identification? What would I say if he died? My mind spun with scenarios. Did I tell them he was a stranger I met on the Graceland tour, or someone who gave me a ride? Did I come clean about his real identity? What if they did a DNA test and discovered the truth about who he was?

Hang on, old man!

A hand on my shoulder gave me a start. "They all gone?" whispered Aaron, who was unexpectedly standing beside me.

"What's going on?" I demanded. "You scared the crap out of me!"

"Move out of the way. You're standin' next to the telephone."

I stepped aside as Aaron reached up and removed the telephone, an old-fashioned rotary model from the 1970s, and handed it to me. Then I watched as he pressed the wooden panel behind the shelf that held the phone and slid it back, revealing a small safe. Aaron quickly gave the dial a few turns, pulled the door open and reached in.

"Son of a bitch! It's empty!" he cursed. "Goddamn, Colonel Parker! Now he's cheatin' me from the grave!"

Hearing the sound of voices, Aaron quickly closed the lock box, slid back the panel, and then took the telephone from me and returned it to its place. Then he slowly began walking toward the front of the plane where he was met by the tour guide and an EMT.

"Sir, I've brought medical help. Do you need to sit down?"

Aaron waved them off. "No, no. I'm fine. Appreciate your kind help, but I'm okay. Just a bit tired, I guess. Happens sometimes at my age. I faint every now and then when I get too excited. Bet you get a lot of that here with people being so worked up at being in the home of the greatest entertainer in all of history."

"Are you sure?" asked the EMT. "I really should check you as a precaution."

"It's not necessary. Our car's parked real close. I'll be fine. But thank you."

The EMT looked at me questioningly to which I shrugged my shoulders in response and followed Aaron down the ramp and back to the ticket plaza. When we arrived, I told Aaron I would return the audio players and meet him at the car. He gave me a distracted wave, still angry at his missing money, and stalked off toward the exit.

I headed to the ticket office where I stood in line with dozens of other tourists waiting impatiently to return our audio players. On the wall next to me, I noticed a bulletin board with a sign above it that said: "The King's Korner." It contained small posters, news clippings and flyers advertising various events for the Elvis faithful. One of them caught my eye and I pulled out my phone to take a quick picture before handing the audio players to a clerk.

When I arrived back at the car, I found Aaron in a stupor slouched in the front seat. "You sure you're doing okay?" I asked quietly.

"I just don't understand," he mumbled as he began to tear. "Mama, Daddy, Priscilla, my baby girl, it was all here. It was just yesterday, yet it was so many years ago. How can it be? How can it be? Oh Lord, what have I done?"

Out of reflex, I put a hand on his shoulder and gently said, "You had to do what you did. There just wasn't any other way. Aaron, it's okay."

"No, it's not! Don't you get it? I had people that loved me, that depended on me. I should have been part of their lives. Instead, I left. I just split."

"No one knows what you were going through—and that's an understatement. You said it yourself, if you hadn't done it, you wouldn't be alive anyway."

"I should'a been with my family. I should'a been with 'em," he said, his voice trailing off.

Let me stop for a moment and ask: Have you ever gone someplace, maybe a shopping mall or amusement park, and seen one of those domino cascades people set up to break a record? You know, where a person has laid out lines of black tiles in a complicated obstacle course with no clear visible end? As I opened my mouth to respond to Aaron, I had a momentary vision of my forefinger softly pushing the first tile.

"You know, maybe it's not too late. Take a look at this," I said, holding up my phone.

"You want me to look at your phone? Why?"

"Not my phone, a picture I took."

"I thought you said that thing was a phone. It takes pictures too?" he said, his voice filled with disbelief.

"Never mind that, just look at this," I said, shoving the phone in front of him.

"Sorry, kid, my eyes aren't what they used to be. I can't read that thing."

"Ok. I'll read it. It says: 'Lisa Marie Presley celebrating the release of her new album *Storm and Grace*. Live at the Roxy in Los Angeles, June 26th. Do you understand what that means, Aaron? That's six days from now. We can drive there. It's the perfect chance for you to see your daughter!"

As I uttered these words, I could see the dominoes falling, running toward an unknown horizon.

Thirteen

Looking back now, I'm not exactly sure what compelled me make the offer to Aaron. There was something instinctive that drew me to him, that made me want to ease his pain and care for him in a way that I had never felt with even my own father. Aaron stared at me without saying a word. Had he heard what I had just said? For a moment, I wondered if the poor old guy had just had a stroke. Then I saw a look of surprise register on his face.

"My little girl's a singer?" he said excitedly.

"Yes, she is. She's got a few albums."

"What kind of music?"

"Mainly rock," I replied, waiting for the inevitable question.

After a momentary pause—boom—there it was: "Is she any good?"

How should I respond? I had only heard a few of Lisa Marie's songs. Personally, I felt they were overproduced and uninteresting and she certainly wasn't the type of artist that my fellow musicians and I discussed. I didn't want to hurt Aaron's feelings, but I didn't want to mislead him either.

"To be honest, Aaron, I haven't listened to much of her stuff. She has a smoky, sultry kind of voice, but she hasn't had any popular hits yet. Some people wonder if her last name has helped her or held her back. Being the daughter of the King is a big weight to carry, especially if you choose to go into the music business."

Aaron considered my response before asking hopefully, "Do you know anything else 'bout her?"

"A few things. Given her last name, she pops up in the news from time to time."

"Well?"

I hesitated before replying, "I think she's been married at least four times, including for a short bit to Nicolas Cage—he's a movie actor—and Michael Jackson."

"Four times? My poor little girl. Michael Jackson? I don't know that other guy, but that name sounds familiar."

"Do you remember a group called the Jackson 5? He was the lead singer."

"You mean that little boy who could dance so well? She married him?"

"Well, he grew up to be a bit more than that. He left his brothers' band and went solo to become one of the most famous entertainers in the world. Many compared him to you—or, rather, Elvis. Some people thought Lisa Marie married him because he reminded her of her father."

Aaron gave me a confused stare.

"He was a pop idol, larger than life. Everyone in the world knew his name. He could act, sing, dance—the man had moves and an almost magnetic sexuality. Problem was, he became a bit of a nut case—or let's just say he was 'eccentric.'"

"What'ya' mean?"

"Well, for starters, he built a mansion in California and named it Neverland—after the Peter Pan story—and filled it with expensive art as well as amusement rides and exotic animals. People always compared it to Graceland. He even had a pet chimpanzee, like Elvis. He lived at the place as kind of a recluse. There were all kinds of crazy stories about what happened there." I held back from going into other details.

"You keep saying 'was' and 'had'. Isn't he alive anymore?"

I slowly shook my head. "No. Jackson was also addicted to prescription drugs. His doctor gave them to him so that he could perform and sleep. That's what killed him a few years ago, just like—"

Aaron interrupted, "How long were they married?"

"Not long. They didn't have any children, but I'm pretty sure she has at least three or four kids by her other husbands."

With that Aaron's face broke into a wide smile. "You mean I'm a grand-dad? I can't believe it! Me, a granddad! Where does she live?"

"I think I read that her current husband is in the music business in

England. They probably live there now. That's why we should try to make that concert in L.A. before she flies back home."

Aaron gave me a knowing look then asked, "Kid, do you remember yesterday when you wanted to know why I was telling you my story?"

"Yeah. You never really answered me."

"Well, ya' discovered the answer on your own. I've come back because I want to see my little girl again. I know it's too late to be a part of her life anymore, and I don't expect to meet her. Too much time has gone by, I'm sure I'm just a hazy memory at this point in her life. It ain't right, what I've done, bein' away from her for so long. I just need to see her again to know she's alright. It's somethin' I gotta do before I pass and I need your help to do that. So, do ya' really think if we drive out to this Roxy place that we might be able to see her?"

I paused for a few moments considering his question. This was something big, even historical. I knew I had to play it out, to see what happened and, if I'm going to be honest, it was also an excuse to avoid dealing with Mo.

"Yes, I do. If we can get the money to get out there, we should be able to find tickets to the show. It looks like it's one of the last concerts of her U.S. tour. Six days should be more than enough time for us to get to L.A. In fact, we'll probably have a few days to spare," I answered, understanding that I had just signed on to see where this little adventure would lead. I know it was odd that someone like me, with an almost allergic reaction to commitment, would volunteer to help Aaron, but it almost felt predestined.

"Far out!" Aaron exclaimed. Noticing my amused smile, he asked, "Do folks not say that anymore?"

"I think you'll need a bit of time to pick up today's slang, but I get what you mean."

"Groovy." Aaron laughed. Then he turned the key and hit the gas. In moments we were heading west out of Memphis and onto I-40.

* * *

For the next eighty miles, Aaron was quiet, which was understandable considering all that he had experienced that day. I was sure it was a lot to absorb, so I kept to myself. It wasn't until we were approaching Little Rock that he spoke again, "Kid, can I ask you a question?"

"Sure, Aaron."

"I still don't understand all those people visiting Graceland. It doesn't make sense to me. Why do they do it?"

"You really don't get it, do you?"

"Get what?"

"You don't understand how famous Elvis is."

"I get that a few of the old folks might still have their memories, but there were a lot of other people there, even some kids," he said with a slight drawl.

"Elvis is part of American culture now, like Abraham Lincoln, the Statue of Liberty, apple pie, and Babe Ruth. And he's not just famous with old people or even just Americans, for that matter. Elvis is known around the world, which is amazing to consider given that he never toured outside the U.S. and Canada."

Aaron continued to look blankly at the road, occasionally glancing at me. I could see that what I was telling him just wasn't registering.

I pulled out my phone and clicked on an app.

"According to this, even today, Elvis has over twelve million followers on Facebook."

"Followers? What's a face book?"

"C'mon you know....Wait a second, that's right. You don't know, do you?"

"Don't know what?"

"Don't know about Facebook."

"Kid, I don't know what you're talkin' about most of the time—and I don't know what that thing is, but it sure as hell ain't a telephone."

"Facebook is one of the world's most popular apps. That's short for 'application', like a computer application."

"I know what a computer is, I'm not stupid. But why does it need to apply for anything?"

I groaned in frustration. "Ignore all that. Just imagine that this phone is a super powerful computer. Almost everyone in the world has one and they're all connected together. Many of the people using these phones belong to a kind of club called Facebook where they share things that they like or don't like. Well, today, more than twelve million of those people are fans of Elvis Presley!"

A confused expression etched across Aaron's face. It was clear this was not making sense to him, so I decided to try a different approach.

"One of the most popular singers of the last twenty years is a guy named Declan MacManus."

"So?"

"So? He changed his name when he began his musical career. Do you know what he changed it to? Elvis—Elvis Costello in honor of the original King of Rock n' Roll who he grew up listening to as a boy in England."

I paused to let this sink in before continuing. "Dozens of songs have been written about Elvis. There's one called *Round Here* by the band Counting Crows, about a girl who wants to find 'a guy who looks like Elvis.' Another band, Dire Straits, had a big hit with the song *Calling Elvis*. Paul Simon, you may remember him, he was part of Simon and Garfunkel, had an album called *Graceland*, and another singer, Marc Cohen, had a hit called *Walking in Memphis* where he sings about following the ghost of Elvis through the gates of Graceland."

"Dire Straits is the name of a band?"

"Yes, but forget about that. Don't you understand what I'm trying to tell you? Even today, people write songs about Elvis."

A thought occurred to me and I turned my phone on again.

"Who ya' calling now?" Aaron asked.

"I'm not calling anyone, I want to play a song for you."

"That thing really does play music too? You're not kiddin'?"

"Here, just listen," I said as I located *Elvis is Everywhere* on my song list, punched play and turned up the volume.

Listening intently, his head cocked toward the phone lying on the dashboard, I saw Aaron break into a broad grin as he listened to the song's lyrics. Finally, he exploded in laughter. "Elvis built the pyramids? Elvis built Stonehenge? Damn, this guy's funny!"

I paused the music.

"Yes, he is. But don't you get it?" I asked. "This song was recorded more than ten years after Elvis died. After that long, most celebrities are well forgotten. But in this song, the musician, a guy named Mojo Nixon, was singing about how people continue to worship Elvis and give him credit for all kinds of crazy shit."

"Is he related to President Nixon? Did you know I met him once?"

"No, he's not. That's his stage name. And, yes, I remember seeing a picture of Elvis meeting President Nixon," I answered, as I thought about what must be the strangest presidential photograph of all time.

"He was kind of an odd cat."

"Before my time. But I know a lot of people thought that. Listen, the point I'm trying to make is that Elvis hasn't been forgotten. In fact, he's more famous than ever! Do you understand?"

Aaron looked over at me and said nothing. I could tell that he was still absorbing what I had said. He looked back out the windshield and we drove on for miles, each of us entwined with our own thoughts and memories.

* * *

It was a half hour later when we pulled over for gas. I filled the tank while Aaron went into the station to use the bathroom and pay. He was gone only a few minutes when I heard the sound of angry voices shouting from inside the station. I walked cautiously toward the commotion only to see Aaron exchanging heated words with a young female clerk.

"I told you, man, it's $32.75 for the gas!" she yelled from behind the cash register.

"Like hell it is. You take me for an old fool?" Aaron responded.

"If you don't believe me, go look at the damn pump!"

"I don't need to. There ain't no way it costs that much to fill up a tank of gas. Hell, you could fill up five Cadillacs for that price."

"Listen, man. If you don't shell out some cash right now, I'm callin' the cops."

"Hope you do. They'll probably arrest you for rippin' off honest citizens like me."

"Honest? You're crazy, you old bastard!" she exclaimed as she reached for her phone.

"Hang on, hang on," I interjected. "Aaron, go to the car, please. Go!" I pointed toward the Caddy.

Aaron gave me a menacing look as he stormed out the door.

"Sorry about that," I said to the clerk as I handed her the money. "My granddad isn't all there these days."

"No kidding! You need to get him some help before he gets himself in real trouble."

"Thanks," I said, as I reached for my change.

I walked toward the car with the clerk's admonition ringing in my ears, opened the front door and sat down. As soon as I shut the door, Aaron lit into me.

"Well? Did you pay her that money?" he demanded.

"Of course, I did. It's what we owed."

"Are you crazy, kid? She's rippin' us off. Ain't no way gas can cost that much!"

"Aaron, look at the pump. What's it say for the price of a gallon of gas?"

Aaron squinted and looked at the pump next to him. "Two dollars and seventy-five cents," he said incredulously.

"Yeah. And we bought a bit more than eleven gallons. Do the math."

"That's for real? That's the price of a gallon of gas now?"

"More or less, depending on where you are in the country."

"How can anyone afford to drive anymore? Oh, my God, I yelled at that young lady. Should I go apologize to her?"

"No, no, no. I don't think that would be a good idea. Better to just leave it alone. And, speaking of the price of things, how much money do you have left? I used almost all of mine to pay for the gas."

"About fifteen bucks. I was counting on getting the money that Colonel Parker stole! I still can't believe that bastard took it! It was my money. He had no right to it. That son of a bitch!"

"It's okay, man. Calm down, calm down. We'll figure something out."

Aaron looked at me, jaw set, his face reddened with emotion. Then he shook his head, turned the ignition and we drove off toward the Arkansas border. For miles, I heard him mumble unintelligibly, as if having a heated conversation with Colonel Parker. It made me momentarily consider that maybe he was unbalanced, just an old man with a mental illness. But in response to that seed of doubt, I thought of everything he had told me and of our experience at Graceland.

I was seven hundred miles from home running from responsibility and the pain I was causing the woman I loved. I was travelling in a decrepit old Cadillac on the verge of breaking down at any moment. My clothes were filthy and I had only a few bucks in my pocket.

But I was riding with the King on the greatest road trip in history.

Fourteen

Another hour passed before we reached Little Rock. I had stopped here once for a night while on tour with one of my first bands and was impressed with the vibe. It was far more youthful than I expected with some good music venues. We even played one named Maxine's, which was located in of all places, a former brothel. I remember thinking at the time that only in America could a person from a poor background like Bill Clinton so quickly outgrow their hometown. Now I realized that I was sitting next to someone who outgrew the world.

As we approached the city center, I saw a sign advertising a downtown Farmers Market, which gave me an idea.

"Hey, Aaron, take the City Center exit and follow the signs to that Farmers Market."

"Why are we going there? I've just spent the past thirty years farmin'. Think I've had more than enough of that."

"Just trust me. I think I know how we can get some money. Seriously, man. Trust me."

Aaron gave me a perplexed look and then turned onto the exit ramp. Minutes later, we pulled up to a plaza filled with market tents and produce stalls, and Aaron parked the car.

"Wait here," I said. "I'll be back in a minute."

I left the car and walked across the street to a pharmacy and, using much of my remaining money, purchased a sheet of poster board and a black felt-tip marker. Returning to the car, I opened Aaron's door.

"Hop out. Let's go."

"Let's go where? What's that for?" he said, pointing at the poster board.

"Never mind," I replied, handing it to him as I grabbed my amp and guitar out of the back seat and shut the door.

"Kid, what in the hell is going on?"

"Aaron, you ever busk?"

"Busk?"

"You know, perform on the streets. It's how I made money the first few years I lived in Austin. You just find a busy location, open up your guitar case and start playing."

"We can't do that—out in the public like that."

"Yes, we can. Look at this market! This place is packed. We just set up on that corner over there and put on a little show. It'll be easy."

"But what am I gonna play? There's only one guitar."

"You don't need a guitar, I've got a microphone that hooks into my amp. You just sing."

"Sing?"

"Of course. Don't you remember the other night at that karaoke bar in Potts Camp? Just do the same thing."

"But you don't know any of the songs I sing."

"Try me. I know about every Elvis number, and plenty of gospel and country songs as well. That's about all my band plays."

"It's a nice idea, kid, but it'll never work," he said as he reached for the handle to get back in the car.

"Listen old man," I replied sharply. "You got a better idea? We only have a few bucks between us. We're miles from your home or mine, driving a car that is likely to break down again at any moment, and with no money to even buy tickets to see your little girl's show, let alone gas to get across the country. Seriously, do you have any better ideas?"

Aaron regarded me in silence for a few moments; then like a petulant child, he grabbed the poster board and marched toward the plaza. I followed him across the street, where we negotiated our way through the crowd and vegetable stands until we found a location that had ample foot traffic and plenty of room for people to watch us play.

"This is a good spot," I said, as a put down my amp, removed my guitar from its case and plugged it and the microphone into the amp. Aaron stood, unmoving, with his hands jammed in his pockets like a nervous kid on his first day at a new school. Placing my open guitar case in front of us, I reached into my pocket and seeded it with my few remaining bills and some change. On the poster board, I wrote in large letters 'NEED MONEY FOR METAMUCIL!' and leaned it against the case. Flicking on the amp, I checked the tuning on my guitar and handed the microphone to Aaron.

"Okay. What's our first number?"

"A. J., I'm not sure. This just don't feel right with all these people."

"Aaron, look at me. You can do this. Just do the same thing you did the other night. Pick a song, close your eyes, and sing. You know how to do it."

Aaron appeared almost terrified, and for a moment I thought he might drop the microphone and run. Then he took a deep breath and surveyed the crowd of shoppers around him carrying bags of fruits and vegetables and bouquets of flowers. He straightened up and looked at me.

"Kid, do you know *Too Close to Heaven?*"

"The old Professor Bradford gospel song? Please, man. You're going to have to do better than that to stump me."

Not wanting to give Aaron time to change his mind, I started fingering the frets, playing the first few notes. I watched as Aaron hesitated. Then, as if by reflex, he pulled the microphone to his lips and began to sing. He was tentative at first, singing as if he was walking on ice. But as he pushed through the song, I witnessed a metamorphosis. It wasn't just the rising certitude in his voice. It wasn't the way he moved, or even how he gestured to the crowd. It was something more. It was that intangible quality that separates true talent from the rest of us hacks. Some call it 'presence' or the 'X Factor'. Whatever the name, Aaron was brimming with it and as he began to let loose, people gathered around us. At first, it was just a few middle-aged couples reliving memories through the songs—Bill Monroe's *Blue Moon of Kentucky*; Lloyd Price's *Lawdy Miss Clawdy*; or Kokomo Arnold's *Milk Cow Blues*. A group of my tribe—that is, pierced nose, gauge-eared, flannel-wearing, cappuccino-carrying, farmers-market-attending twenty-somethings—soon joined them. Other shoppers put down their bags to stop and watch; some sat on a nearby lawn and began clapping in rhythm to the music.

When we launched into Big Boy Crudup's *My Baby Left Me*, a young father grabbed his infant daughter and began to dance with her on his hip as she giggled with glee. A number of other couples also joined in and began to dance.

As the crowd grew, so did Aaron's confidence, along with the pile of bills in the guitar case. After a dozen songs, he owned the audience. Speaking into the microphone, he asked, "A. J., you ready to shake it loose?" Before I could reply, he pulled the mic away from his face, turned to me and mouthed two words: *Hound Dog.* In one quick motion, shocking for a person of his age, he corkscrewed toward the audience and growled the open lyric.

That was all it took.

The rest was pure pandemonium. It was as if a flash mob had exploded in the Farmers Market. Around us everyone was singing, swinging, dancing, and clapping, all channeling something from their pasts. And Aaron…well, let's just say he was in another place. He sang with a fervor and intensity far beyond what he had shown singing karaoke. In fact, it was a performance beyond anything I had ever witnessed from any entertainer in my years in music. And, for God's sake, this was in a farmers market!

Unfortunately, the growing size of the crowd not only paralyzed the foot traffic entering the Farmers Market, but also attracted the local officials who, when they discovered we didn't have a permit, shut us down despite vocal objections from the crowd. As I flicked off the amp, I looked over at Aaron. Microphone in hand, he was being taught the intricacies of the high five, forearm smash, and fist bump by well-meaning fans as the crowd slowly dispersed.

"Damn, kid. Don't people just shake hands anymore? Every time you meet someone it's like there's some secret code ya' need to know. Everybody seems to do somethin' different," he groused.

I collected the money from my guitar case, jamming my pockets with coins and rolls of bills. Then I packed up our gear and we headed toward the car. People around us called out as we wove our way through the crowd.

"Wish my grandfather rocked like you!"

"You guys playing anywhere local?"

"Do you have any CDs for sale?"

That last one stumped Aaron a bit. He leaned toward me and asked, "I remember one of my accountants tellin' me about those, but why would we sell those when we play? Don't make sense."

I considered clarifying this one for Aaron, but let it pass and loaded my gear into the car. Then I sat down on the front seat and counted our earnings. I was astounded.

"Aaron, we just made two hundred and twenty-seven bucks! I've *never* made that much working the street." I handed him half the money and Aaron put it in his pocket, grinning at my excitement. Then he started the car and we pulled away from the curb threading our way through downtown Little Rock and back to the highway.

"We've got to keep doing this!" I declared. "Do you know how much we can make? Hell, if we can pull in more than $200 for an hour in Little Rock, there's no telling what we can do in other cities! It's a bit out of the way, but we could clean up in the French Quarter in New Orleans. A few days there and we could earn enough to cover anything. We need to work on our song list. Do you have any numbers you want to add?" I couldn't contain my enthusiasm and began to reel off titles. Suddenly Aaron pointed ahead.

"Look! That gal's in trouble!"

Stomping on the gas, he accelerated down the block, throwing me back in my seat. Without warning, he abruptly swung a U-turn and over to the opposite side of the road alongside a young woman.

"Are you okay, darlin'? Who's chasing you?" he asked anxiously, leaning out my window glancing over his shoulder. "Get in, we'll help you."

The woman looked at us and recoiled in fear. In one quick motion, she spun around and sprinted down the street in the opposite direction.

"What in the hell are you doing?" I yelled, jerking the steering wheel back toward the other side of the road.

"That gal's being chased by someone! We need to help her."

"No, she's not. She's jogging!"

"She's running down the street in some kinda' underwear. Someone must be after her. She needs our help!" he cried as he looked back in her direction.

"What do you mean underwear? She's wearing a sports bra and yoga pants! That's what most women wear when they exercise these days."

Aaron was stunned. "You mean gals go out in public in those clothes? On the streets? Where everyone can see 'em?"

"Yes, of course, look around," I said, pointing to a number of other women wearing similar clothes.

Aaron's head turned as he stared at each of them intently. Slowly, a broad grin rolled across his face, like the kind you see when a baby first tastes a piece of chocolate. Then, he looked back at me and drawled, "Well, ah guess some things have definitely changed for the better."

Fifteen

It was just after sunset, as we motored toward Amarillo, when my phone vibrated with another text. I reached out and picked it up from the dashboard. Flipping it over, I looked at the screen and saw an ultrasound picture with a message from Mo:

> Stop being such a world-class prick and call me—you jackass! And, BTW, it's a girl!

Even now, years later, it's hard for me to describe what I felt at that moment. Wonderment? Fear? Awe? Anxiety? My eyes began to water as I stared at the picture. Then, it really sunk in. I was going to be a father. I was going to have a baby girl.

"You alright? What's wrong?" Aaron asked, looking over from the steering wheel.

I spoke the words tentatively, as if trying to convince myself of their truth. "I'm going to have a daughter."

"Damn, kid, congratulations! I didn't even know you were married!"

I immediately regretted sharing this information and tried to shut down the conversation.

"I'm not. Yesterday, at the bar...I didn't tell you everything. Never mind, it's a long story."

Aaron was silent for a few moments before asking, "A. J., how long 'til we get to L.A.?"

"About three or four days, I guess. Why?"

"Well, it seems like we've got plenty of time for your story."

I watched the night sky settle over the desert of the Texas panhandle. I felt the hypnotic rumble of the Caddy's tires and the gentle sway of its ancient suspension rocking me like a child. I looked out at the vast, lonely desert, and the words began to flow.

"I told you about moving around the country with my fucked-up family, right? Well, I continued my traveling even when I was on my own until eventually finding my way to Austin which was the best thing that ever happened to me. I don't know if it was the people, the music, the food trucks, or the Lone Star beer, but it was the first place I began to feel a sense of community—a feeling of home. Something I'd never had in my life."

"Sounds kinda like Memphis always was for me," said Aaron. "It was that special place that I could always come back to no matter what. Is Austin where you first got serious about your music?"

"I never really thought about it that way, but, yeah, that's probably true. Before Austin, playing was just something to keep me from feeling alone. I think I told you I was part of a few bands in college, but those groups were short-lived, usually only put together for a dance or a frat party. Most of the time, it was just my guitar and me."

Aaron nodded, and I knew he understood.

"When I got to Austin, everything changed from the moment I arrived. It was one of those days that you can only find in Texas in August—unbearable humidity with booming explosions of thunder. I ducked into a bar for a cold beer and to reconsider my choice of locations. Next to me, nursing a drink, was a guy about my age and we struck up a conversation. Turns out he was a drummer for a band called the Armadillo Assholes—kind of a Tex-Mex group. They needed a lead guitarist and within a few days I was part of the band. I don't know if it was the same for you, but I've always found local bands to be like high school cliques; everyone always wants to be part of the 'in' group. I'm no different. After I played with the Assholes for about six months, I joined a more popular band, Armstrong's Testicle."

Aaron interrupted, "Wait. Are those are really the names of bands?"

"Yeah, the last one was named after one of Austin's more infamous citizens. He was a professional bike racer who lost a nut to cancer. I played with them for about two years before they broke up. After that, I joined my current band, Sweet Lil and the River. We play a lot of blues, folk and old country stuff. We've got enough of a following to tour a few times each year, but most of the time we play in the Austin area."

"What's all this have to do with having a baby?"

"Well, life was good in Austin, really good. I had no real obligations other than three or four gigs a week, and enough money for rent, guitar strings and beer. It was stress-free and everything was fine, until I met Mo."

"Mo?" What kind of name is that? Like the guy who was one of the Three Stooges?"

Now it was my turn for a laugh. "No, no, it's short for 'Maureen'. Believe it or not, she prefers 'Mo'. I guess that tells you something about her."

"Is she your gal?"

I hesitated. "I think...I hope so. Guess I'm not sure at the moment." I paused and looked out at the last vermillion rays of daylight brushing the barren landscape. "I still remember when I first met her. I was playing with Sweet Lil and we were finishing our set at this bar, the Broken Spoke. Damn, she looked hot. I remember she was wearing a pair of tight Levi's and a starched white blouse. Her hair was in these long brown ringlets that rested on her shoulders. When I first saw her, she was lost in concentration. Not, unfortunately, on the handsome and gifted lead guitarist on the stage before her," I smiled and pointed my thumb at my chest. "Instead, she was focused on a stack of school papers she was grading while drinking a beer and tapping her boot to the music. I tried over and over to make eye contact with her from behind my Fender without success. Finally, after we finished our last song, I mustered up a bit of courage, stepped off the stage, sat down on the stool next to her and stuck out my hand. 'Name's Armitage,' I said, 'but everyone calls me A. J.'

"I still recall the way she slowly looked up from a paper covered with red scribbles and sized me up for a moment. Then she put down her pen and shook my hand. 'I'm Maureen. But everyone calls me 'Mo'. By the way, it rhymes with 'no.'"

Aaron let out a snort. "Sounds like a funny gal."

"Yeah, she is. And despite what she said, we clicked immediately and three weeks later I moved in with her. A month later, I moved out. A few months later, we were back together. Then we broke up again. It was kind of the choreography of our relationship. I'd feel trapped, convinced that she was tying me down and find some excuse to leave. It was always something trivial or stupid, any excuse for me to avoid growing up. Then we'd see each other at a street festival or nightclub and our dance would start again. You know, Aaron, we were kind of like magnets—either pulled together by a strong bond or powerfully repulsed."

"But she's someone important in your life. I can hear it in your voice. Kind of reminds me of the way I felt when I was first with Priscilla. There were things she did that drove me crazy, but I couldn't resist her. Ya' know what I mean?"

I nodded.

"What makes your lady special to you?"

I thought for a moment about Aaron's question. I'd never really attempted to put the feeling into words. I just knew I liked being with her, that I was something better when she was part of my life.

"Well," I began, "I guess one thing is, with the exception of her on-and-off relationship with me, she is one of those people who is always happy, someone who seems to find joy in every aspect of life. Physically she can do almost anything, whether it's salsa dancing or mountain climbing. I mean for God's sake, for my birthday, she gave us a gift of bull-riding lessons!"

"Sorry, kid, did you say bull-riding?"

"Yeah, I know, I had the same reaction when I opened my birthday card and saw the gift certificate. It's a Texas thing. Anyway, there was no way I was going to climb on an angry horned animal that weighs more than a car and ride it. At least that's what I thought until the following weekend when Mo and I spent two days learning how to ride a bull."

"Really? You actually rode a bull?" said Aaron with a look of amazement.

"Well," I admitted, "not for very long. At the end of our training we had a contest with the others in the class to see who could stay on their bull the longest. Mo's time was 11 seconds for which she received the first place trophy. My time was 1.4 seconds for which I received a separated shoulder and five stitches when I fell off the bull and it stepped on me."

Aaron grimaced. "Ouch!"

"No kidding. But that's life with Mo. It probably doesn't sound like it, but she's also the most feminine woman I've ever dated. She's the kind of girl who thinks nothing of wearing her old, ratty, red Lucchese cowboy boots with a black cocktail dress. On her, it looks awesome."

"You said she was grading papers. Is she a teacher?"

"Yeah, she's a professor at the University of Texas. She's been teaching freshman composition there for the last five years. No surprise, she's one of the most popular instructors on campus."

"She sounds like a great gal—smart, funny, beautiful. So let me ask you one question."

"Yeah?"

"Why aren't you with her right now?"

Wow, I thought. Who was this guy? It was like I was talking to a shrink again. I let out a deep exhale.

"You sure you want to hear all this?"

"Like I said, kid, we got plenty of time."

I looked out the window at the first stars of the evening and smiled. The constellation, Sagittarius, was just breaking over the horizon. I knew how to identify exactly one constellation and that was Sagittarius. It was Mo's birth sign. On summer nights, when I was feeling horny, she'd block my moves by handing me a glass of wine and pulling me outside by the hand and say, 'First, show me'. Then I'd have to demonstrate that I could locate the constellation as an act of enduring fidelity, for which I would be rewarded with a very passionate kiss.

"Kid?"

"Sorry. Why aren't I with her? Well, we're in our late twenties—you know, that time in life when it seems like all your friends are getting hitched and having kids. I could see in her eyes that she thought it was time for her as well. But I couldn't do it. Hell, I still feel like a kid myself. Any time the conversation turned to marriage, I'd redirect it to something else. Maybe someday I could tackle marriage, but...I don't know, I just could never see myself as a parent."

I stopped for a moment, recalling the last time I saw her. "Last Sunday, Mo met me at the door after I came home from a week playing in Lubbock. She had a look on her face that I hadn't seen before; it was kind of a mixture of joy and anxiety. She helped me off with my jacket and had me sit down on the couch next to her. Then she asked me about my gig, but before I could begin to tell her anything she blurted out that she was pregnant."

For minutes, I looked out at the landscape rolling past in the dim evening light, but all I could see was Mo's face as she shared the news with me. In her deep blue eyes edged with tears there was apprehension and fear, but also confidence that she had in the power of her love for me, confidence that was, in the end, sadly misplaced.

Aaron broke my reverie in a soft voice. "Kid? You okay? What happened after that?"

"I'm embarrassed to tell you that I didn't say a word. It was like I had an emotional blackout. I just stared at her. Then I reached over grabbed my guitar and stuff and walked out. That was a week ago."

"So when I picked you up back in Mississippi, you were runnin' away from being a daddy? Is that why your phone thing has been buzzin' so much?"

"Yeah," I admitted.

"But, you're gonna be a daddy! How can you not be sure you want that? It's the only thing that's pure and real in life. What's wrong with you, kid? You know, some nights when things were at their darkest—with the drugs, and all my bad ways, those times when I felt alone and trapped; on those nights, I'd walk down the hall to my little Lisa Marie's room and watch her sleep. That's all I'd do. I just sit on the floor besides her bed and watch her. The soft pinkness in her cheeks, the gentle rise and fall of her chest…I'd get so close I'd inhale the moist sweetness of her breath. She was so beautiful— a little angel in the moonlight. Looking at her, I could feel love flood my heart. It filled me with such happiness, I'd just sit there and cry. How could you not want that?"

"I guess I'm just scared. I haven't been able to stick with anything in my life other than my guitar. Like I told you, my own dad split when I was in high school. And before that he wasn't much of a parent. How am I supposed to know how to be a father?"

"Son, I felt the same way, but there's just something that happens when you become a daddy. Don't know exactly what it is, but when you first hold that little baby you feel it—somethin' you can't describe. It's this connection, this bond, and slowly you begin to realize that nothin' else really matters. *Nothin'*. At least, I think that's how it is for most folks. For some of us," he gestured toward his chest, "it takes a bit longer to come by that understandin'."

I thought about what Aaron had said, turning it over in my mind. Up to that point, my life's fulfillment was found in a tight, fourteen-song set before a packed house. For a moment I imagined holding that little girl, tossing her in the air, blowing kisses on her stomach, listening to her giggle with glee. As I did, an unfamiliar swell of warmth and happiness washed over me—instantly replaced by a tidal wave of fear. Reverting to form, I sought refuge in avoidance.

I sighed. "It's getting late. We should find a place for the night."

Sixteen

We drove on for another twenty miles before we reached Amarillo where Aaron pulled off the highway and into the parking lot of a Motel 6. We parked, walked into the office, and rang the desk bell. And rang it again. And again. Finally, some punk kid sauntered in from a room behind the desk, irritated by the disturbance. You know the type—mid-twenties, hair dyed raven black, heavy eyeliner, multiple ear gauges and tongue piercings, tats on both arms, and a heavyweight attitude.

"Yeah? What do you want?"

"We'd like a room for the night. Two beds, please."

"That'll be thirty-nine bucks. Cash or charge?" he asked with an air of disdain and complete boredom.

"Cash, please."

As I pulled the bills out of my wallet, I noticed Aaron staring intently at the desk clerk with a quizzical look.

"What happened to you?" he asked in a tender voice.

"What do you mean?" replied the clerk.

"Those holes in your ears and that thing in your tongue. Don't that hurt? And all those tattoos and you're wearin' makeup? What's goin' on?" he asked, sounding genuinely concerned.

The clerk looked at Aaron in astonishment, then he exploded, "Fuck you, old man!"

Quickly, I pushed myself in front of Aaron, blocking him from the clerk.

"I apologize," I said. "My grandfather's not all there. He doesn't mean to be insulting. Honestly. He's just a touch senile. Can we just get the key and I'll get him out of here?"

The clerk glared at Aaron for a few moments with a look that bordered on hatred, then slowly handed me the room key.

"Thanks," I said as I grabbed Aaron by the elbow and pushed him out of the office.

"What in the hell are you thinking?" I snapped, once we got outside and began walking to the car.

"What do ya' mean?"

"Insulting that guy."

"How was I insulting him? Did you see how he looked? He's done all that stuff to his body. What do you think happened to him?"

"Happened to him? He has tattoos and piercings. So what?"

"You act like that's normal."

"Of course it's normal," I replied. "Most of my friends have them these days. Here, look." I stopped and rolled up my sleeve to show him my ink, a small Fender on the inside of my left arm.

"You mean you want to do this to yourselves?" he asked, eyeing my tattoo with a look of disbelief.

"Of course, it's the style these days."

"Y'all are crazy. What the hell is wrong with you?"

"Nothing's wrong with us—it's part of who we are. It's a way of showing our identity, that we're different." Realizing Aaron hadn't meant to be insulting, I tried to lighten the mood.

"You know, when you think about it, kids today are just following a trail blazed by a young man from Tupelo more than sixty years ago. You may recall that his hair was dyed black as well," I needled.

"Wait a second. You can't blame this on me," Aaron responded, waving his hands. "I didn't tell people to mutilate themselves!"

"No, but Elvis was the first person to show kids that they could be themselves, that they didn't have to act like everyone expected. He was the original rebel! From him came the Beatles, the Stones and the Who; then the metal bands, the hair bands, the glam bands; Billy Idol, Devo, and Marilyn Manson to the musicians of today—Green Day, Radiohead, and Pearl Jam. Elvis was the first entertainer who was so popular that he was known by only one name. Now there are a bunch of 'em, like Prince, Madonna, Eminem, and Beyoncé. All of them are part of a musical history that goes back to the moment when that young man first stepped into Sun Studios in 1953."

"Those are all entertainers and bands? 'Course I remember the Beatles and the Rollin' Stones—"

I interrupted. "Did you know the Stones are still playing? They just came through Austin last year."

"Those guys are still around? Really? Do they still have that same crazy guy, the guitar player?"

"Are you talking about Keith Richards?"

"Yeah, yeah, that's the guy."

"He's still playing, and some say even better than ever."

"That can't be! That other stuff may be true, but there's no way that guy is still alive. I remember meeting him a couple of times with the rest of the band. He was always drinkin' and doin' drugs and other wild stuff back then, completely looney! I figured there was no way he'd make it to thirty." Aaron shook his head skeptically.

"What about the Beatles—did they ever get back together? Never expected them to break up the way they did. Ya' know, they came out to visit one time when I was in L.A. doin' movies. I think that was the only time I met 'em. They were gettin' big in the U.S. back then. Good group of fellas. I really liked that guy, John. There was somethin' special about him. They still playin' too?"

"No, they never got back together. Paul McCartney and Ringo still perform with their own bands. George Harrison died a few years ago, I think of cancer. And, John Lennon," I paused. "He was shot to death outside his apartment building in New York about thirty years ago by some lunatic fan."

"Shot? By a fan?"

"Yeah."

Aaron looked at me in stunned silence, confusion and sadness rippling across his face. Was he remembering his time with Lennon, or was he considering what could have been his own fate? I didn't know, because he didn't say anything further. He just slowly opened the trunk of the car and pulled out a few odds and ends of clothing and walked toward our room. If this was his reaction when he heard about John Lennon, I thought, how would he respond when he learned about everything else that had happened since he disappeared into the hills of Mississippi?

Seventeen

Aaron was strangely quiet as we made our way toward Albuquerque the following morning. It was one of those New Mexico days when the sunlight attacks you the moment the sun breaks the horizon. As we drove, the temperature quickly climbed into the high 80s. Aaron seemed oblivious to the smell in the Caddy. But as the mercury rose, so did the odor of the ammonia from the chicken shit embedded in the carpet and upholstery. Finally, I couldn't take it anymore.

"Aaron, do you smell that?"

"Smell what?"

"The chicken shit in this car!"

Aaron wrinkled his nose and sniffed. "Not really."

You're kidding—aren't you? It smells like this car is composed entirely of chicken shit."

"Smells like bein' on a farm to me."

"I've been on a farm. That's not the way a farm smells. It's the way a chicken coop smells. A chicken coop filled with decades of chicken shit!" I exclaimed. "Seriously, Aaron, can we drive this thing through a car wash? I'm getting dizzy from the smell."

"Son, I normally like my cars shiny and clean, but I want this one to stay dirty like it is."

He said nothing further, so I volunteered, "Because you don't want to draw attention to it? Because someone might figure out who you are—like I did?"

Aaron looked over at me and nodded.

An hour later, we reached the outskirts of the city and pulled in for gas at a station that had a remote self-washing area with large industrial vacuum cleaners.

"C'mon, man," I pleaded, "Can I at least vacuum the car before we get gas? No one is going to notice. Please, this car really reeks!"

Aaron looked around slowly. Seeing no one in sight, he nodded in agreement.

It took twenty minutes and ten dollars in quarters before I was finished. Aaron sat quietly on a bench and watched as I worked. Occasionally, he would turn his head nervously to check for approaching strangers. Even though upholstery was now free of feathers and bird crap, the vacuuming hardly made a difference with the smell—the chickens had taken their toll on the Caddy. Aaron pulled the car up to the pump and filled it while I went into the station to grab a few snacks and to pay the cashier.

I returned to the car and slid onto the passenger seat, placing the bag of food between us. "Well, you happy now?" Aaron inquired.

"To tell the truth, I don't think the vacuuming made any difference. But I found something that will help," I answered with a smirk.

With that, I reached into the bag and pulled out a cardboard auto air freshener. This one was a scent-embedded photo of Elvis Presley resplendent in high-collar white jump suit and violet-colored lei around his neck from his 1973 Hawaiian comeback concert.

I thought Aaron's eyes would pop out of his head as he watched me pull off the plastic wrapping and hang it from the rearview mirror.

"They sold them in the gas station. In case you're wondering, I went with the pine scent. I thought it would remind you of home."

Aaron turned the key and pulled onto the road without a word. But I took great pleasure in watching for miles as his focus alternated between the road and the air freshener swinging from the mirror like a hypnotist's pocket watch.

* * *

We were approaching downtown Gallup before Aaron spoke again. At the time, I was asleep with my head on the dash so that my nose was in closer proximity to the air freshener. His voice brought me back to consciousness.

"What else has happened?"

"Huh? What do you mean?" I asked with a yawn.

"What else has happened since I've been gone? You told me about the Beatles—what else has happened? I know I missed some things…"

Where should I begin? I thought. Politics? Sports? Music? How could I tell him everything he had missed during a period longer than my entire life? Would Aaron believe that the Red Sox had finally won a World Series? What about YouTube? *Survivor*? Cargo pants? Would he believe that for twelve of his missing years a President named "Bush" had been in the White House? Before I could respond, Aaron interrupted with another question.

"Also, why is everyone so fat? Look at all these folks," he said, pointing at a crowd walking by. "Look at how big they are! And, damn it, you can't blame that on me!" He paused before adding, "Even though they sure look a lot like I used to."

"No, this one doesn't have anything to do with you. Americans have been eating crap for decades. It's all the fast food—it seems like there's a McDonalds, Burger King or Taco Bell on every corner. Even if there isn't one of those, you can always find a place to grab a Big Gulp or Starbucks."

"Son, I'm almost too frightened to ask. What's a Big Gulp? Or Starbucks? One of 'em sounds like a porno and the other like somethin' from a science fiction movie."

I laughed. "Big Gulps are these enormous soft drinks that people buy at convenience stores. The cups are about the size of a bucket. Starbucks is a chain of coffee shops that serve these sweet coffee drinks with names like 'Frappuccinos'. People drink them like they're crack."

"Crack?"

"It's a kind of cocaine, a drug. I'm trying to say that people are addicted to the drinks."

"Can we get some? Coffee, I mean. I haven't had a good cup in a long, long time."

"Sure," I pointed. "There's a Starbucks up ahead in that strip mall. Like I said, they're everywhere."

Aaron navigated the Caddy through the crowded parking lot until we found an empty spot, parked and went into the store. Like most Starbucks, this one was packed with people working on laptops, reading newspapers, and drinking coffee. As we stood waiting in line, Aaron read the drink menu with a growing look of consternation.

"May I take your order?" asked a perky young barista when Aaron finally approached the counter.

"Honey, I can't make heads or tails of what you have on the board up there. I just want a cup of black coffee. Do you have that?"

"Yes, sir! Today we have a few specials. Would you like the Guatemala Casi Cielo, the Komodo Dragon Blend or Pikes?"

"Are any of 'em coffee?"

She laughed, thinking Aaron was teasing her. "Yes, sir, they're all coffee. The Komodo has an earthy taste with a hint of spice; the Casi Cielo has more of a citrus taste with a cocoa finish; and Pikes is our signature medium roast."

"Ma'am, I just want a cup of coffee. I have no idea what you're talkin' about."

"Why don't I get you the Komodo. Most people love it. Would you like decaf or regular?"

Aaron shifted awkwardly. "Regular, I suppose."

"And will that be a venti, grande or tall?"

"Please, ma'am, I just want a cup of coffee."

"That's the size, sir. Do you want a small, medium or large?" she asked patiently.

"Large, I guess."

"Sleeve?"

"What do you mean 'sleeve'?" he asked in an agitated voice. "Do y'all have some kind of dress code? Besides, I'm wearin' 'em!"

"He'll have a sleeve," I interrupted. "The coffee will be hot. Thanks."

"Ok," she said looking strangely at Aaron, "that'll be two fifty-seven, please."

Aaron glanced at me and whispered loudly, "Two bucks for coffee? Next thing ya' know, they'll be chargin' for water!"

I was tempted to point out the bottles of water for sale in the display case, but thought he would lose it completely.

Aaron handed the cash to the barista who rang up the order and went to pull the coffee before returning. "Sir, here's your coffee. Sir?" Aaron stood motionless, his gaze focused on the display of CDs on the counter, one of which was titled, "Elvis Presley—Boy from Tupelo."

I jabbed him in the ribs. "Hey, your coffee."

Startled, Aaron looked up and grabbed the cup. "Thank you, ma'am."

I followed him as he quickly exited the building, looking back as if to see if anyone was staring at him. As we walked across the parking lot, Aaron asked excitedly, "Did you see that? There was a thin little box that looked like a tiny LP of Elvis songs. What was that?"

"Remember in Little Rock when that guy asked if you sold CDs? That's what he was talking about. We call it a CD, it's short for 'compact disc.' It's like a small record."

"But it was of Elvis songs. That coffee shop was selling Elvis songs!"

"I keep trying to tell you—Elvis is still one of the biggest recording artists in the world."

Aaron shook his head. "I still can't believe it. After all these years. How can that be?"

* * *

We drove slowly through the city along sidewalks packed with pedestrians as we headed back toward the freeway. Aaron eyed them like he was a bird of prey.

"Son, I got another question for you."

I looked at him and waited.

"I know this is going to sound a bit weird…but are some of those folks…" He gestured to the people walking by. "…Robots?"

"Robots?"

"Or is there some kinda mind control thing goin' on?"

"What? What the hell are you talking about?"

He looked closely at my face, as if he was inspecting it.

"You don't have 'em, but it seems like most everyone else does."

"Has what?" I asked, completely perplexed.

Aaron lowered his voice to a conspiratorial whisper and gestured toward his ears. "The wires."

"The wires? What wires?" I asked as we pulled up to a stoplight.

"Can't you see 'em? Look at their ears, son—their ears! Look at that guy!" he pointed surreptitiously at a man in a business suit, waiting at the crosswalk for the light to change.

I glanced at the man and instantly burst into uncontrollable laughter.

"Why you laughin'? What's so funny?"

It took me a few moments to catch my breath and respond.

"Those are called ear buds. They're like tiny headphones. Here, I'll show you." I reached into the pocket of my jacket, pulled out my ear buds, and plugged them into my phone.

"Put these in your ears. This one goes in your left ear and this one goes in the right."

Aaron looked at them warily before delicately placing one in each ear, steering with one hand. I searched through my library and selected Springsteen's *Fire*, a song he was said to have written for Elvis, and hit play. Instantly, Aaron's face lit up in astonishment. A minute later his eyes crinkled and his face broke into a warm smile as he started singing, "Cause when we kiss…"

Pulling the ear buds out of his ears, he said in a loud voice, "Hey, that guy's pretty good. He ever release any other songs?"

Now it was my turn to laugh again. "Yeah, just a few."

"So all of those folks are listen' to music?"

"Most of them. But, some are listening to books or podcasts…kind of like recorded radio programs that you can play whenever you want. You can also use these for phone calls."

Aaron shook his head in amazement. Then he asked, "Can I hear Lisa Marie? I was goin' ask you yesterday when you played that Nixon song, but I didn't know if I was ready for it."

"Hang on a minute," I said as I downloaded a dozen of her songs into a playlist. "Here you go. Give it a try now."

He nodded and awkwardly placed the ear buds back in his ears as I again hit play. For a moment, nothing happened. Then, for the first time in more than thirty years, Aaron heard his daughter's voice. He looked at me with a rapturous expression, his eyes beginning to tear, and then began tapping his hands on the steering wheel, his head bobbing in time to the music. He continued this way for the next few hours as we traveled through the desert, chasing the setting sun, saguaros lining our way west.

Never once did the smile leave Aaron's face.

Eighteen

We reached Flagstaff late in the evening and found a room at a place called the D-Lux Motel. Regretfully, there was nothing deluxe about it. Not even close. In fact, the name bordered on false advertising. It was a threadbare hovel, but the price was right, and it had a room with two beds. We'd had a long day of driving and I could tell the miles had taken their toll on Aaron. After we checked in and threw our stuff on the beds, I said, "You've done all the driving, why don't you take the first shower."

Aaron looked at me, the fatigue showing in his face. "Much obliged. I could use a hot shower."

As Aaron walked into the bathroom, I flopped back on the bed and turned on the TV. Mindlessly, I flipped through the channels thinking of Mo's last message. I only felt one emotion: fear, bordering on terror. My thoughts formed an infinite loop that I couldn't seem to break. How could I be a father? I wouldn't know what to do. Could I raise a child and still be a musician? What if I ended up being a loser like my dad and I screwed up my daughter's life? Did Mo expect us to get married? It was enough of a commitment to raise a child, but could I be a husband too? Everything that came at me was a question, but answers were nowhere in sight. On top of this, I felt ashamed of myself and worried about how she was handling the pregnancy. I knew we had to talk, but I was once again incapacitated by fear.

In the mist of my anxious internal debate, something on the television caught my eye. It was the opening scene of *The Naked Gun*, a movie I had loved since I was a child and adolescent humor at its finest. Watching Lieutenant Frank Drebin wipe the birthmark off Gorbachev's forehead had me convulsing in laughter and distracted me from thoughts of fatherhood.

Then, it hit me—Priscilla Presley was the co-star of the movie! As if on cue, Aaron walked out of the bathroom with a towel around his waist while drying his hair with another.

"What's so funny?"

I hit the pause on the remote. "This movie. It's about twenty years old, but it's still one of the funniest I've ever seen. I've watched it at least a dozen times." I paused. "I think you'll be interested in it for another reason."

"Why is that?"

"Tell you what, it just started. Why don't you finish cleaning up and watch the rest of it? Just hit the button that says 'pause' when you're ready. I'll go over to that place across the street and get us a pizza and some drinks."

Aaron looked questioningly at me as I shut the door and walked to the pizza parlor, wondering how he would react when he saw Priscilla on the screen. Should I have warned him? Was he still in love with her? Did he realize she was still alive? As these thoughts raced through my mind, my phone vibrated. I pulled it out of my pocket. I had missed three calls from Mo, and there was a text:

Goddammit, you asshole.

I deserved her wrath. I was a piece of shit for not calling her, but I was a frightened piece of shit with no idea what to do. She was the only woman who had been able to get me to talk about my screwed-up family. Didn't she understand how difficult this was for me? I wanted to call her, to ask how she was feeling, but was certain the conversation wouldn't stop there. Faced with uncertainty, I flicked off the phone and jammed it into my pocket, wishing that I could bury my emotions as easily.

* * *

Forty-five minutes later, I returned to the room with a large pepperoni pizza and a couple of soft drinks. From the edge of the bed, Aaron turned toward me as I opened the door. Tears filled his eyes.

"Are you okay?" I asked.

"Damn, son. This is the funniest movie I've ever seen!" He looked down at the TV remote and carefully pressed the pause button. "I haven't laughed so hard in a long time. And Priscilla's in it! 'Course you knew that already. She's good, really good. She's a better actor than I was, that's for sure. Is that what she's doin' now?" He paused for a moment and then quietly added, "I guess I've been too scared to ask…is she okay? Is she still alive?"

"Yes, I'm sure she's still alive."

A look of relief flooded across Aaron's face. "Thank goodness. There were a couple of times I almost asked you as we were drivin', but I couldn't bring myself to do it. I may have had a number of girlfriends, but she was my only wife. I was worried she might've passed before me. Do you know anything else about her?"

"I'm not sure what she's doing now. She did a few movies like this one. I think I also read somewhere that she's still involved with running Graceland. She and Colonel Parker fought it out in court for control of the estate, including Graceland. She won—"

"That son of a bitch," Aaron interrupted. "I knew he was only after my money."

"Otherwise, she's been out of the public eye."

"I hope she's had a good life. You know, the smartest thing she ever did was to leave me. I had no idea how to be a husband, especially when there were gals everywhere who were interested in me. Marriage is tough enough as it is, but bein' a celebrity made it impossible. But no matter how tough things were with us, at least it gave me my little girl, Lisa Marie."

Listening to the certainty in Aaron's voice, as he again spoke about his daughter, only increased my confusion over my own anxiety at becoming a father. How could something be so powerful that it would extend over distance and years of absence? Why didn't I feel the same? Would I ever?

"Aaron, I don't know how to ask this, but how can you feel so strongly about your daughter when you haven't seen her in more than thirty years?"

Aaron turned to me. His pale blue eyes locked on mine. For a moment, it was as if he was looking into me, seeing all of my insecurities and fears. "Son, it's something too hard to explain. But I think you're gonna discover the answer to that question very soon." Then he gave me a gentle smile, grabbed a piece of pizza, and resumed the movie.

Nineteen

It was clear the next morning that Aaron was not looking forward to another long day behind the wheel. He didn't appear motivated to get up, even when I suggested breakfast. Instead, he sat in bed, staring at the TV and flipping through channels, while I went out and found us some coffee and donuts.

"A. J.," he asked when I returned, "what's with all these TV programs? They don't really seem to have much of a story to them or any actors that I've heard of."

"Like what? Give me an example."

"Well, there was one show that was about buyin' houses, another was about fixin' houses, another was about decoratin' houses, and a few of 'em were about housewives. This one," he gestured to the screen, "is about some gals in a family with a name that sounds like they're from outer space."

"The Kardashians?"

"Yeah, that's the one. Beautiful gals, but why exactly are they on the television? What do they do?"

"You're not the first person to ask that question. The Kardashians are a family in Hollywood. One of the girls was in a sex video a few years ago that became public."

"A sex video?"

"Her boyfriend filmed it." Waving my phone, I said, "Remember how I told you that these are really computers that are all connected?"

Aaron nodded.

"Well, somehow that video became available to everyone on their phones and computers."

"How embarassin'."

"It probably was at first, but she and her family turned the publicity to their advantage. They started a TV show about their daily lives in Hollywood. In the process, they've become big name celebrities and grown incredibly wealthy."

"Do any of 'em sing?"

"Nope."

"Are any of the musicians?"

"Nope."

"Dance?"

"Nope."

"Tell jokes?"

"No."

"Are they in any movies?"

I shook my head, "Just that video."

"Hang on a second. Let me make sure I understand this. One of 'em makes a video while she's havin' sex and they end up all gettin' a TV show without havin' any entertainin' ability?"

"I guess that's about right. And since then there have been a bunch of shows about all the mundane aspects of people's lives—cooking, home remodeling, gardening, making clothes, fixing cars. It's called Reality Television."

Aaron turned his head back toward the TV where Khloé was arguing with Kim about some bit of drivel. Looking at the screen, he shook his head, "Looks like I missed out. Life in Graceland would've made one hell of a reality show."

* * *

As we checked out and walked toward the car later in the morning, Aaron handed me the keys. "Son, you mind drivin' for a spell? I'm feeling a bit fatigued." I had asked several times over the previous days if he wanted me to share the load of driving, but each time he said almost the identical thing, "I've always loved to drive, and it's been a long time since I was behind the wheel." Now, he was giving me a chance. I sank down deep in the still-rancid-smelling driver's seat, turned over the engine, and steered the car toward I-40. Was this all some kind of hallucination? I had taken some drugs in my time, but have never experienced anything quite so fantastical. Was I really driving Elvis Presley's Cadillac, with the King riding shotgun?

I glanced over at Aaron. He had fallen asleep, his head pressed against the passenger window. I tried to look at him objectively, with a critical eye, as if we had just met and I hadn't heard his stories or seen him sing and dance. How would Elvis look at the age of seventy-five? The heart-shaped face, the piercing blue eyes, the full lips, and the thick head of hair—they were all there, under a layer of wrinkles and gray hair. I had to sneak a photo to prove this wasn't all a dream.

Slowly, I inched the phone out of my jacket pocket and turned it on. If I could just get one good shot. Glancing away from the road, I extended my right arm and held the lens in front of Aaron's face, framing the photo. As I did, the car drifted onto the rumble strip, shaking Aaron awake.

"Wha...what ya' doin?" he asked as he groggily raised his head and looked up at me.

"Um—just checking to see if I have any more messages. Nope! Doesn't look like it," I said awkwardly as I quickly put the phone away.

Aaron didn't appear to notice my embarrassment. I glanced in the corner of the rearview mirror and watched him sit quietly, squinting out in the distance as the desert blurred past. What was he thinking about? The years of his daughter's life that he had missed? The money and fame he had surrendered? Was he wondering whether he had made the right decision to escape from the public eye, or was he thinking something deeper? I soon had my answer.

"Son, what's Viagra?"

"Viagra?" I choked back laughter, "Why do you ask?"

"When you were out getting' pizza last night and I was watchin' that movie—the one with Priscilla in it—there were these commercials about somethin' called Viagra." With his thumb, he gestured over his shoulder. "That last sign advertised some doctor in Vegas who could prescribe it."

I began to laugh again, then caught myself. Before I could reply, Aaron, sensing my hesitation, implored, "C'mon, man, what's it for? Must be important. Is it for people who have heart problems? Have they cured cancer?" he asked excitedly. "Or is it for colds and things like that?"

"Nope, there still aren't any great medicines for those."

"Well then, what's it for?"

"You're not going to believe this," I paused. "It's for erections."

Aaron looked at me blankly.

"It's to help men get wood."

Nothing.

"Have you ever heard the expression 'laying pipe'?"

Silence.

"Some men, especially as they get older, have problems getting...hard," I said awkwardly. "This drug is to help them with that."

Aaron's face flushed with embarrassment before he managed to ask, "You mean it's for gettin' a boner?" Then he burst into uncontrollable laughter. Breathlessly, he exclaimed, "The big medical discovery of the last thirty years is to help men get boners?" He broke into laughter again. It was infectious, and before long I was laughing so hard my eyes were watering and I had trouble catching my breath.

"That's one pill I've never needed!" Aaron exclaimed. "Of course, it has been a long, long while. May need to check into how I get some of those. You know, back when I was a star, I did a TV commercial about getting the polio vaccine...raised the number of people getting the shot by like eighty percent. Now, maybe, I could do a spot for Viagra!"

He laughed again and then in a more serious tone said, "You never did answer my question. What else has happened while I've been gone?"

"It's kind of a big question. I'm not even sure where to start. What do you want to know?" I asked as I looked out over the big hood of the Caddy.

"You've been alive most of the time I've been gone. Why don't you start with the major things since you were born."

I paused and thought for a few moments. "Well, your friends the Stickley boys weren't making up stories. What they said is true. In 2008, Barack Obama became the first black president of the United States."

"Enough kiddin' around. I'm serious. You might be able to get me to believe there's a colored president, but there ain't no way his name is 'Barack Obama'. Sounds like some kind of cartoon superhero."

"No, really, that's his name. His mother was American and his father was from Kenya."

"A. J., I mean it," he implored, "I really want to know what's happened. Quit makin' up stories."

"Well, if you aren't going to believe that, I'm not sure what you will think about everything else I have to tell you."

With that I began to recount the historical events of my lifetime. I started with 9-11, the wars in Iraq and Afghanistan, and the recent protests in the Middle East that were becoming known as the Arab Spring. I explained the fall of the Soviet Union, China's industrial ascent, Y2K, Enron, the Internet, Google, smart phones, and the recession of 2008. Along the way, I found myself telling Aaron about Tiananmen Square, the end of Apartheid in South Africa, the O. J. trial, Bill Gates and personal computers, Harry Potter, the shooting of President Reagan, climate change, Ugg boots, Pee Wee Herman, the discovery of the Titanic, and cable TV.

I'd like to believe this was all presented in a cogent, organized manner, but trying to tie everything together was impossible. I'd think of one event and others would spring to mind. I bounced around from topic to event to person, for almost three hours. During this time, Aaron said almost nothing. He just looked out the window or occasionally at me—like when he leered after hearing about Clinton, Lewinsky and the blue dress—but for most of the time, he was silent.

"I think that's most of the major stuff during my lifetime. I'm sure there are others that I've forgotten. If I remember them, I'll let you know, but that should be a pretty good start."

"Guess I gotta lot of catchin' up to do," Aaron replied, and then he was quiet again until we approached an intersection with a turnoff sign that read "LAS VEGAS – 216."

"Are we really that close to Vegas?" Aaron asked.

"Yeah, it's only a few hours away. Why?"

"I think I'd like to go there. You said we have a few days before the concert and I haven't been to Vegas in a long, long time. I had some of my best shows there. I owned that town," he said confidently.

"Aaron, we've already spent much of the money we made in Little Rock. I'm not sure it's such a good idea. It's probably better that we conserve our cash and just head straight to L.A., get a hotel and lay low for a few days until Lisa Marie's show."

"Head to Vegas, A. J.," he commanded. "Trust me. It's where fortunes are made."

Twenty

I hit the turn signal and turned off as Aaron had instructed and for the next few hours we motored up I-93. There's a whole lot of nothing in this part of Southern Nevada. It's just rocks, sky, and asphalt. As we drove through towns like Boulder City and Henderson, I had to fight the urge to shut my eyes and give in to Aaron's metronome-like snoring. When we reached Sin City, the people, buildings and traffic were almost an affront to my brain. I gave Aaron a nudge to rouse him.

"Hey, we're here. Wake up, Aaron."

Aaron lifted his head from the headrest, gazed out the window, and yawned.

"This is Vegas? Las Vegas, Nevada?" Aaron asked excitedly as he looked at the city's versions of the Eiffel Tower, Statute of Liberty, and Luxor Pyramid. "You sure you didn't get lost and drive to Disneyland? Damn, I don't recognize anything. Is that where the Dunes was? I think the Flamingo used to be over there."

"Sorry, that was before my time, Aaron."

"The place is so built up. Nothin' looks the same."

We were down to only about sixty dollars in cash—hardly enough for a few days in this city. We needed more money. To make things worse, we were driving a car in traffic with plates that hadn't been renewed since before I was born. I wasn't sure what Aaron would do if we got pulled over by a cop for expired tags. Things were not looking good.

I drove aimlessly down the Strip, wondering what we should do, while Aaron chattered unceasingly. When I saw a guy walking with a guitar on his back an idea hit me. I turned up Frank Sinatra Boulevard where I located a multi-level parking garage and we drove up the ramp to the top floor. I parked the car in a remote, secluded spot and turned off the engine. Turning to Aaron, I asked, "Are you up for another street performance?"

"I don't know, man…"

"Listen, we don't have much money left. I've been to Vegas once before and I saw musicians busking on the street overpasses. Tourists use them to get from hotel to hotel. They have lots of foot traffic. Unless you've got any other ideas, it's about the only thing I can think of to make some money. Besides, man, we're good together! I know you felt it in Little Rock."

Aaron took a moment to consider what I had said. Then he nodded, and we grabbed our gear, and stepped toward the elevator where we made our way along a walkway lined with glass panels etched with life size photographs of various Vegas celebrities—Sinatra, Cher, Siegfried, and Roy—and one with that famous image of a young Elvis Presley gripping a microphone, his legs splayed, his hips in full motion. I dropped my bag in front of the stainless steel elevator doors and hit the call button wondering how Aaron would react when he spotted it. In the door's reflection I could see him standing behind me turning his head from side to side looking at the celebrities. His eyes locked in on the panel depicting his younger image. He cocked his head, gave it a puzzled look for a moment, then grabbed an imaginary microphone and stiffly mimicked the same pose before being startled by the bell announcing the elevator's arrival.

We entered through the rear door of the Aria hotel and continued until we reached Las Vegas Boulevard, and climbed the stairs to the Harmon Avenue overpass. We walked until I found an open spot in the middle of the thoroughfare and opened my guitar case and propped the Metamucil sign against it. Leaning the amp against the wall, I plugged in my guitar and handed the microphone to Aaron.

"You ready to go?"

Aaron looked at the push of people passing by—couples on a short holiday, a group of Asian businessmen, a tour group holding miniature German flags, and an assortment of college students blowing off steam. He turned back to me nervously.

"*Evil Hearted Man?*"

"The Josh White tune?"

Aaron nodded.

"You got it." I hammered the opening notes, smiling at the people walking past. Then Aaron joined in. With that, we were off and rolling. Aaron grew more and more confident as he sang, calling out songs by Junior Parker, Bill Monroe, and Kokomo Arnold.

A crowd began to form, mostly retired couples enjoying the soundtrack of their youth. After twenty minutes of playing, more than thirty people were packed in a semi-circle around us, and bills were piling in my guitar case.

Aaron was clearly in his element, hard wired into something from his past. As the crowd clapped, he turned to me and said in a loud voice, "Son, do you know any Elvis tunes?" He grinned at me, reached into a plastic bag he had carried from the car and pulled out a worn white bath towel that he had likely swiped from our motel the previous night. He draped it around his neck and used the end to blot his forehead dry. Then he looked my way and mouthed the words *Let's Play House*. I closed my eyes and began to run my fingers over the strings as I listened to Aaron sing. It was the voice of someone fifty years younger. His body may have aged, but his voice sounded the same, like thick, rich tupelo honey, and the crowd and I were delivered back in time.

Seamlessly, we next launched into *That's All Right*. It was then I spotted the drunken college kid pushing his way to the front of the crowd, which by now had grown to more than fifty people. He had one tattooed arm draped over an attractive blonde chick wearing cutoffs and a halter top. With his other hand, he held a red plastic barbell-shaped glass filled with a margarita and a long straw. The kid was probably in his early twenties, and judging by his buzz cut and build, was likely a football player or wrestler. He wore a sleeveless t-shirt with 'Property of University of Alabama' printed on the front. He was sunburnt and had no discernable neck. His obnoxious behavior had all the signs of a kid celebrating his twenty-first birthday or first vacation in Vegas.

Aaron shifted into *Love Me Tender* and the crowd grew quiet as he began singing, his movements transformed from those of an arthritic septuagenarian to a graceful athlete. He held the microphone delicately by its base and moved through the crowd. It was amazing how this old man could grab an audience. Everyone grew quiet, until all you could hear was his voice against the muffled sounds of the traffic moving below us. As he sang, Aaron looked into the eyes of the women around him and made a connection. It didn't matter if they were fifteen, fifty or eighty-five—he had them. For that matter, he had mesmerized everyone around us. Everyone, that is, except for the inebriated college kid who kept yelling things like, "I've got something tender!" before breaking into drunken laughter.

After his second or third outburst, the kid lost his balance and started to fall over, dragging his embarrassed girlfriend with him. The only thing that broke his fall was an older couple standing next to him. The kid almost knocked them down as he struggled to regain his balance.

What occurred next happened so quickly that, at first, I wasn't sure it really happened at all. I replayed it in my mind for days afterward like it was the Zapruder film, breaking it down frame by frame to verify what I thought I had seen. By the time Aaron reached the song's dramatic coda, he had worked his way through the crowd until he was standing only a few feet in front of the kid and his girlfriend. As they straightened up from their near fall, the kid pointed his drink at Aaron and yelled, "He's just like an old Elvis dude!"

Aaron faced the drunken kid as he hit the final notes of the song, one hand holding the microphone, the other reaching skyward like a revivalist minister. Then, in a single motion, his hand flashed down and landed a quick chop to the side of the kid's neck, dropping him like a sack of beef as Aaron followed through with an exaggerated bow. It happened so quickly, most in the audience didn't notice.

"Thank you, thank you all very much. Looks like someone had a bit too much Vegas!" he roared, gesturing toward the young man on the ground.

As the crowd laughed, he put his hand over the microphone, turned to me and whispered, "Told you I had a black belt."

Encouraged by the crowd, Aaron decided we should do one more number. We closed with a spirited version of *Jailhouse Rock* surrounded by people singing, dancing, and shaking, and a young woman trying to revive her unconscious boyfriend.

As we were packing our gear at the end of our performance, a dude in a tight-fitting suit and wrap-around sunglasses approached us. My first thought was, *cop*. I'd been shaken down so many times while street performing that

I could spot them a mile away. I readied myself for the squeeze, but instead I heard the guy say to Aaron, "You guys are good. Much better than the performers I see out here most of the time. You ever play to a larger crowd?"

"Yeah, I've entertained bigger crowds, but it's been a while," Aaron answered.

"My name's Blake Hamilton," he said, shaking our hands. "I'm in charge of floor entertainment at the Aria. Here's the thing. I'm in a bit of a jam tonight. The guy who normally does the 8 p.m. Paul Anka covers flaked on me. I've got no one for his spot. I was thinking you two might want the gig? All I need is a sixty-minute set."

"What's in it for us?" I asked.

"How about $200 for the night? You two split it anyway you want."

Before Aaron could respond, I said, "How about $400 and you throw in a hotel room?"

I knew it was an outrageous request. Hell, I'd never made more than a couple hundred in an evening, but I could sense this guy's desperation and, after all, I knew the true value of the street performer standing next to me.

Blake looked down at his feet for a moment before reaching out his hand. "What the heck. I'm in such a bind, I'll even make it a suite!"

Blake wrote something on a card and handed it to us. "Give this to the clerk at the front desk. They'll set you up. Meet me at the round bar near the Blackjack tables. Be there at 7:45 sharp."

As Blake shook my hand, I tried to keep from losing it over our good fortune. A well-paying gig with the King of Rock and Roll *and* a suite for the night in one of the best hotels in Vegas—life could not get better. I looked over at Aaron as he bid goodbye to Blake, expecting him to share my delight, but he looked unimpressed, almost indifferent. It was as if this was nothing new to him. Just another performance.

Twenty One

Aaron and I returned to the car, grabbed our clothes and the rest of our gear, and walked to the lobby of the Aria where we checked in as Blake had instructed. Collecting our room key, we took the elevator to our Sky Suite on the 20th floor.

I'll admit, I was a bit apprehensive, maybe even insecure. I wasn't used to staying in luxurious places like this. When I was on the road, anything more than sleeping on a vinyl bus seat felt like the Four Seasons. This was clearly going to be a different experience. Opening the door, I dropped my duffle bag and guitar in the entryway and looked around.

"Check this out! Can you believe it? I've never even lived in a house this big!" I yelled as I wandered through the suite. "Holy shit, it's got four flat screens! And a Jacuzzi! And a kitchen! And look at that view!"

"Yeah, it's nice," Aaron replied in an unexcited voice.

"That's it? It's 'nice'? This place is over the top!"

"Well, when I worked in Vegas before, I had my own suite at the International. Took up the entire floor. Even had a grand piano. Wonder if it's still there? But," he added, "I guess this ain't bad."

I found a bedroom, dropped my stuff on the floor and pulled the cash out of my pockets and counted it on the bed.

"Hey, Aaron," I yelled, "we just pulled in $120 for less than a half-hour of work. How sweet is that!"

There was no reply.

"Aaron? Aaron?"

I quickly walked out of my room and down the long hall, concerned that Aaron had wandered off somewhere. But as I entered the living room,

I found him standing silently, silhouetted by the floor to ceiling window. In his hands he was holding a *Top Things to Do in Vegas* hotel guidebook, which he stared at intensely.

"Aaron?" I asked. "Are you okay? Aaron?"

"Look at this," he said, tapping his finger on an advertisement for Las Vegas weddings. "They have a place here where you can get married by a guy dressed up as Elvis. Can you believe that? It just doesn't make sense. I know what you said, but how would anyone getting married today even remember Elvis? Most of them weren't even born back then. Hell, why would they *even* want to get married by Elvis, 'stead of a preacher? Seems pretty silly."

"I don't know what else I can say. I keep trying to get it through to you. Elvis is still famous, more famous than ever!"

"Son, that just can't be. I've been gone. Haven't done any shows or records or movies in decades. Young people would have no way of knowin' me, and to the old timers, I've got to be just one more forgotten singer from the past."

"But don't you get it? Elvis has become way more than just a singer. He's an American—no, a global icon. You can go anywhere in the world and find people wearing t-shirts with pictures of Elvis, watching his movies, or playing his music. Advertisers use Elvis all the time. You saw all those people at Graceland! Elvis has become an ageless symbol of freedom, rebellion, youth, sexuality—"

"I'm okay with that last one." He grinned.

"—and fun! Which is why some people want to take their marital vows before a minister wearing a sequined jumpsuit, black pompadour, and aviator sunglasses."

Aaron just shook his head and turned back to the guidebook.

* * *

After grabbing a shower and a quick bite to eat, Aaron and I walked to the bar that Blake had described and found him anxiously looking at his watch and waiting for us.

"Room okay, boys?"

"Great, thanks," I replied.

"Good, good. So here's the situation. We'll set you up on a corner of the floor. A. J., you can plug in back there. Aaron, we have a floor mic you can use. I just need a sixty-minute set—you can take a quick break after thirty. It's a Q-tip crowd on nights like tonight, so stick with some of the old country songs I heard you sing this afternoon. Any questions?"

"Q-tip?" Aaron asked.

"White hair. You know, retirees, oldsters, geezers—your generation. Okay? Ready? Let's get going."

Aaron gave a quick salute and we headed out to where Blake had indicated. The bar was filled with what looked like a busload of retirement home gamblers, sprinkled with the normal Vegas detritus: a bachelor party smoking cigars and throwing back shots of Patron, aging hookers looking for a score, and down-on-their luck gamblers, wondering once again why they had made that last bet. No one took notice as we set up.

I finished tuning my guitar and looked at Aaron. "You ready to go?"

He hesitated for a moment, "Son, I know what Blake told us, but I think I'd just like to do all Elvis songs tonight. I'll just call 'em out and we'll see where it takes us. Let's start with *Are You Lonesome*. Bet ya' know that one, right?" He smiled.

Aaron's suggestion caught me by surprise. For the last few days, he had avoided attention, and especially any connection with Elvis. Now, he seemed to be gradually accepting, even embracing it. Was it because he was performing again? Did it have something to do with Vegas?

While I was wondering at the change in Aaron, he turned and faced the room.

"Evenin' folks. My name's Aaron and this is my friend A. J. We're very, very happy to be here with you tonight at the Aria. It's been a long time since I've been to Vegas. So much has changed here—for that matter, everywhere," he said, shaking his head. "But for me, the one thing that's still the same is the music. Tonight, we'd like to share some of that with you."

With that, I slowly strummed the opening chords to *Are You Lonesome* and for the next thirty minutes, Aaron drifted effortlessly from ballad to ballad. As he sang, a crowd slowly formed on the floor around us. It reminded me of when I was in elementary school and we first studied magnetism.

We'd point a horseshoe magnet toward a pile of iron filings, which slowly broke off and moved toward the magnet. Aaron was that magnet, and the crowd was drawn to him like those iron filings. The women were the first to gather near us—it didn't matter whether they were Gen X or geriatric, there was a connection, something visceral between them and Aaron. I'd see them lean in, focus on him and gradually begin to sway. They were followed by the retirees and the elderly couples, doubtlessly struck by the eerie way the older singer behind the microphone sounded like something from yesteryear. Then the college kids joined the crowd. Two of them got up from the bar and started slow dancing in front of us as Aaron's voice gradually filled the room and pushed aside the noise of the casino.

The songs he called out were progressively up-tempo: *A Little Less Conversation, Stuck on You, Blue Suede Shoes.* Aaron's hair and face were ringed in perspiration as he paced the crowd—working it, willing it, pulling everyone in the room toward him and the conclusion of the set.

Finally, Aaron told the audience, "Well, we thank y'all for joining us. It's getting kind of late and I've got to get young A. J. to bed, but we'd like to leave you with this last one." Then he looked at me and whispered, *Can't Help Falling*, and I began to play.

Aaron was the consummate professional working his audience into a lather and then bringing them down slowly with a ballad to close the evening. It was something you learned only after many years of entertaining. I watched with growing admiration as Aaron finished the song, gave a dramatic bow, smiled at the audience and said, "Thank you, thank you very much."

The room responded with boisterous applause. A few people even gave us a standing ovation. Aaron waved, grabbed his towel and stepped off the stage, wiping his face, while I packed up my equipment. As I closed my guitar case, a slender man approached me. He was wearing sunglasses and a black t-shirt layered with several gold chains. His dreads flowed down past his shoulders.

"Hey, bro. S'up?"

"Hey," I replied.

"You dudes can bring it."

"Thanks."

"Name's Roscoe. My boss saw a couple of your songs when he was walkin' through the casino. He sent me to see if y'all would stop by and play a few at a party in his suite tah'night."

"I don't know. It's getting kind of late."

"He said he'll make it worth your while—C-note for each song. You just need to play two or three, but he wants them all to be Elvis songs."

"Seriously?"

"Truth. Suite 2514," he said writing the number on a piece of paper. "See y'all there."

"Okay, I'll check with Aaron. But I think we should be able to stop by. Thanks."

I walked over to the table where Aaron was resting, slowly nursing a Pepsi and occasionally exchanging a few words with well-wishing bar patrons. "What did that guy want?" he asked.

"You'll never believe this. He wants us to do a few songs at a party his boss is throwing tonight in one of the suites. And get this—he'll pay us a hundred dollars a song."

"That's nice, son, but I'm gettin' kind of tired. Been awhile since I did a real set."

"Aaron, all we have to do is show up, do a few songs and collect our money, and you'll be in your bed. C'mon, man. We need to stockpile some cash to see us through to California and to get tickets to Lisa Marie's concert."

Aaron considered for a moment. "Well, ah guess so…might even be nice to go to a party. Okay, let's do it."

I flagged the waitress for a beer and talked to Aaron for a bit before Blake bounded over to us. He pulled up a chair and sat down.

"Wow, you guys are good. I didn't realize you were an Elvis impersonator. I've heard a stream of 'em for years—mostly guys a lot younger than you—but I've got to tell you Aaron, you really nailed it." He paused before continuing, "What are you boys doing tomorrow night? I could set you up with a couple of other musicians and you could do the floorshow in the Alibi Cocktail Lounge. We just remodeled it and added a small stage. It's a bit more upscale and holds a few more people than this place. How's that sound?"

I looked at Aaron, but before I could respond, Blake interrupted, "It's a Saturday, so you would need to give me a 90-minute set, but I'll pay you seven-hundred dollars. And you can have the suite for another night."

Before I could say another word, Aaron stuck out his hand to Blake and in a slow drawl said, "Guess, we'll be seein' y'all tomorrow night."

Blake shook Aaron's hand, gave us the details and walked back into the casino. This was crazy, I thought. Yesterday, we were almost broke, and today we had landed two gigs in the space of less than ten minutes. Aaron must have sensed what I was thinking, because he looked at me, slapped me on the back, and said, "I told ya', A. J.—Vegas is where fortunes are made!"

Twenty Two

Aaron and I ate a snack at the bar before heading up to the party on the 25th floor. When the elevator opened, we followed the sound of a pounding bass line to a suite where an enormous bouncer was stationed outside the door.

"Roscoe sent us. We're the band," I announced.

The bouncer eyed us questioningly before opening the door and gesturing us inside. The suite was every rapper's fantasy, high ceilings with crystal chandeliers and floor length purple velvet curtains overlooking a stunning view of the Vegas skyline below. It was like something out of a music video. The room was populated with beautiful women—some in cocktail dresses, others in gold lamé bikini tops, tight shorts, and stiletto heels—and men wearing all shades of black, adorned with dreads, cornrows, and enough ink to fill a case of toner cartridges. Some couples were oscillating in rhythm to the music, others were throwing back glasses of Cristal and Cîroc. A silver-blue cloud of high-grade ganja smoke hung overhead.

I felt a tap on my shoulder. Roscoe was standing beside me.

Leaning into my ear to be heard over the music, he pointed at an area on the floor and said, "Y'all can set up there." I nodded, and we wove through the bodies until I found a place to open my guitar case and plug in my amp. As I did, I sensed the energy dissipating from the room as all eyes turned toward us.

I was struck by an overpowering sense of foreboding, that we were somewhere we shouldn't be, that we were not welcome. This was a mistake, I thought. There was no way these people wanted to hear some crooner from the past. I could feel the fear rising in my chest, but if Aaron felt the same, he didn't show it. He stood beside me, quietly surveying the room with a bemused smile. I was about to suggest to him that we quickly leave, when a door swung open on the opposite side of the suite. Through a cloud of blue smoke emerged a man with beaded cornrows framing his face, wearing Ray Bans and multiple layers of gold chains. His arms were draped over two scantily-clothed young women. In one hand he held a cartoon-sized joint.

I recognized him at once. "Holy shit, it's Snoop."

"Snoop?" Aaron asked.

"You know, Snoop Dogg."

"What?"

I was about to explain when Snoop stepped out onto the main floor of the suite. He waved a hand and the music was silenced. Two men brought a large chair onto the floor and placed it behind him.

"Listen up, y'all," he said. "I know you think we is all gangsta and shit, but I bin tellin' you fur years that the original gangsta was this Elvis dude. None of y'all believe me. But I sampled his *Suspicious Minds,* and me and my homie Pharrell, even ripped a song a' his called *I Got Stung.* You mutherfuckers think it's all West Coast and shit. But y'all is wrong. Elvis was the original gangsta and he came from the South. I can't prove it to you 'cause the cat's dead…died about thirty years ago. But when I was walkin' through the casino yesterday I heard these boyz. They be representin' that Elvis sound. So shut up, mutherfuckers, and listen!" With that Snoop sat back in his chair, sparked up his joint, and pointed at us.

My eyes were fixed on Snoop's outstretched finger, my body frozen with fear. We were expected to play Elvis songs to this crowd? This was a musical mismatch of epic proportion, like asking The Clash to perform at the Vatican Christmas party. We were screwed…unless I thought of a way to get us out of here. As my mind spun through possible excuses and methods of escape, I heard Aaron quietly say, "*Jailhouse,* then *All Shook Up*; we follow that with *Suspicious Minds* and then *A Little Less Conversation* for an encore."

Encore?' What the hell was he thinking? The secondhand smoke had to be affecting his brain. I looked around the now silent room and all I saw were blank stares. This was not going to go well.

Aaron began to count off, "one, two, three…." There was a confident calmness in his voice that liberated my fingers from my fear and I began to play as Aaron launched into the song. The ferocity and power of Aaron's voice filled the room, and I noticed a number of people react with surprise. By the second verse, someone joined in with rhythmic accompaniment using a wooden end table he pulled between his legs. When it came time for the song's celebrated guitar solo, I found the courage to step in front of Aaron and let it rip. Around me, I saw heads bobbing and feet tapping. A group of women began dancing in synchronization and my fear was replaced with amazement.

After *Jailhouse Rock*, we seamlessly shifted into *All Shook Up*. Within moments Aaron was enveloped by a group of gyrating women, all clapping their hands in unison. Aaron was in his element. He moved from woman to woman, looked into their eyes and sang to each as if they were the only two people in the room. They melted.

From there we hurled into *Suspicious Minds*. Upon hearing the first verse, Snoop shouted, "Oh, yeah. I got this one." He stood up, took a deep pull on his joint, walked up to Aaron and held up his hand to stop the music. "Shit, home boy, youz good, but let's try this one West Coast Style. I'll freestyle, then you sing the refrain. White boy," he said, looking at me, "you just play. Let's go."

I did as Snoop instructed, and began playing as he rapped:

> "Desert through the glass
> All you can see,
> But we briggin'
> West Coast to L.V."

Snoop handed the microphone to Aaron who seemed to know intuitively how to respond singing the refrain from *Suspicious Minds*.

Snoop took another drag of his joint before handing it to Aaron and taking back the microphone. I watched with surprise as Aaron reflexively took a small hit, while Snoop sang:

> "The original gangsta,
> Not from our 'hood,
> But he be bringin' it,
> Bringin' it good."

The microphone was exchanged for the joint as three girls moved behind Aaron serving as spontaneous backup singers as they again sang the refrain.

Snoop took the microphone back, and again handed Aaron his joint. This time, Aaron took an even deeper pull—so deep that Snoop's eyes widened as he pointed at him and sang:

> "This old man be flexin',
> He really fly,
> And same as all you bitches,
> He like to get high!"

With that the crowd broke into laughter as Aaron and his backup singers followed with the chorus.

And so it continued, with Snoop and Aaron trading off lyrics—and hits of the joint—until the song reached its crescendo. Snoop and Aaron took exaggerated bows as the crowd applauded and yelled for one more. Snoop nodded at Aaron and walked back into the crowd as Aaron told the audience, "I'm an old fella and don't understand half of what you folks are sayin', but I do appreciate your company tonight." Turning toward the backup singers, he added, "And, damn you gals look fine! A. J.," he said with a wink, "I'm thinkin' it's time for a little less conversation…"

Seamlessly, I segued into the opening of *A Little Less Conversation*. Aaron followed with a voice filled with power and intensity, transforming the room into something between a wild frat party and a modern version of Soul Train. Women gathered around us, shaking everything they had. The men, including Snoop, were dancing as if on pogo sticks, gold chains and designer baseball caps flying from side to side. The place was a writhing, vibrating, pulsating mass of motion with sweat flying off the dancers and onto the floor. Standing behind us, our amateur backup singers danced flawlessly in unison and sang the chorus in harmony as if we had performed together for years while Aaron worked the room like a politician at a musical fundraiser. He would flirtatiously dance with a young woman, encourage someone to join him for a chorus, hold the microphone out to showcase our tabletop drummer, and act with exaggerated surprise at a dancer displaying a particularly challenging move. The man positively owned that room.

When at last the song ended, a very exhausted Aaron held up his palms to an electrified room indicating that he was done for the night.

Aaron turned to me. "Son, would you find me a Pepsi or a glass of water, please?" Then he walked over and dropped down onto a couch. A minute later, I returned from the kitchen with glass of water and a bottle of beer, right as Snoop plopped down next to Aaron.

"I know you be chillin' now, but that was the shizzle, old man! Snoop Dogg be lovin' what youz bringin'."

Aaron gave him a tired smile. "I think that means you thought it was good?"

"Hell yeah. Ol' Snoop Dogg sayin' that you waz wacked."

"Wacked?"

"Yeah, wacked! You tore the mutherfucker up!" he said as he took a long pull from a joint before handing it to Aaron, who looked at it, took a puff and then offered it in my direction. I shook my head and held up my beer nearly dropping the bottle when I heard Aaron ask, "When am I gonna see this dog y'all keep talkin' about?"

"Dog?" asked Snoop.

"That Snoop Dogg you keep talkin' about," Aaron answered, as he inhaled from the joint. "I always loved dogs."

"Snoop Dogg? That's me, man, you know what I'm sayin'?

"Your name is Snoop Dogg? You keep talkin' like it's somethin' or someone else. Why don't you just say 'I'? And who names their kid Snoop Dogg?"

"Dig this, man. My real name is Calvin. Calvin Cordozar Broadus, Jr. Ain't no way you do what I do with a name like Calvin Cordozar Broadus, Jr. So people call me Snoop Dogg."

Aaron pondered this for a moment before handing the joint back to Snoop, "Guess it was kind of the same for me," he said slowly. "Folks called me 'Tupelo Tornado', 'Hillbilly Cat' and things like that. 'Course that was when I first got famous."

"Say what?"

"Yeah, when I was first startin' out in show business, before the records and the movies, they gave me all kinda names—'Sideburns,' 'The Big E,' 'Fire Eyes'…there were a whole bunch of 'em."

"What you sayin'? You waz in movies?"

I looked at Aaron and realized that he was exhausted—exhausted and stoned. If I didn't get him out of here, he was going to spill his crazy story to everyone. Quickly, I interrupted, "Snoop, it's been an honor to play for you tonight. In fact, it's been kind of a dream for me. But my grandpa here is looking pretty exhausted, and I think I need to get him back to his room."

"Nah, nah, I'm fine, A. J.," Aaron responded in a faltering voice, slowly waving his arms in a flailing motion.

Snoop remained quiet, observing us suspiciously as I picked up my equipment with one arm and hoisted Aaron off the couch with the other. "C'mon, gramps. It's time to go. You've had a long night."

"Really, really, really, man. I'm fine." Aaron replied, in a cadence and tone familiar to me from many a high school and college party.

"Thanks again, Snoop," I said as I pushed Aaron toward the door and through the people now twisting to another loud staccato rap number. Aaron continued to complain as we walked down the hallway and toward the elevator. He even tried to break free of my grip and return back to the suite. Growing frustrated, I pushed him against the wall and looked into his glazed eyes.

"Aaron, listen to me."

"What?"

"You're blazed, man. Baked. Do you understand me? You're stoned."

Aaron began to giggle. "Ya' mean this is how you feel when ya' smoke pot?"

I nodded and smiled.

"Why the hell didn't I try it earlier," he exclaimed through growing laughter. "It's a lot a better 'n all that other stuff I used to take!"

I put my arm around his shoulders and joined his laughter before noticing a large man with a shaved head striding out of the suite toward us.

"Snoop said youz forgot somethin'," he said.

I looked down at my guitar and amp. "I don't think so."

Then he held out five folded one-hundred-dollar bills. "He told me to give youz a little extra," he said, his face breaking into a broad smile composed entirely of gold teeth.

We thanked him and watched as he walked back into the suite. Then Aaron turned to me with a mischievous look. "A. J., did ya' see his teeth? Did ya' see 'em? It reminds me of this James Bond movie I saw right before I left to live with Rholetta. One of the bad guys in it had metal teeth like that 'cept I think they were silver."

"They call it a 'grill'."

"A grill?" he asked with a snicker.

"Yep. Some people now, especially rappers, get gold covers made for their teeth. I guess it's kind of a status thing."

Aaron looked at me with surprise. "Well, don't that beat all. I guess if Elvis was still around he'd have a grill made of diamonds!" Then he doubled over in laughter as I helped get him into the elevator and back to our room.

* * *

I couldn't sleep that night. My head raced as I replayed the events of the evening. I had just performed a set with the King of Rock n' Roll and played a private party with him before one of the world's most famous rappers. While in my dreams, I may have fantasized of performing with others, this was a night that would go down in the history of music. Future generations of musicians would analyze and discuss it.

As I lay in bed, my mind spun with random ruminations like the reels of a slot machine. But when my thoughts finally came to rest, they were not of Aaron or Snoop Dogg but of my mother. It's strange how the brain works. I hadn't thought of her for many months or even longer. It had been years since Mom's death, and we were estranged toward the end. Yeah, I made a few half-hearted attempts to get her sober after I moved to Austin, but they were ineffective. I can rationalize my failure now. I was young, and maybe I couldn't handle the situation alone. Dad was long gone, and Mom didn't really have any friends. But the truth was, I just couldn't give enough of myself. Not even to help my own mother.

An alcoholic mother, an abusive father, and a rock star who had deserted his family—yeah, I had some *great* models for the stability and commitment that Mo wanted. It was no wonder I couldn't return her call.

Twenty Three

We were both a bit wrung out the next morning and it wasn't until after 10 a.m. that we finally got our asses out of bed and moving. We wandered out of the Aria and onto the Strip under a bright desert sky, the kind that radiates light of such intensity that it pierces your skull. Just what one needs after a long night of performing. After walking only one block, we quickly concluded that we needed to ease into the day a bit more slowly, and detoured into a casino for breakfast. A note for all of you who have never been to Vegas—when you see a sign offering the "$3.99 Breakfast Gambling Special," know that it is appropriately named because what you're gambling on is the extent of your heartburn. I took a few bites and pushed away the tasteless caloric mass, choosing to stick with black coffee instead. Aaron, on the other hand, shoveled through his mound of eggs, bacon, and hash browns like he was trying to rescue a loved one trapped in an avalanche.

"Slow down, man. We're not in a hurry. We have an entire day to kill."

"Sorry," Aaron mumbled between mouthfuls, "it's been a long time since I've had this much to eat. For years, I've been eatin' only what I could grow or hunt. This is a meal like back in the old days in Memphis!"

"Think it might have anything to do with what you were smoking last night?" I teased. Aaron was silent except for the sound of his silverware scraping an almost clean plate.

"So, what do you want to do today? Do you want to grab a show?" I prodded.

"Nah, don't think so."

"We could take a tour to see Hoover Dam…"

Aaron just looked at me blankly.

"Want to do some gambling?"

Aaron smiled. "I was never one to gamble. I had plenty of other ways to throw my money away."

"How about going shooting? They have shooting ranges here."

"Shooting in Vegas? Why would anyone want to come here to do that?"

"Well, I think I remember that Elvis did. I thought I heard some story about how he shot up a T.V. in his hotel when he was staying here."

"That's all it was—a story. There were a lot of those about me back then. I suppose some of them mighta been true. I was so drugged up I couldn't think straight most of the time. But I'm pretty sure that one was made up. I've always liked to have guns, but these days I only use 'em for huntin'."

"Any other ideas?" I asked.

"Well, I guess it would be nice to visit the International. Don't mean to brag, but I sold out over eight hun'red consecutive shows there. Not sure if it's still a record, but it was back then. Think I'd kind of like to see it again."

"You mentioned that place yesterday, but I've never heard of it. It may have been knocked down and replaced with another hotel, but let's take a walk and see if we can find it."

* * *

Las Vegas Boulevard is a fascinating place under normal circumstances. It's a confluence of cultures, economic diversity, ages, and lifestyles funneled onto a single street. Everyone is united by the search of a quick win, whether it's money or love. But walking the Strip with Aaron was downright surreal. It was mind-boggling to imagine how the tourists would react if they knew the true identity of the old man walking beside me. That would be one story that certainly wouldn't "stay in Vegas." I could only imagine what the experience was like for Aaron. It seemed every few yards, I'd notice he was missing and look back to see him transfixed by something: the fountains of the Bellagio, the Eiffel Tower at Bally's, the pirate ships in the Treasure Island lagoon. He was a tourist from another time, trying to absorb the strangeness around him within the context of his memories.

Aaron appeared not to notice the jostling crowds. He moved as if he was in a dream. The only thing that snapped him out of his reverie were the hawkers on the street corner who would hand him cards with pictures of naked women, advertising, "Girls, Girls, Girls to Your Room!" Aaron would reflexively accept them, then stare at what he was handed with the surprised look of a young boy finding a *Playboy* magazine in a pile of recycled newspapers. Eventually, his repeated embarrassment overcame his innate Southern politeness and he learned to walk past with his hands buried in his pockets.

The costumed street people drew most of his attention. I think Aaron recognized Superman, Spiderman, and Wonder Woman, but you try to explain SpongeBob SquarePants to someone who has been removed from society for more than three decades. For that matter, try explaining it to me. Walking among these characters, Aaron was in a fantasy world, moving around with a dazed smile plastered on his face.

Two young women dressed as showgirls really caught his eye. Both were wearing enormous feathered tiaras that covered more surface area than their clothing, which consisted of little more than sequined G-strings and pasties.

"Hey, handsome! Welcome to Las Vegas," one of the women purred. "Why don't you come over and get a picture with us—your grandson can take it."

Before I could warn him that this was a scam that was going to cost us money, Aaron joined the girls and slipped an arm around each of their waists.

"Is this your first visit to town?"

"Nah," said Aaron, "I used to come here a long time ago, back in the sixties and seventies."

"You can't be that old," said one of the girls flirtatiously.

"Well, I am!" Aaron responded proudly. "I'm seventy-five."

"No, you're not! Not with biceps like this!" said the other girl in mock astonishment as she squeezed his arm.

Aaron was positively radiant. "Take a picture, son. Use that phone thing of yours." Then he turned to the girls. "A. J. has this special little telephone that takes pictures, plays music, and all kinds of other stuff. You should have him show it to you!"

The girls looked oddly at Aaron and giggled. Then they kissed him on both cheeks as I snapped the photograph. Aaron gave them both a hug and headed off toward another character, while I followed behind, handing out a five spot to everyone he left in his photographic wake.

The first Elvis impersonator we encountered brought Aaron to a full stop. The guy was short, his stature exaggerated by his high bouffant. He looked like a cartoon caricature as he dramatically thrust his hips at passersby. With an exaggerated sneer he beckoned to female tourists, "I got some burnin' love for you, baby." Aaron stood motionless, like a hunting dog focused on its prey. I could sense his anger rising. Hurriedly, I grabbed his elbow and pushed him along the sidewalk as he continued to stare back at the impersonator.

"Did you see that? Did ya' see him?" he growled.

"Yes, I did. Get used to it. You'll see a lot of guys like that in Vegas."

"But he didn't look anything like me. It was like he was just wearin' a costume, and he was actin' rude!"

"I've been trying to get you to understand! Elvis isn't a person anymore! He's something much greater. To some people he's nostalgia, a reminder of how things used to be, to many he's almost a spiritual deity, and to others, like that guy, he's just a way to get a laugh and make a few bucks."

Aaron looked at me for a few seconds, his face quivering with changing emotions. Then he shook his head, pulled his elbow free from my hand, and stalked off ahead, and down the Strip.

Twenty Four

We walked a few more blocks before we located a tourist information kiosk. A slender man in his late sixties was manning the booth, sitting on a stool reading *The Racing Daily*.

"Excuse me," I said. "My grandfather hasn't been to Vegas for decades. He used to stay at a hotel called the International and wanted to see the place again. Can you give me directions to it?"

The man looked at me over his reading glasses as Aaron continued to stare back in the direction of the Elvis impersonator. "The International properties have changed hands several times. When did you say your grandfather was last here?"

"It would have been during the mid-1970s."

"Ah," he smiled. "Those were the Elvis years. My wife and I used to go see his show at the International on all our special occasions. My wife, may God rest her soul, worshiped Elvis." His eyes began to glisten before he looked down the street and pointed.

"The place now belongs to Hilton. It's called the LVH – Las Vegas Hotel and Casino. Keep walking past the Venetian and Wynn properties, then take a right on Riviera. You'll run right into it."

"Thanks," I said.

"It's still quite a hike. You want me to call a cab for your grandfather?" the man offered.

"No, we've got plenty of time, and I think he's enjoying reliving memories."

I turned and walked back to Aaron. Given all that had happened in Vegas over the last thirty years, I wasn't really sure whether he was reliving memories or just trying to make sense of the city where he spent so much time. When I reached him, I put a hand on shoulder, "The place isn't called the International anymore, but it's still around. I've got directions. You ready to walk some more?"

Aaron nodded, and we merged with the flow of tourists down the Strip.

* * *

As we walked, I'd look over at Aaron and try to imagine what he was thinking. Was he shocked by the changes around him? Overwhelmed by the sensory assault of the crowds, the traffic noise and the buildings looming over us? Or was he lost in thoughts of the past: memories of performances, celebrity friends? I couldn't tell. He wasn't saying much of anything until he started looking up at the marquees lining the street.

"A. J., what's a Carrot Top?" he asked.

"Where do you see that?"

He pointed up to a sign high above the street.

"He's a red-headed comedian. That's his nickname."

"Blue Man Group?" he asked, as he gestured to another.

"They are a group of, I guess you would say, comedians, who perform in skin-tight blue suits that cover their entire body."

"Thunder from Down Under?"

"Male exotic dancers from Australia."

"Men?"

"Yep. Kind of male strippers."

Aaron looked at me in disbelief, "Cir-que-do-so-le-eel?"

"Cirque du Soleil? It's a circus with acrobats and comic performers."

He hesitated before asking, "Where's the music?"

"What do you mean? There are all kinds of musical reviews on the Strip."

"No, no. I don't mean musicals. Those are just plays with singin'. Where's the real music? Used to be that every casino would have someone—Sinatra, Dean, Sammy, Tom Jones, Louis Prima. People would come night after night to hear 'em sing. Vegas was the one place in the world where you could see all of 'em. What's happened to all that?"

"I guess music's changed. There's more of it and it's more accessible than it was in the past. People have music with them when they exercise, when they walk, ride the bus, drive a car, or work. It's everywhere, because of these," I said holding up my phone. "Now people can listen to music all the time. Just how you were listening to it in the car."

Aaron turned to me. "They listen to it, but do they hear it?"

"What do you mean?"

"Music used to be special; you went to hear it with someone that was special to you. You shared something. You'd get dressed up and go to a club. The ladies would wear a dress and the men would put on a tie. Maybe you'd enjoy a drink and a meal before the show. When the singer came out, you'd sit real close to your gal and get lost in the song. If the singer was good, you could feel the emotion. The singer's style and phrasing got to you. It was the same thing when you listened to an LP. You'd invite a friend over to hear it and look at the cover together taking turns reading the liner notes. Back then, the music meant something. It brought people together. It wasn't just background like the music in elevators."

As we walked, I considered what Aaron had said. "I think the difference is that now music is democratized."

"Democratized? I'm not followin' you."

"Remember when I told you about the Internet? Well, now musicians can record their songs and put them on the Internet where anyone can buy them. Some musicians just set up a site—think of it as a store where people can go to from anywhere in the world—and use it to sell their music and publicize their concerts. My band, Sweet Lil, does this. Certainly not all of it is music that 'means something' or 'brings people together,' as you say. In fact, much of it is crap. But now everyone can have their voice heard. You don't need agents, record companies or distributors, just an Internet connection."

"So, no labels, no agents, no RCA—no Colonel Tom Parker?"

"There are still big recording companies, but now there are other ways to get your music heard."

"Damn," Aaron declared, "Maybe I started in the business too soon."

It took us another hour to hike to the LVH. We probably could have done it faster, but Aaron was mesmerized by everything around us. He stopped every time we came across an Elvis impersonator and we passed at least four of them on the way. When we finally reached the hotel, we walked into the lobby and I went up to the front desk and asked if it was possible to take a tour of the suite where Elvis had lived.

"I'm afraid not," replied the clerk.

"It's not for me, it's for my grandfather," I said, pointing to Aaron, who was gazing around as if in a trance. "He's a big Elvis fan—used to come see him here all the time."

"I would if I could, sir, but it doesn't really exist anymore. The Elvis Suite was divided into rooms years ago, with new furnishings. Truth is… there isn't a trace of Elvis left other than a plaque that says 'Elvis Suite,' and currently we have guests staying in all the rooms."

"Thanks," I said, a bit dejectedly, and walked back to where Aaron was standing and gave him the news.

"Well, I guess that's more like what I expected. Hard to believe they would keep all that expensive real estate dedicated to a singer from thirty years ago," he murmured, his eyes betraying a touch of disappointment.

"Hey, I've got an idea," I said. "The desk clerk mentioned a car show outside the Orleans Casino. Do you want to go to that? We still have plenty of time before our gig tonight."

Aaron's face lit up, "Now you're speakin' my language! I miss my cars. Let's go."

* * *

Aaron may have loved cars, but car shows bore the shit out of me—probably because I've never owned one. I didn't even get my driver's license until I met Mo. I got tired of her teasing me all the time about her having to drive everywhere. So, for her birthday, I surprised her and passed the driver's test. I gave her a copy of my license as a gift. Before you get too judgmental about me being cheap, Mo appeared to like this present much more than her gift from the previous year—a set of matching beer mugs I filched from a bar where I was playing.

Aaron, however, was in his element, wandering up and down the aisles, pointing at cars like a kid in a toy store. "A '75 Dino! I had one of those.

Look, a '56 Eldorado, had one of those too. Wow, a Stutz Blackhawk. That was one of the last cars I ever bought. See that one—that's an MGA. I had a red one. Fun car, it's the one I drove in the movie *Blue Hawaii*."

"Aaron, how many cars did you own?"

"Don't rightly know. Probably, hun'reds."

"Hundreds?" I exclaimed.

"Yeah, I guess so. Course if you count all the ones I gave away, it would be a bunch more." He paused and looked at me for a moment. "You know how some people send birthday cards? Well, I'd send birthday *cars*. All my friends got 'em for their special occasions. Once I bought a pink Cadillac for my mama and she never even learned to drive! It just sat at home and every now and then Daddy would take her for a spin around the property," he said with a laugh.

At that moment the loudspeakers rang out: "Thank you Ladies and Gentlemen for joining us at the Viva Las Vegas Car Show, the premier event for the automotive enthusiast. Today, we've got a real treat for you! A crowd favorite here in Vegas, please look high overhead and put your hands together for the Flying Elvises!"

Upon hearing those words, Aaron's head whipped around like the chick in that old *Exorcist* movie. He stared at me in shock as the crowd started clapping and shouting, but I could only shrug my shoulders in response.

We watched as a small white plane slowly circled high above us over the parking lot. *Viva Las Vegas* blared from tinny loudspeakers as a dozen jumpers streamed out of the plane; a few seconds later, chutes blossomed above each of them. As they slowly drifted toward the parking lot and came into focus, I could see they were dressed in matching, caped, baby blue sequined jumpsuits with dark sunglasses and exaggerated black pompadours. Within minutes, Elvis look-a-likes were dropping to the ground around us as the speakers began playing *Hound Dog*. The crowd roared in laughter as each jumper detached his parachute and immediately began an exaggerated impression of Elvis.

One of them walked straight toward us with a melodramatic strut. Stopping directly in front of Aaron he asked in an imitation Elvis voice, "What's your name old timer?"

"Aaron," came the tentative response.

"Well, Aaron, you look like you might be old enough to remember seeing the King of Rock n' Roll."

"I might' a seen him a time or two," Aaron replied with a sly smile.

"Well, then," he shouted, swinging his hips wide and shooting his arm out toward the crowd, "bring it like the King!"

Aaron stood immobile for a moment as I inched toward him, trying to anticipate how he was going to react. Was he going to yell an insult at the performer or run away? I stared at him uncertainly. Finally, I detected a slight twinkle in his eye as Aaron slowly began to mimic the motions of the impersonator to the roaring response of the crowd.

"Not bad, not too bad. But, really, is that all you got?" the impersonator shouted above the music as he continued to exaggerate his dance moves and gestures.

Aaron looked at him blankly for a moment before repeating the motion and then enhancing it by suddenly pivoting from side to side on the balls of his feet. The impersonator feigned awe and responded by mimicking Aaron's moves. People begin to gather around the two of them, laughing and clapping as they watched an Elvis Presley face-off. Each took turns adding something to their routine—karate kicks, spins, head rolls, hand gestures—as the song approached its coda. Finally, Aaron energetically repeated all of the previous moves, then came to a sudden halt, drawing the crowd's rapt attention. He thrust his finger to the sky while rocking his hips in perfect time to the music, before slowly unveiling a full Elvis Presley lip curl. Riotous laughter exploded around us as the song ended, and the impersonator waved a white handkerchief in surrender. He made a show of taking off his cape and placing it around Aaron's shoulders as the people around us shouted their approval. Aaron beamed through it all.

Gradually, the crowd began to dissipate and we headed back to the Aria. It was a long walk, but Aaron was vibrating with energy and excitement, and I knew he would have no difficulty making it. As we walked along the Strip, the cape never left his shoulders. He seemed to flaunt it as we retraced our way past the tourists and Elvis imitators. It was if Aaron wanted to announce that the real King had returned.

Twenty Five

Aaron was changing. Maybe he was just adjusting to everything around him, but I felt it was something more. Only days before, he disbelieved Elvis's popularity. Now he seemed not only to accept, but embrace it. We had driven almost two thousand miles in a car that reeked of fermented chicken shit because he didn't want to draw attention. Now, he was performing Elvis songs and even repeating his signature dance moves. What the hell was happening and where would it all lead?

We showed up at the Alibi Cocktail Lounge at 7:45 p.m. and met backstage with Blake.

"How ya' doing, gentlemen? Did you have a good day in our lovely city? Are you still happy with the room?"

"Wonderful," I replied. "We just did a bit of sightseeing. And the room is great. Thanks."

"Good, good…Listen, you guys were so successful last night, I was thinking tonight we'd try to take it to the next level."

"What did ya' have in mind?" drawled Aaron.

"Well, I've got a couple of other musicians who can back you up—Frank Jeffries on bass and Mitch Haley on drums. Real professionals. They've played for everyone."

"That sounds okay," I said, "but how are they going to know what to play? We don't have time to work through a set list."

"Well," Blake paused, "I was thinking maybe this evening you could do just Elvis songs. You ended up playing them last night and it worked pretty well. I'm sure they know *his* catalog. How's that sound?"

I looked at Aaron, who nodded. "Sure, no problem," I said.

Blake stood quietly for a moment. "Aaron, there's one more thing…I was thinking how 'bout you wear this?" With that Blake turned around and pulled a powder blue sequined jumpsuit and a long white scarf from a rack behind him. He handed it to Aaron.

Aaron looked at the clothes and then Blake. "You mean you want me to dress like Elvis Presley? Are you going to want me to dye my hair or wear some silly wig too?"

"No, no, nothing like that. You can be a senior citizen version of Elvis," he said with a smile. "You know, like if he was still alive."

Aaron ran his hands over the sequins lost in contemplation for what felt like minutes. Then he looked at Blake, chuckled, and said, "Sure, what the heck."

"That is really outstanding! I know it will be a great show. Just one more thing, can you please try to tone it down a bit tonight?"

"Tone it down? You mean we were too loud?"

"No, no, the volume was fine," he paused. "This may sound strange given that I'm asking you to wear an Elvis costume and giving you backup musicians, but can you not be so good? Last night was great, but some of the dealers said customers were leaving their tables to watch you. It was like you were a real entertainer, not a lounge act."

Aaron grabbed the clothes and in a voice oozing with Southern sincerity, said, "Yes, sir, we'll tone it down, no problem." Then he headed toward the dressing room, flashing me a mischievous smile as he walked past.

While Aaron changed into his outfit, I introduced myself to Frank and Mitch as we began unpacking our instruments. Frank looked like he was in his mid-sixties; Mitch was perhaps a few years younger. They came across as the stereotypical aging musicians trying to hang onto popular relevancy. Frank sported a grey perm and a gold crucifix earring. Somehow, he had jammed his pear-shaped torso into a set of stylish skinny jeans, topped off with an expensive Robert Graham shirt. Mitch wore wire frame granny glasses and a ponytail, despite being nearly bald. He had on black biker boots, jeans, and a puffy white shirt that looked decades out of date. Despite appearances, I discovered that these gentlemen were the real thing, professional musicians.

"How long have you been playing?" Frank asked.

"Only seriously for about six years, since I moved to Austin."

"Where have you played there?" asked Mitch.

"Just about everywhere around town—Threadgills, Antone's, The Continental Club. Now I'm with the house band at Stubbs."

"We've played most of those. Austin's great for music—and musicians. Seems like we never had any trouble making money there. You done any touring?"

"Only the last couple of years," I said. "We usually hit the road for a month or two in the summer. Mainly it's just small dives, but sometimes we get to open at nicer places. Last year we played Tipitina's in New Orleans, Tootsies in Nashville, and the Folly Theater in Kansas City."

"Those are all good gigs, man."

"They were for us—even if we weren't headlining. But I'm not sure where it's all going. We haven't gotten close to signing with a label."

"Hang with it," Mitch said. "If the music's important, you just keep plugging away until you get that break. You just gotta stick with it."

"How long have you guys been playing?" I asked.

"Professionally for more than forty years," he answered, shaking his head. "Hard to believe. Isn't that about right, Frank?" Frank nodded as he opened his case and pulled out a bass guitar.

"Frank and I met as session musicians in Alabama at Muscle Shoals."

"Wait a second. Muscle Shoals?" I interrupted. "When did you play there?"

"During most of the seventies."

"You're kidding! That's when it was going off! It was the epicenter for music back then… Aretha, Wilson Pickett, the Staple Singers."

Mitch grinned, looked at Frank and exclaimed, "This youngster knows his music." Then he turned to me and continued. "We recorded with all of them, including Dylan, Dr. Hook, and a bunch of others. Even got to tour with the Stones and Elton a few times."

"Yeah, that was the life," said Mitch. "We traveled on planes, not buses. Nice food in the dressing rooms, free booze, and the girls… Damn, the girls were even interested in hacks like us." He laughed and elbowed Frank.

"How'd you end up in Vegas?"

"A friend asked us to join his band here about twenty years ago. He told us a lot of recording executives were coming from L.A. to sign talent. It was a regular gig at the Aladdin, which gave us the chance to stop traveling—and keep up on alimony and child support." He grimaced.

"Two divorces for me; three for Mitch. The road is hard on relationships, and even harder on the wallet!"

"Do any of your kids play?"

"No, I think they all wanted to get as far away from music as possible. As tough as it is on your wife, being the child of a professional musician is worse. Your dad's never at home, and when he is he's playing gigs at night and sleeping all day. Worse yet," he said, directing his eyes in Frank's direction, "he's always got his bandmates coming over, drinking and raising hell. It makes it hard to form—what do they call that, Frank?"

"A parental bond," Frank replied.

"Yeah, right," said Mitch. "That's it. A parental bond."

"Are you still in the band?" I asked.

"Nah, we broke up. For years we thought we were going to get signed. We'd have a great set and someone from a label would come up afterward and give us a business card, saying he was interested in recording us. It happened a few times, but nothing ever came of it." Mitch's voice trailed off.

"Anyway," Frank continued, "Mitch and I are still hoping we'll get a break. We may be getting a bit worn around the edges, but we can still bring it. In the meantime, we pick up work where we can from Blake and others in addition to our day jobs."

"Day jobs? I thought you were full-time musicians. You guys played at Muscle Shoals!"

"Hell, that doesn't mean shit. You need something more than that to pay the bills around here. I drive a limo; Mitch runs a roulette wheel at the Bellagio. And like I said, we play other gigs when we can get them. Sometimes it's a corporate event or convention, sometimes it's casino jobs like we're doing tonight."

Just then, Aaron stepped out of the dressing room wearing his jumpsuit with the white scarf draped around his neck. The transformation was striking. It wasn't just the costume—it was his bearing. Unlike the sometimes-disoriented seventy-five-year-old I'd traveled with for the last week, the man standing next to me was intense and focused.

"Ok, boys. How's this work?" he asked in a commanding voice as he turned to Mitch and Frank.

"Well," Mitch responded, "usually, we play about two minutes of set-up music during which Blake will come out and introduce the act. The stage has two overhead lights that track the movement of the microphone. If you hold it and walk around, the lights will follow you."

"A. J., you can plug in opposite me," Frank added. "Everything's set up on the floor tonight. You won't need your amp, just your guitar. It's not a bad gig. Free drinks and food—just flag a waitress. We've got a tip jar on the corner of the stage closest to the bar. Some nights you can do pretty well if a drunk high roller drops by."

Mitch broke in, "I overheard what Blake told you. He's right, don't go big. If you attract too many gamblers from the tables, the pit bosses get up-set and Blake will never hear the end of it. Now how about the songs? You goin' to just call 'em out?"

Aaron reached into his sleeve and pulled out a folded piece of paper covered in scribbles. "I put together a set list. It should come out to about sixty minutes. Let's see how things go, and I'll call 'em after that. Why don't you boys take a look at it and make sure you know 'em all."

Frank, Mitch and I reviewed the list. All of the Elvis classics were there and even a few I had forgotten. It was a reminder of the breadth and vol-ume of his work; the man was a hit machine back in his day. Noticeably, the songs Aaron had selected were all ballads and slow tempo numbers. It appeared that he really was taking to heart Blake's admonition.

Despite this, I had a feeling that Aaron might have other plans.

Twenty Six

We walked onto the stage at about 8:15 and began setting up our equipment. I plugged in where Frank had indicated and began to tune up while looking out at the club and the still-sparse crowd. It was definitely a step up from the night before. The stage was small and raised a couple feet off the ground, but it was surrounded by a richly-appointed lounge. The crowd was a bit more upscale as well. A dozen nicely dressed couples were dining at the tables around us, a group of kids my age were laughing in a booth, and at the bar, a number of gamblers were throwing back just one more for luck before hitting the tables.

When all was ready, Frankie gave the nod, and we played a soft melody for about a minute before Blake jumped on stage and grabbed the microphone. "Ladies and Gentlemen. Welcome to the World-Famous Alibi Cocktail Lounge. It's great to have you all here with us this evening. Tonight, you are going to be part of music history! Why, you ask? Well, let me tell you. When people think of Vegas they think of one thing…"

"Yeah, strippers!" yelled one of the kids from the bar.

"One person comes to mind…."

"The asshole dealer who caused me to bust!" yelled another to a smattering of laughter.

"That person is the Man from Memphis," continued Blake, "the one with the Blue Suede Shoes. I'm talkin' about the King of Rock n' Roll! Now, I know what you're thinking. That the King died over thirty years ago. But tonight, I'm here to tell you…I'm here to tell you…I'm here to tell you…." Mitch pounded the drums to a crescendo as Blake shouted, "that Elvis lives!"

With that, Blake replaced the microphone and the curtain pulled back, revealing Aaron in his blue jumpsuit. He strutted on stage to a smattering of applause. As he walked past me toward the microphone, he turned and grabbed my aviator sunglasses hanging from the neck of my hoodie. He flicked them on his face in a single motion, like he was opening a switchblade. Then he gave me a quick smile, strode to the microphone and called out, "One, two, three," and we started into *It's Now or Never*. From there, following the set list, we played *Are You Lonesome* and then *In the Ghetto*.

At first, the crowd paid little attention, but the applause built with each song and people gradually began to detach from their conversations to watch Aaron. As they did, I could see him grow more relaxed. Between songs he gradually began to talk about Vegas in the 1960s and 1970s, including stories about Howard Hughes, Sinatra and the Rat Pack, Evel Knievel, and Liberace. Some of them were poignant, others hilarious, but they were all personal. The audience ate it up and steadily the room filled.

It was about then when Aaron began to go off script. He started calling more upbeat songs: *All Shook Up, Return to Sender,* and *Blue Suede Shoes.* It was in the middle of that last number when I saw an agitated pit boss talking to Blake and gesturing angrily toward Aaron. Moments later, Blake jumped on the rear of the stage and leaned over Mitch's shoulder and said something to him. Mitch nodded and continued drumming until the end of the song when he gestured to draw Aaron and me closer. "Guys, I warned you. The pit boss is pissed off. He says we've got to tone it down."

Aaron flashed a devilish smile, slowly nodded his head and walked to the top of the stage. Then he looked back and said, "I'll call the rest of 'em out from here, boys. Ready? Let's do *That's All Right Mama*." Given the upbeat nature of that one, I was surprised to hear him choose it, but I just looked at Mitch and Frank, shrugged, fingered the frets and started playing.

From there, the evening became a blur. We played a couple more up-tempo numbers in rapid succession. It was as if Aaron was daring the pit boss to make a move. I remember in the middle of *C.C. Rider*, Aaron pointed to me and said, "Take it, A. J., make it hurt, son," and I spontaneously reeled off one of the most epic riffs of my life ripping at the strings like I was the love child of Nancy Wilson and Jimmy Hendrix.

I could tell Mitch and Frank felt the same as I did. We were on fire that night. And as with them, my eyes were constantly following Aaron. You never knew what he was going to do, whether it was reaching out to a woman in the audience, calling for a solo, or performing karate kicks with surprising exuberance for a man in his mid-seventies. As a joke, I pulled the "Need money for Metamucil" sign out of my guitar case and leaned it against the microphone stand while Aaron was singing. The gesture caught him by surprise and he erupted in laughter in mid-chorus. He whispered to a waitress, who handed him a black Sharpie out of her pocket. With a big flourish, Aaron crossed out the word Metamucil and wrote "Viagra." The crowd roared in approval and we launched into *Jailhouse Rock*.

We had been playing for almost ninety minutes when I glanced over at the casino floor. It was nearly empty except for a few solitary dealers standing guard over their tables. It seemed everyone in the casino was crowded around the lounge. Gamblers, dealers, tourists, and drunks of all ages were moving with abandon as the song ended. Calls for more followed while Aaron mopped his face and neck with his towel. Then he raised his hands to quiet the crowd. "Thank y'all for joinin' us here at the Alibi Cocktail Lounge and for bein' such a great audience. We'd love to play more, but I'm an old man and need my sleep." To which two attractive middle-aged women yelled in unison, "We'll help you get to bed!"

Aaron chuckled, then turned to me and asked, "A. J., you know what I'm thinkin'?"

I nodded and gestured to Frank and Mitch to follow my lead as I hit the first few notes of *Viva Las Vegas*. Watching us, Aaron smiled, spun around and belted out the first line of the city's informal anthem. Almost in unison, everyone in the lounge jumped to their feet and started clapping and dancing. As they did, the few remaining gamblers on the floor started leaving their tables and crowding into the room. When Aaron hit the final chorus, the club was crammed with people singing "Viva Las Vegas!" at the top of their lungs.

I've watched hundreds of club performances and played in my share of many them. To this day, I've never seen anything like that night playing with Aaron. The room had the energy of a mosh pit at an AC/DC concert, but with fewer tattoos and more hair product and collared shirts.

After the song finished, Aaron thanked everyone and stepped down from the stage. He looked happy, but completely drained. Mitch, Frank, and I waved to the crowd, packed up our instruments and followed him. We gave each other high fives as we stepped backstage where Blake was waiting.

"You guys were incredible!" Blake exclaimed. "Hell of a show. Did you see the way the crowd reacted? I haven't seen anything like that in years. It was as if the real Elvis was out there!"

"Thank you," said Aaron, who was slouched in a chair with a white towel around his neck, suddenly looking every bit of his years.

"I know you mentioned something about having to get to L.A., but what about staying here? I can set you up with a regular show on a bigger stage."

"That's right nice of ya' to offer," Aaron quietly interrupted, "but we're on our way to Los Angeles to see my little girl. I've only got a few days to see her."

With that, he stood up and headed to the dressing room to change his clothes, running the towel through his wet grey hair as he walked away.

Blake called after him, "Well, think about it if you ever come back this way. Seriously, you guys were great. You've got my card. Call me anytime you want a regular gig."

"Thank you, sir," Aaron replied over his shoulder as he walked away. "You never know. I may just take you up on that some time. I've heard Vegas is great place for entertainers to get their careers started."

Twenty Seven

Frank, Mitch and I toweled off back stage and divided the tips. I didn't know when I would see them again, but our performance was a shared bond that none of us would likely forget. It was that kind of evening.

"Wow, Aaron can really bring it," Mitch exclaimed. "How old *is* he? I've never seen anyone who can fire up a crowd like that."

"I really don't know," I answered. "I just met him recently."

"Well, stick with him," advised Frank. "I'm not sure where it will lead, but the guy has serious talent. He could play anywhere in Vegas. Maybe even get a recording contract."

"Thanks, guys. I'll pass it on to him."

We exchanged contact information and said our goodbyes and then Frank and Mitch walked out onto the casino floor as Aaron, now changed into his street clothes, returned from the dressing room.

"A. J., looks like you could use a drink."

"You've got that right," I responded as we walked through the crowd toward the bar. The going was slow as a number of patrons wanted to pat Aaron on the back, give him a hug or shake his hand. In the space of ninety minutes, the man had become celebrity. We finally found a couple of empty stools near the corner of the bar and sat down; I ordered a Johnnie Walker on the rocks and a Pepsi for Aaron. Then we huddled together over our drinks and reviewed our set. It's a ritual for professional musicians, a way of coming back down after the emotional high of a particularly good performance. For me it was the unbelievable chance to learn the thinking of one of the world's most famous showmen, to understand his decisions on song changes, the tempo of the performance and directions to the band.

While in the midst of discussing a particular song transition, we were overcome by a cloud of Shalimar and the sound of jingling metal bracelets as the two women who were flirting with Aaron during the show squeezed in on either side of him.

"You were *so* good," fawned Blonde Number One, as she placed a heavily manicured hand on Aaron's shoulder.

"Thank you," said Aaron in an amused voice.

"I saw Elvis when I was a teenager. He was so handsome and sexy. Tonight, it was like you were him," said Blonde Number Two as she tossed her hair to the side and flashed a seductive smile. "My name is Connie and my friend is Bonnie," she said, offering her hand.

"Pleased to meet you, ma'am. My name is Aaron and this is my friend A. J."

"Bonnie, he called me ma'am. He is *so* cute."

"I know. I told you he was," Bonnie replied.

"Can we buy you ladies a drink?" Aaron offered.

"I'll have an Apple Martini."

"I'll have a Sex on the Beach."

"Bonnie, you only order that drink for the name," giggled Connie.

Aaron flagged a bartender, "Could we get an Apple Martini, and um, ah… Sex on the Beach…" He laughed out loud and then recovered. "A Pepsi, and…" he looked my way.

"Another, please," I said shaking the cubes in my empty glass.

Observing the interplay between Connie, Bonnie, and Aaron was similar to one of those BBC animal shows narrated by David Attenborough. It was like watching two lionesses circling in on an unwitting water buffalo. It was clear that Aaron's new lady friends had one thing on their minds, and it was equally clear that he was dangerously outmatched.

While listening to their flirting and staring at my fresh drink, my phone rang. I looked at the screen. It was Mo. I held the phone and stared at it for several rings until Aaron, seeing the name on the screen, gave me a nudge. "Son, I think that's a call you need to take." I nodded reluctantly and took my drink over to an empty booth and answered the phone.

"Hi, honey. Can you hear me? It's kind of noisy here."

"Thank God you're alright!" gasped Mo, her voice filled with relief that quickly gave way to anger. "You are such a fucking asshole. Where are you?"

"I'm in Vegas."

"Vegas? Las Vegas? Las Vegas, Nevada? What in the hell are you doing there?"

"It's a long story… a really strange one."

"Well, are you okay?"

"Yes, I'm okay. How are you?"

"How am I? Hmm…let me think about that. How about hurt, abandoned, afraid, lonely, deserted, confused? Let me know if you want more. English professors are good with adjectives. Oh, and you can add nauseous to the list. Morning sickness sucks!"

"I'm sorry, honey. I really am."

"I don't want you to be sorry. I want you to decide what the hell you are going to do. You're either in or you're out—permanently. This is happening whether you like it or not. You need to make a decision."

I took a deep swallow of my drink and waved to the waitress for another. "A. J.?"

"I heard you. This is just all so unexpected. I'm just trying to… process it."

"Listen, you bastard. It's unexpected for me too. But I know that I love you. I also know that I'm the best thing that's ever happened in your life. And I'm about to make it even better by replicating my incredible chromosomes in another human being. So you can either be part of something amazing and enduring, or you can *process* it for as long as you want. Either way, you're going to be a father!"

She hung up abruptly and I sat staring at the screen as the waitress set my drink on the table. Could I really settle down? Could I spend my life with Mo? Would she want to be Mrs. Shanks? She'd probably want to hyphenate. But, her last name was Banks. Mrs. Banks-Shanks? She'd never go for that. Maybe she would want to keep her maiden name. How would I feel about that? We hadn't even talked about it. I shook my head. Crap, I'm focusing on the wrong thing! I'm going to have a child. How am I supposed to be a father? What does a father even do? I tried to imagine what it was like, but my own dad had provided no template for me to consider.

I had no memory of Dad really being there for me. Not just in clichés, like reading to me, teaching me to ride a bike, or taking me to park or a movie. He was just emotionally absent, never seeming to care about my life, my interests or my aspirations. I grew up convinced he viewed me like a piece of furniture that was always in the wrong place, always in the way. One thing was clear: I couldn't do worse than him. The man set a very low bar for parenting.

As I finished my drink, I looked back to the bar where Aaron had been sitting. He was gone, and so were Bonnie and Connie. Surprised at their sudden departure, I quickly drained the rest of my glass and threw some cash down on the bar. Where the hell was he? I searched the rest of the club without success. Then I paced the casino floor, through the aisles of slot machines and Blackjack tables anxiously looking for Aaron. What if I'd lost him? The truth was that I'd quickly grown to like Aaron and in a way I hadn't experienced before. The bond I felt with him after even just a week together far exceeded anything I'd ever felt even for my own father. Panic set in as I thought of the idea of him traveling on his own. What if Bonnie and Connie were hookers taking him somewhere to rob him? Should I alert hotel security? But what would I tell them? What had happened to him?

The drinks and worry were beginning to hit me hard. I staggered through every part of the casino floor until I spotted a bored dealer, standing Sphinx-like besides her empty Blackjack table.

"Have you seen a handsome elderly man, possibly accompanied by two middle-aged blonde women?" I anxiously slurred.

"Sir, you've described at least half of our patrons," she replied in a monotone voice.

Suddenly, I felt completely exhausted. The gig, the drinks, talking to Mo...I had nothing left in the tank. I needed sleep. The thought made me consider checking our suite. Maybe that's where he was. It could be that Aaron hadn't seen me and went up to the room to sleep. I tottered over to the elevator, got in, and slumped against the wall staring at the numbers as it rose toward our suite. God, what if I'd lost him? Shit, where was he? Where *was* he?

Relief flooded my body when I unlocked the door. The lights were on in the suite and Aaron's clothes were strewn along the hallway floor leading to the closed door of his room. Instantly, panic gave way to intense fatigue. I turned off the light switch and stumbled into my room where I passed out on my bed, fully clothed.

Twenty Eight

I awoke with a piercing headache—the kind that feels like someone is using a melon baller on the inside of your skull—and little memory of the previous evening. I placed my feet tenderly on the rug, trying to hold my dry heaves at bay. Pulling off my wrinkled, sweat-stained shirt and hoodie, I grabbed a crumpled t-shirt out of my duffle and threw it on. The fabric brushing over my head felt like a metal rake on my scalp. I needed an aspirin and some coffee.

Christ, I needed a fuckin' gallon of coffee.

Pulling on my shoes, I headed down the elevator. Casinos are strange, soulless places in the early morning, like something out of the movie *Zombieland*. Everything is operating—lights flashing, slot machine bells and chimes sounding—but there's not a human being in sight. In a corner of the floor, I found a small café. Behind the counter a large, middle-aged woman was sitting on a stool leaning against the wall.

"Looks like you had a night. Need coffee?" she asked tenderly.

I nodded.

"Large and black?"

I nodded again.

"The croissants here aren't bad. They might soak up some of that alcohol."

I slowly raised two fingers. She poured coffee into a large mug and placed it in front of me along with a plate of croissants.

"This chaser's on the house," she said, smiling maternally as she slid a package of aspirin toward me.

"Thanks," I replied in a hoarse croak.

As I sipped my coffee, I thought about the previous evening. Despite the pain in my cranium, I was in near rapture realizing that I had played in a real show with the man who many said had invented rock music. If I had any lingering doubts, they had disappeared. Aaron was Elvis. His voice, his mannerisms, the way he worked the crowd. There was just no way any imitator could be that good. I chewed a piece of croissant as the night came flooding back, replaying the many highlights of the show. But my happy reverie was abruptly displaced by thoughts of my conversation with Mo. I went over every painful word of it feeling her sadness, anger—and my fear.

I let out an involuntary sigh, ordered a couple of extra cups of coffee to go and took the elevator back to the room, thinking it was about time to wake Aaron. As I unlocked the door and entered the suite, I heard the unexpected sound of muffled giggling coming from the direction of his room. Raising my hand to knock, the door opened, revealing the two women from the night before. What were their names? Carol? Betty? They pushed quickly past me, carrying their heels and purses looking a bit disheveled and embarrassed. I watched them go down the hallway and out the door before looking back to Aaron's room. He was sitting on his bed wearing nothing but an ancient set of yellowed boxer shorts. A broad smile rolled across his face. I laughed and handed him his coffee.

"How you doin' this mornin', son'?" he asked.

"I should ask the same about you," I teased.

Aaron ignored my response.

"You walked away to take that call and I never saw ya' again. How'd it go?"

I shook my head. "Not well. Not well at all." I paused. "She doesn't deserve what I'm putting her through. I know I'm hurting her and it's eatin' me up. But I'm not ready to be a father. Hell, I can barely take care of myself. And I've got to focus on my music career."

Aaron gave me a serious look for a moment. "Ya' know A. J., I once thought my career was the most important thing in the world. The people around me—my agents, my producers, my crew—they all made me feel like it was everything. Turns out, it wasn't. Not by a long shot. Yeah, I had the fans, the money, and the fame, but at some point I finally realized that bein' a daddy was more important than any of it. Years after I'm long forgotten by everyone, I want to know that at least I will be remembered by my little girl."

I considered what Aaron had said as I sipped my coffee and looked out at first rays of sunshine reflecting off glass facades of the Vegas skyline. It was going to be a hot one today.

"How are *you* feeling this morning?" I asked.

"Son, I haven't been this sore in years. It must've been all those karate kicks last night."

"You think that's what it was? The karate kicks? Sure it wasn't anything else?" I needled.

Aaron grinned, then his face grew serious.

"A. J. can I ask you a kinda personal question?"

"Sure," I answered hesitantly hoping that the subject would be something other than a certain pregnant girlfriend in Austin.

"Are women…" He paused. "Different these days?"

I wasn't quite sure how this was a personal question, but nonetheless I launched in to an explanation of the feminist movement and the advances that women had made in business, society, and politics over the last few decades. It was then that Aaron interrupted my little dissertation.

"No—I mean physically."

"Physically?"

"Yes, physically."

"I really don't know what you're talkin' about, Aaron."

"Those gals last night. They just felt, well… different."

"How so?"

"Their breasts," he whispered.

"Oh!" I responded with a laugh. "Yeah, they looked like they had had some work done."

"Work? What do you mean by that?"

"Plastic surgery. A lot of people get plastic surgery today. Some get wrinkles removed, some do it to make their stomachs look flatter or their butts rounder. And plenty of women get their breasts enlarged."

"You mean gals now have surgery not because they have somethin' wrong, but just to have bigger…boobs?"

"Yeah, it happens all the time, especially in places like Vegas."

"Silliest damn thing I ever heard. I like women who feel like how God made 'em, not some doctor."

"But," I smiled, "I'll bet last night wasn't too bad."

He playfully growled, "Still the King. Still the King," before adding, "And I didn't need any of that Viagra stuff." Then he burst into laughter so loud it made my head pound.

* * *

A couple hours later, I checked us out of our suite with great reluctance. God knows when I would stay in a place like this again. I could really grow accustomed to marble floors, down duvets, and flat-screen televisions. We walked to the parking garage and loaded ourselves into the car.

"Ready to go?" I asked.

Aaron nodded, but I noticed he looked pensive. He absently handed me the keys.

"You doing okay? Something on your mind?"

"I'm just thinkin' about seeing Lisa Marie again. Guess I'm not sure what's goin' to happen. Maybe it's a mistake."

"Well, there's one way to find out," I said, as I turned the key.

For the next three hours, we traveled through the Mojave with the top down, each of us lost deep in our thoughts and imaginings. The desert can have that effect. The thrum of the car's engine, the dry hot air blasting on your face, and the hypnotic flashing of Joshua trees sent an emotional semaphore signal to lost memories. Mine were of Mo. The way she nestled her face on my chest when we slept, the delight she found in even the most mundane aspects of my musical career, the way she could seamlessly traverse from the world of college professor to Lone Start pounding line dancer. I marveled that she could put up with all my shit. Now this amazing woman wanted me to be a parent with her, to raise a little girl together.

God, I was such an asshole.

My ruminations were interrupted when we reached the L.A. basin and traffic slowed to a crawl.

"What's all this? Is there an accident?" asked Aaron.

"Nope. It's L.A. traffic."

"L.A.? The sign says we're still 45 miles away."

"Los Angeles is a bit bigger than when you were probably last here. And, this," I said, waving my hand dramatically "is the legendary L.A. rush hour."

Aaron looked at the cars creeping along the freeway. "This may be Los Angeles, but it don't look like anybody's rushin' round here. In fact, that reminds me, I been meanin' to ask you about the cars."

"What about 'em?"

"They all look the same! It's like car companies are usin' the same cookie cutter. Used to be cars were all different sizes and shapes like the old ones we saw at the car show in Vegas; a Cadillac looked different from a Lincoln and a Rolls Royce looked nothing like a Ford. Now they all look the same, like round blobs with no personality. What happened?"

"Remember when we stopped at that station outside of Little Rock? The one where you were so surprised by the price of gas?"

Aaron nodded.

"That's your answer. It's the high price of gas. Fuel economy is driving car design these days. The more aerodynamic and lighter the car; the more fuel efficient it is."

"But they look so boring. Even the names are dull," he said as he read the nameplates of passing vehicles."'328i,' 'F150,' 'IS 250,' '300.' Those ain't names, those are numbers. 'Eldorado,' 'Blackhawk,' 'Mustang,' 'Thunderbird'—now those are names of cars you want to drive!"

"You've got a point, but a lot has changed since you disappeared. Do you remember much from when you were here in Southern California? You must have spent some time in Hollywood."

"Yeah, plenty, performin' on TV and makin' movies, but it's been a long time since then." He chuckled as if a thought had just occurred to him. "My singin' first got attention here when I was on the Milton Berle Show. You probably won't have heard of him. He was a comic who had what they called a variety show. It was one of the first times I was on TV and I decided to make it special. After all, I didn't know if I'd get another chance. So when it was my turn to perform, I gave it a little bit extra. I think I sang *Hound Dog*. Folks back then hadn't seen anythin' like the way I danced. They began to call me 'Elvis the Pelvis'. Ain't that funny? All because I moved my hips around. I'm guessin' nowadays entertainers do that kind of thing all the time."

"And more."

"More? What ya' mean?"

"Well, let me give you an example. There's a band called the Red Hot Chili Peppers. They've got a bass player named Flea."

"Flea?"

"Yeah, Flea. It's his stage name. Flea is known for wearing a single white athletic sock when he performs."

"He wears only one sock? That's a bit strange."

"No, you don't understand. That's all he wears."

Aaron shot me a confused look.

"He comes out on stage buck naked except for a sock covering his… how can I put this delicately… his dick."

"Son, you're kiddin' me."

"No, I am not. A few years ago, the Chili Peppers played a series of concerts that was billed as the 'Socks on Cocks Tour.'"

"You gotta be making this up. That can't be true. I don't believe ya'."

"Aaron, you ever hear of the Butterfly Effect?"

"What in the hell are you talking about now?" he asked, growing agitated.

"It's a scientific theory that says everything is causally interrelated. So, for example, that something as slight as the flapping of a butterfly's wings can eventually cause a hurricane."

"I swear to God, I don't understand anything you're sayin' right now. It's like you're speakin' in tongues."

"It's the idea that seemingly inconsequential actions can eventually cause something much more significant to happen."

"Okay, but what's that have to do with what you were just talking about—that guy with the sock on his…"

"You remember the way you first moved your hips on the Milton Berle show?"

Aaron nodded.

"That was the musical equivalent of the flapping of butterfly wings."

Twenty Nine

We pulled onto Hollywood Boulevard late in the afternoon. It was pure entertainment watching Aaron's head swing from side to side as we drove as if he was viewing a match at Wimbledon. It seemed he couldn't let anything escape his eyes—billboards, tourists, hookers, street hawkers, business people—each seemed to trigger a flood of memories for him.

"Did I ever tell ya' I had a place in Beverly Hills? Wasn't as big as Graceland, but it had a real nice view. Priscilla and I lived there when I was filmin'. There was a park somewhere near here where me and the boys used to play football when we were on a break from movie makin'. Oh," he exclaimed, "and there used to be this great deli we'd hang out at. It was always open. Think it was called Canter's or somethin' like that. We'd work up an appetite after a day on the set and end up there for bagels and lox…"

The vibrations of a throbbing bass line halted Aaron midsentence as we slowed for a stoplight.

"What in the hell is that?" he asked anxiously looking over his shoulder at the car pulling alongside us. It was a late-1950s Chevy Impala convertible that had been lowered and covered in a bright lime green paint job with an abstract design on its hood. The car's woofers announced its arrival as they blared rap music at eardrum splitting levels.

Aaron reacted by throwing his hands over his ears and gawking at the car's driver, a young man wearing a black sleeveless t-shirt, and a red baseball cap with its brim turned sideways. The driver, sensing Aaron's stare, slowly looked over at him, and pressed a button on the car's dashboard with a finger wrapped in multiple gold rings. In response, the front of the Impala began to rise and then oscillate vigorously. The rear of the car followed, until the car began to dance from wheel to wheel on the pavement. With his hands still cupped over his ears, Aaron exploded in laughter until the driver again pressed the button and the car gently stabilized and lowered its suspension. As the light turned green, the driver pointed toward Aaron's Cadillac and gave him a thumbs-up before driving slowly away.

As we pulled forward, Aaron asked through his laughter, "What in God's name did I just see?"

"It's a low rider—an example of Los Angeles street culture. Cars today may look the same, but there are still many people like that guy, who express themselves through what they drive. Think of it as today's version of a hot rod, except instead of making the cars go fast, people intentionally drive them slow, and modify them so they can hop around and add sound systems like what you just heard."

"To be honest, I don't know what I just heard, but it was loud enough that everyone could hear it. Sounds kind of like that stuff they were playin' at Snoop's party."

"Yeah, it is. It's called rap."

"Weird name. Why's it called that? Is it 'cause people want to wrap their hands around a person's throat until they turn that noise off?"

"No, not 'wrap', like wrapping a package, 'rap', like rapping…you, now street talk. It's a type of music."

"Music? Son, I may have been gone awhile, and I know many things have changed, but that ain't music."

"No, really it is. In fact it's some of the most popular music in the world today."

"It sounds angry. Why would people want to listen to angry music?"

"Why do people listen to sad music like the blues?"

Aaron paused. "I think I see what you mean, but I still think that's a ridiculous kinda music."

"Didn't you record a song called *Fever?*"

"Yeah," he replied proudly. "It was a pretty big hit."

"Are you going to try to tell me it was written about being sick? No, it was about sex! Get my point? Music has always been about our emotions. Rap is the sound of inner cities and the people who live there, people who have a lot to be angry about, like poverty, violence, drugs and racism."

"Maybe so, but it still ain't music."

"That's because it's not music for you. Let me try to explain it this way. My mom used to tell me the story of when you first appeared on the Ed Sullivan Show."

Aaron gave me a big smile. "I'll never forget it. That's when I first really showed the world who I was. The kids went crazy for me after that one."

"I'm sure they did. But what about their parents, the older generation?"

"They always complained about my music, said it was some kind of noisy racket—or worse."

"That's kind of my point."

"What d'ya' mean?"

"To the parents of your fans, you were the sound of youthful rebellion. But because they were older, they didn't understand you or your music."

"No doubt about that!"

"It's the same with rap music. You don't like it because you don't come from the community it speaks to. You didn't come from the inner city. You didn't grow up in urban poverty or subject to discrimination. So you can't connect with what you are hearing."

"I guess I kinda get your point, but let me ask you; do you like it?" Aaron asked tentatively.

"Rap? I understand it, but, no, not really," I replied, as we pulled away from the intersection. "Then again, I come from a different place and have my own baggage."

* * *

We drove for a few more blocks before I realized how hungry I was. We had driven for most of the day without stopping for food other than some snacks from a gas station. At a stoplight, I pulled out my phone and found a couple of nearby restaurants that looked good.

"Hey, are you hungry? Let's grab a bite to eat. There's a sushi place a few blocks away that has good reviews."

I noticed a questioning look on Aaron's face before he nodded.

I turned onto La Brea and found a parking spot about a block off Hollywood Boulevard. While Aaron pulled up the top, I put my guitar and amp in the trunk and then we headed toward the restaurant. Aaron was quiet as we crossed the street as if something was on his mind.

When we got to the corner, Aaron regarded me with a serious look before asking, "I know I'm askin' a lot of questions, A. J., but I've got another one for ya'. What's a 'sushi place'?"

"You don't know what sushi is?"

"Nope. Never heard of it. Sounds like some kind of Indian thing."

"Indian? Oh, you mean like Sioux Indians? No, it's Japanese. You know, raw fish."

"Raw? People eat raw fish? That sounds awful. What happened to hamburgers?"

"Sushi is really popular."

"There is more than one of these places?"

"Sushi restaurants? For sure, they're everywhere now. In fact, there are probably more sushi restaurants than there are McDonalds. Here's the place. C'mon in and give it a try."

Aaron regarded me dubiously before we entered the restaurant saying, "Well, at least we'll save money. It must be cheap, after all, they don't even cook the food."

It was over an hour before we left the restaurant and turned toward our car. Aaron refused to even attempt to use chopsticks, but he was a surprisingly adventuresome eater, provided I didn't tell him what he was eating in advance. Once he got started, he wanted to try everything—miso soup, tempura, sashimi, seaweed salad, different rolls—there was seemingly no limit to his appetite.

As we stepped out of the restaurant, he rubbed his stomach.

"Son, that was some good eatin'. How'd you pronounce that one dish— Eye Koo Rah Goo Kan?"

"Ikura Gukan. Salmon Roe."

"Yeah, that's it. It's good stuff. But, I wonder how they get them eggs out of the fish." He laughed. "It's not like they're chickens and you can just pick 'em out of the straw."

"Or the backseat of a Cadillac," I joked. "I'm glad you liked it."

It was while walking toward the car a few minutes later that I began to sense that we were being followed. Maybe I was getting a bit paranoid traveling with Aaron, worried that he would be unexpectedly discovered, but I just had a sense that someone was trailing behind us. Turning my head over my shoulder, I saw an older man and woman walking a few yards behind Aaron. Each time I glanced back I saw them and noticed that the woman, who looked like a solid Midwestern type, kept speaking animatedly to her rail-thin companion as she gestured toward Aaron.

Finally, when we approached a gray gazebo-like structure on the corner, I stopped and confronted them. "Excuse me, do you need help?"

With a surprised look, the man responded, "We're sorry to bother you, but my name is John Dressler, this is my wife Ann. We saw you and your…?"

"Grandfather," I answered, looking in Aaron's direction.

"Yes. Well, we saw your grandfather in the restaurant and Ann is convinced we know him."

"Are you by any chance from Terre Haute?" Ann asked, turning to Aaron. "That's where we're from. We're out here on vacation."

"No, ma'am. I'm from Mississippi," Aaron replied softly.

"You didn't work for Ford, did you? John spent his career running the Ford dealership in town. I was thinking maybe we met at an auto show or Ford dealer convention."

"I'm afraid not. I've been farmin' for decades."

"But, you look so familiar. I know I've seen you before."

"If she says she's seen you, then she's seen you. Ann never forgets a face," John declared proudly.

"I'm really sorry folks, but I don't think we would have met," Aaron replied with a trace of nervousness.

Ann snapped her fingers and pointed at him, the fat wings below her arms flapping. "I know! Have you ever done any entertaining?"

I looked over to Aaron and saw his face blanche. I wondered how he'd respond, then saw that his eyes were transfixed downward. I followed his gaze and quickly noticed what he was staring at. We were standing on one of the stars embedded in the sidewalk as part of the Hollywood Walk of Fame. The name on this one—Elvis Presley.

Quickly, I grabbed Aaron's arm. "I'm sorry Mr. and Mrs. Dressler. It was nice to meet you, but Grandpa and I have had a long day and we need to find a motel for the night. Hope you enjoy your vacation."

With that I quickly ushered Aaron down the street and toward our car. "Wait," Ann yelled, "you didn't answer my question."

"Walk fast," I whispered to Aaron.

"Come on, John!" Ann commanded. "They're hiding something. I know it!" I looked back to see Ann pulling her husband in our direction.

"C'mon, pick it up," I urged Aaron.

With a glance over my shoulder, I saw the Dresslers were gaining on us. We began to walk more briskly. They picked up the pace in response. We were engaged in an escalating speed walking competition through the streets of Hollywood like some kind of *Monty Python* sketch. For such a heavy-set woman, Ann could move, even as she dragged her reluctant husband behind.

Thankfully, we won, though by the narrowest of margins. The leaf springs of the Caddy let out an ancient groan as Aaron and I jumped in the car and quickly slammed the doors shut. I put the key in the ignition and hit the gas, and we drove down the street, leaving the Dresslers behind, staring after us with a perplexed look.

Thirty

"Well, that was bit too close for comfort," Aaron said with a loud sigh of relief as he steered down the road. "What are the chances? You know, I heard somethin' about my Hollywood star a long time ago. I think it might'a been when I was in the Army. Never got a chance to see it all these years, and today I'm standin' on top of it. Ya' know, it's a strange world."

"It is, indeed," I agreed, thinking back on the previous week.

Aaron continued to recount his Hollywood memories as we drove around, while I looked for a motel with vacancies. It seemed that every corner awakened some story from his time making movies. The tale might be about a late night drink with Sinatra, or a quiet tryst with a young starlet, or working on the set of *Double Trouble* or *Charro*, but the stories flowed without pause. Finally, we found the Holloway Hotel, located on Santa Monica Boulevard, about eight blocks from the Roxy. It was a bit out of our price range, but Aaron liked it because of its proximity to the IHOP next door. I was feeling a bit overwhelmed after listening to Aaron's patter, so after we checked in, I just left my stuff in the car and flopped on the bed to watch T.V. while Aaron showered and dressed. I must have drifted off, because the next thing I knew, Aaron was shaking me awake.

"Son. Son. Wake up."

"Sorry, I must have nodded off. You ready to go?" I asked, groggily.

"Yeah, I guess. Do I look ok? I gotta admit, I'm feelin' a bit nervous."

I straightened the collar of his flowery shirt—the one he had bought in Potts Camp.

When was that? Could it really have only been just days ago?

I looked at Aaron. "You look great, man. Really great," I said reassuringly giving him a slap on the shoulder. Aaron's smile indicated he took some comfort in my words and we left our room, got in the car, and I pulled us out toward Sunset Boulevard. As I drove, I pointed out some of the landmarks around us, trying to distract Aaron from his nerves. But he remained distant, clearly dwelling on something else.

"Aaron, what's the matter? What's wrong?"

"I don't think I can do it," he murmured.

"Can't do what?"

He turned his head toward the road, his eyes focused on something that wasn't there. He hesitated for a moment, then swallowed loudly, and words began to cascade from deep within some hidden reservoir of emotions.

"I'm scared, son. I don't know if I can see her, don't know if I can see my little girl. It's been too long. Too many years; too many miles. I left that part of me more than thirty years ago. Probably nothin' more selfish than a man leavin' his child. And, yeah, I know I had to do it to survive, but that don't make it hurt any less." He paused and took a deep breath before continuing. "For years, I'd lay awake at night imagining what she was doing, imagine snuggling next to her so I could sleep. I'd help one of Rholetta's neighbors with a horse and it'd remind me of the time I was teachin' Lisa Marie to ride. I thought of all the fun she would have had livin' there with me and Rholetta. Sometimes I was missin' her so much I'd think about getting a message to her. Came close to sending one with the Stickley boys a couple of times. I was going to have them call her from a pay phone, but what would they say? Plus, I figured they'd probably be too drunk to do it," he said, shaking his head dismissively. "After many years, the pain started to go away. I guess I grew a callus around that part of my heart. It's protected me all these years. Until now."

I glanced at Aaron. Suddenly, he appeared old and frail, as if the life had ebbed from his body. As I looked at him I felt this surprisingly intense need to comfort him, to help him as a son would help an aged parent.

"Well, I guess you could always bail. That strategy's worked pretty well for me in the past."

He looked at me and blinked.

"Bail?"

"Split, leave, turn back, you know, give up. It's kind of my specialty. Like what I'm doing now, when I'm about to be a father."

A giant shudder ran through Aaron's body and I heard him sigh deeply. "No, man, that ain't right for you or for me. I've come this far. I've gotta' play this one to the end. Let's get there before I change my mind."

We drove silently for another few blocks until I turned down Hammond Street and found a place to park. Aaron ran a comb through his hair and inspected himself in the rearview mirror before we locked the car and headed down the street.

We had walked for about five minutes before I stopped and drew Aaron's attention to the marquee of the Roxy across the street. In prominent block letters it said: LISA MARIE PRESLEY—STORM AND GRACE TOUR.

Aaron's eyes locked on the sign and an expansive smile broke across his face.

"My little girl's an entertainer," he said with a slight shake of his head. "I mean ah' heard the songs you played for me. She's gotta beautiful voice an' all, but I never thought it was real, that she was an entertainer, until now." Aaron's eyes were riveted on the marquee as we walked across the street. He was so distracted that I had to put a hand on his back to shepherd him through the traffic and toward the ticket booth, where a few people were milling about looking discouraged.

A handwritten note taped to the Plexiglas window of the booth explained why.

"Damn!" I exclaimed. "The concert's sold out."

To say I was disheartened was an understatement. I thought of all that we had done since leaving Graceland. The miles of driving in Aaron's mobile chicken coop; the music and our performances; the relationship we had built. Aaron's quest had become mine as well. In my mind, I had begun to believe that the last chapter of this story would be one of reunion and love. Now, I felt only profound dejection. The disappointment was obvious on Aaron's face as well, but I also detected a trace of relief. He looked at me, and then the marquee before saying, "Well, I guess it wasn't meant to be." Then he turned and sadly started walking back in the direction of the car.

Shit! After all we had been through, things couldn't end like this. I banged on the window of the ticket booth, hoping to draw someone's attention, but all was quiet in the building. As I turned to look back at Aaron, I spotted a disheveled young man wearing a dirty gray sweatshirt on the other side of the street. He was holding a small scrap of cardboard with scrawled handwriting that said: *"Need tix? We got 'em."*

"Wait up, Aaron. I think I see a scalper!" I yelled as I ran across the street. Aaron stood waiting under the marquee for a few minutes until I returned.

"Well, I've got some good news and some bad news."

"What's that, son?"

"Well, the good news is that I scored us some tickets."

"That's wonderful. Thanks, A. J....But what's the bad news?" he asked.

"The bad news is that your little girl is expensive; these two set us back $500," I declared as I flashed him the tickets.

Aaron let out a shout of happiness and grabbed me in a powerful hug, proclaiming, "I guess she takes after her Daddy!"

Thirty One

We killed more than an hour eating at the Rainbow Grill, a diner next door to the theater waiting for the show to start. I had a beer and fries; Aaron gorged himself on something called a "Sinful Sundae." The guy seemed to be packing it in every time we stopped for a meal and I swear he looked several pounds heavier than when we first met earlier in the week. I wondered if he was slowly reverting to the behaviors of his gluttonous past.

As we ate, we watched the large crowd that lined the sidewalk in front of the restaurant, leading to the Roxy. Anticipation constricted our conversation and we finished our food in silence. Then I paid the bill, and we joined the line as it slowly shuffled into the storied venue. The voices of the concert patrons blended together in a cloud of ambient chatter that was indistinct except for a single word that stood apart whenever it was spoken: "Elvis." I wondered if Aaron heard it, too. But whenever I glanced at him he was always looking ahead vacantly as if trying not to draw attention.

When we entered the Roxy, it was my turn for memories. Only a few years earlier, I had performed here as part of the first of two opening acts for Elvin Bishop. Thankfully, most in the audience were too young to remember Elvin "Fooled Around and Fell in Love" Bishop; they were there for Elvin "the blues guitar legend" Bishop. And on that night, the man delivered.

Up to that point in my career, I thought I was a pretty fair guitar player. Hell with the false humility, I thought I was a massive (but yet undiscovered) talent. All the proof you needed was that I was performing at the Roxy on the same stage where all the musical gods had appeared—B.B. King, The Clash, Springsteen, Neil Young, Prince. I kept that in mind as I hammered through each of my solos, the crowd milling into the theater. As I played, I was certain that Elvin was backstage, listening to me blister the notes, that he and the sparse audience were astonished at the way I had mastered the strings. "Who is that guy?" I imagined them asking. The euphoric feeling lasted all of an hour, until Elvin took the stage and began his set. I still remember the way he looked at me as he brushed past. It was a glance that said, 'Step aside, son, I'm the headliner.' Listening to him that night filled me with reverential awe, and the realization that I still had miles to go before I would make it in the music business, and walking through the theater with Aaron now only rekindled those feelings of professional insecurity.

Unfortunately, the scalper hadn't had a pair of tickets seated next to each other; I'd only been able to purchase a couple of singles. I had hoped that I would be able to get someone to trade a seat so that my "grandfather" and I could sit together, but after asking several people, I had no luck. In the end, we were located about five rows apart, Aaron closer to the stage, and me seated behind him. It wasn't ideal, but at least I could keep an eye on him during the concert.

* * *

I'll admit that Lisa Marie Presley has never made her way onto my playlist. It's not that I disliked her music. I simply never bothered with it, assuming any popularity she had was due to her father's monstrously long coattails. After watching her performance that night, I realized that I could not have been more wrong. The woman knew how to sing. If her last name had been anything but Presley, she would have been a top-selling artist. When she wrapped her hand around the microphone, she carried the audience away with melodies of grief, pain, longing, and lost love. The way she sang made me want to put my arms around her shoulders, just as I would reflexively shelter a young girl who had suffered a profound loss. Where Elvis was a ball of fire, exuding energy and passion, Lisa Marie was an ember of smoky sensuality. I know that I was not the only one who was moved by her music that evening. The Lisa Marie faithful crowded the floor and swayed their heads and bodies in rhythm to each ballad. Looking a few rows ahead, I watched Aaron, his eyes locked on Lisa Marie wherever she moved on the stage. Her ninety-minute performance that evening was so captivating that the intensity of his stares and the tears streaming down his face went unnoticed by those around him.

Toward the end of the evening, Lisa Marie leaned into the microphone and said, "I'd like to finish tonight with a song that was written as a duet. It would only sound right for me to sing it with one other person." Her voice trailed off as she added, "Unfortunately, he isn't with us tonight." She turned to the band, counted off, reached for the microphone and did a moving rendition of *In the Ghetto*. I looked at Aaron and saw the flash of his broad white smile cutting through the darkness, moisture reflecting from his cheeks.

At the conclusion of the song, Lisa Marie waved and walked off stage with her band. As she did, the crowd rose in unison for an encore and I glimpsed Aaron clapping his hands loudly over his head, talking animatedly to the people sitting on either side of him. A few minutes later, Lisa Marie returned to the stage alone, holding nothing but an acoustic guitar. She sat on a stool before the microphone and looked out at the audience.

"Thank you. Thank you all very much. I hope you've enjoyed this evening. I know I have. I thought I'd play you one last song. It's one I wrote for my Daddy. It's called *Nobody Noticed*."

I caught a glimpse of Aaron. His seat was in a row just on the edge of the spotlight, less than twenty feet from Lisa Marie, his face caught between shadow and illumination. At any moment, I expected him to do something dramatic—to yell out to her or approach the stage—but he sat mesmerized and unmoving until the moment when Lisa Marie sang a lyric about her desire to have spent just a little more time with her father. Through the swaying bodies and forest of illuminated smart phones, I saw Aaron's head drop into his hands and his body began to tremble with emotion.

Quickly, I began to push myself through the other fans standing beside me and up the aisle toward his seat while Lisa Marie sang of her unending love for her father. By the time I squeezed in next to Aaron, she had finished the song, waved to the crowd and walked off stage. Reaching out to him, I asked, "Are you alright?"

An attractive young woman sitting next to Aaron turned to me as she clapped and leaned into my ear. Over the applause of the crowd, I heard her say, "I thought *I* loved Lisa Marie. Your grandfather must be a serious fan."

"Yeah, something like that," I replied, putting my arm around Aaron and helping him to his feet.

I towed Aaron alongside me and toward the exit, moving through the crowd as we walked into the cool evening air on Sunset Boulevard. Gently, I led him to the side of the exit doors and against the wall of the building.

"Aaron? Aaron, are you alright? Talk to me, man."

Aaron wiped a sleeve against his nose before responding, "Did you see her? Did you see my little girl? She's all grown up. And she's beautiful. Looks just like her Mama. She sings like an angel, too." Then he paused, a forlorn expression covering his face, and began sobbing. "What have I done? Oh, Lord, what have I done?"

"If you hadn't left, you would have died. You know that," I said, as I gave his shoulders a squeeze. "At least now you've had the chance to see her again, to know that she's okay, that she's become a beautiful, talented woman."

Aaron suddenly stopped sobbing and looked up at me. "I know I told ya' that I just wanted to see my little girl. But, now… I want to do more n' that."

"Do more than what?"

"I want to do more than just see her. A. J., I want to meet my daughter. I want to be her Daddy again."

"What…are you serious? Aaron, I don't know how we can do that. You can't exactly call her and say: 'Hi daughter. I didn't really die. Sorry for being out of the picture for thirty years. Would you like to grab a cup of coffee and catch up?' She'd think you were some deranged Elvis fan. Besides, like I said, I'm pretty sure she lives in England now. Unless you're thinking of us performing on a cruise ship, I don't know how we could afford that trip."

Aaron looked at me with pain etched on his face, his blue eyes filled with the tears of someone confronting the realization of what he'd lost. As I looked at him, I thought of my own father. It had been years since I had heard from him. Had he remarried? Did he have another family? Did he ever think of me? Had he ever missed me as intensely as Aaron missed Lisa Marie? How would I ever know? We really hadn't spoken since Mom died. The laughter of some fans interrupted my thoughts. Suddenly, I had an idea. I put my hands on Aaron's shoulders and gave them a shake.

"Aaron, I don't know how to get us to England, but there still may be a chance for you to meet Lisa Marie. C'mon, follow me."

Thirty Two

I moved into the stream of people filling the sidewalk and turned around the corner of the theater, looking back frequently to make sure that Aaron was close behind. Things grew quieter as we reached the rear parking lot, where a few barricades cordoned off an idling black stretch limo. Surrounding it were a couple of dozen people waiting anxiously. Some looked like security and press, but there were a few fans as well.

"What's all this?" Aaron asked as we squeezed through the small crowd, toward the front of the barricades.

"I played here a few years ago. This is the exit they use for the stars so they don't have to wait for the crowd to clear out front. I'm guessing this is Lisa Marie's ride." I gestured to a black painted door under a small neon exit sign. "With any luck, she should be coming through that door in a few minutes."

As we waited at the barricade, an increasing number of press and photographers pushed in alongside us. One of them was a large, greasy-haired man in his late forties, wearing multiple cameras from straps around his neck. He shoved in next to me. Standing beside him was a guy about my age, wearing jeans and a wrinkled white shirt. He was holding a Nikon camera with a lens the size of a small howitzer. In the still night it was not difficult to hear their conversation.

"Hey, Mark. Didn't expect to see you working this late."

"You know how it is, Justin. You gotta do what it takes to earn the dead presidents."

"But I heard you just had a great score. Wasn't that your picture of Lohan coming out of the Avalon that I saw in the *Star*?"

"Made ten thousand on that one," he said with a laugh.

"Ten grand? Nice! That your biggest?"

Mark assumed a sage look and pulled a toothpick from his pocket.

"It wasn't too bad but, nah, it's not my biggest. A few years ago, I got Clooney coming out of his girlfriend's house at three in the morning. I honked the horn and he looked right into the lens and I caught him square. Perfect. Twenty-five large from *People*."

"Think we can get something like that tonight?"

"Good luck with that! I've been trying to get a decent one of LMP for years. Hollywood's finest always like to complain about us. How we're invading their privacy, how we only shoot them at their worst, blah, blah, blah. Fuck them! They want the publicity—they can't be picky. Narcissistic bastards. They know they need us."

He pulled a chunk of food out from between his teeth and dropped the toothpick to the ground before continuing, "Presley's different. She doesn't need the pub or the money. She sings because she likes to sing. Must be a daddy issue," he snarled. "So she always does a quick exit surrounded by security and almost never even stops to sign autographs. Just blows past people and into her limo. She leaves so fast it's impossible to get back to the car to follow her. Yep, she just doesn't want to play ball, the bitch."

I could sense the fury rising in Aaron as he listened, his eyes riveted to the rear stage door. Putting a hand on his shoulder, I whispered, "Ignore him. The guy's an ass." Aaron turned toward me, and I saw him flexing his fist.

"Well maybe we'll get lucky tonight," said Justin.

Mark replied in a conspiratorial voice, "Tonight, my friend, luck's gonna have nothing to do with it."

"What do you mean?"

He lowered his voice so that it was barely audible. "It took me years, but I finally have someone on the inside. It cost me plenty, but one of her security detail gave me her route out of Hollywood. He wouldn't tell me where she's staying, but at least I know which streets she'll be taking," he said with a short laugh.

"How can I get in on this?" asked Justin excitedly.

"Not a chance."

"C'mon, man, I'm just getting started in the biz. I need a score. Please, Mark, just this once. I need something to make a name."

The big man stared at his companion for a few seconds. "I guess with two of us we could increase our chances. Tell you what I'm going to do, I'll let you in, but if I get the shot you get nothing, and if you get the shot, my cut is seventy-five percent."

"What? That's bullshit, Mark."

"Take it or leave it. I'm guessing twenty-five percent of a good Presley pic is still more than you've made this entire month." He reached into his pocket and pulled out another toothpick, his eyes glued to the backdoor of the theater.

After a few seconds, Justin stuck out his hand. "Okay...deal. Now, what's the route?"

Mark shook his hand and in a hushed voice said, "Right on North San Vincent, left on Beverly, right on La Cienega ..."

Aaron tried to squeeze against the barricade, moving toward Mark and Justin, but I blocked his path and gently held him away.

"Did you hear those bastards? What are they plannin' to do to my girl?" he said through gritted teeth.

"They're paparazzi."

"What—zi?"

"Paparazzi. They're photographers, but instead of working for a newspaper or magazine, they work freelance. They take pictures and shop them to whoever will pay the most."

"They sound like scum," said Aaron, disgusted.

"They are. It's not enough that they take the pictures, sometimes they make the pictures."

"What d'ya' mean?"

"The photos that are the most valuable are the ones where they catch a celebrity doing something wrong, like getting stopped by the police for a D.U.I., or flipping off the camera. Many of these guys lie in wait and surprise them at an embarrassing moment—like when an actor is cheating on a spouse—or they aggravate them so the celebrity snaps and does something they regret when their picture hits the paper. In some cases, it's even worse..." I paused before asking, "While you were living up in the hills, did you ever hear of Lady Diana?"

Aaron shook his head.

"She was British royalty back in the 1980s. Young, super attractive, and popular with the press—kind of the world's sweetheart. After she and Prince Charles were divorced, the paparazzi hounded her relentlessly. One day, she and her boyfriend were in a car with a royal bodyguard, driving through a tunnel in Paris. Some paparazzi raced alongside them, trying to get a picture. The bodyguard became distracted, lost control, and crashed, killing her, her boyfriend, and the driver. So, yeah, these guys are scum."

Aaron looked horrified. Just then, the stage door flew open and Lisa Marie walked out into an explosion of camera flashes. She was wearing a black full-length coat, a pair of large sunglasses, and a floppy hat pulled low over her eyes. Four burly guards formed a protective wall of human flesh around her as she moved quickly in the direction of the limo. Aaron and I were pressed against the barricade when the crowd, which had grown to about forty, surged toward her. Voices around us began yelling.

"Lisa Marie! Lisa Marie! Look this way! How about a picture?"

"Have you kicked the drugs yet?"

"Is it true that you belong to the Church of Scientology?"

"Do you think the reason you've been married so many times has something to do with your father?"

"C'mon, Lisa Marie, just one!"

"Did you divorce Cage or did he divorce you?"

"How much did Michael Jackson pay you to marry him?"

"Did you guys really have sex?"

The phalanx of bodyguards pushed along the barricades toward the car through a tunnel of outstretched arms, holding microphones, cameras and mobile phones. Out of the corner of my eye, as Lisa Marie passed in front of us, I saw Aaron lean over the barricade and shout something quickly toward her. In a flash, a bodyguard leapt forward and shoved Aaron back and into my arms. Lisa Marie's head snapped around and she looked directly at Aaron before her bodyguard opened the door and pushed her into the limousine. Seconds later, the car moved through the crowd and up the alley before turning onto Sunset Boulevard.

As the crowd ran after her, I lifted Aaron to his feet. "What just happened, man? Did she recognize you? What did you say to her?"

Aaron looked at me and in a slow drawl uttered a single word, "Moriah."

"That's what you said to her?" I asked excitedly.

"Yeah. I knew I wouldn't have long, so I tried to think of sumthin' short that only she and I would know. Remember when we were at Graceland and I mentioned teachin' her to ride a horse there? Well, Moriah was the name of her favorite horse. Of course, her guards pushed her into the car before anything could happen."

I grabbed Aaron's arm.

"Wait a second, there's still a chance. Our car is parked around the corner and we know the route she's taking. If we get lucky with the lights—c'mon let's go!"

Thirty Three

Aaron and I ran up the alley and down the street to where the Caddy was parked. I threw the keys to him and climbed into the passenger seat as Aaron slid behind the wheel.

"You drive," I said. "I'll navigate."

Aaron started the car and we accelerated onto Sunset Boulevard.

"Let's go! Let's go!" I implored. "I think I see them up ahead at the next stoplight." Aaron wove between cars until I saw the limousine a block ahead of us.

"Keep well behind them," I cautioned. "We don't want them to see that we're following."

"Got it!" Aaron yelled, as we continued tailing the limo from a distance. We had traveled another three blocks when suddenly two cars accelerated around us—a black SUV and a beat-up, late-model Olds Cutlass. I looked at the drivers as they flashed by—the two paparazzi! Aaron noticed them as well.

"It's those guys!" he yelled, pointing at the cars. "What did you call 'em? Pappa-rot-see?"

The cars closed in quickly on the limousine, flicking their high beams and honking their horns. As they did, the SUV accelerated alongside the passenger side of the limo and I watched the driver raise a camera toward the window. A strobe lit up the car, the bright flash causing the driver to swerve. As the limo driver recovered, the Olds pulled along the other side. The driver leaned across the passenger seat, holding out a camera and firing off flashes. The limo swerved again, almost hitting the SUV.

"They're gonna cause an accident; they're gonna hurt my little girl!" yelled Aaron, pounding his fist against the steering wheel.

The traffic light turned red as the cars reached the end of the block. The limousine and the paparazzi came to an abrupt halt at the crosswalk as cars flooded the intersection. We were only a few cars behind the limo, which was lit up by a continuous stream of strobes as the paparazzi yelled and waved their cameras, trying to get a good shot. With each flash, I could see Lisa Marie illuminated through the tinted windows, her body turned away, her hat pulled down low.

"I'll call the police," I said and began pressing 911.

Without warning, the limo driver accelerated through the stoplight and across the intersection between a break in the cross-traffic, leaving the other two cars stranded, waiting for the light to change.

"That was pretty smart!" exclaimed Aaron.

The light turned green, and the paparazzi screeched after the limousine. We followed with the rest of the traffic.

"Hold on, A. J.," Aaron commanded as he floored the gas on the ancient Cadillac. The car belched a cloud of smoke as the carbon burned off its ancient cylinders and the big V-8 came to life.

"What are you doing?" I yelled.

Aaron didn't say a word, focusing on closing the distance with the two other cars. He wove through slower-moving vehicles as the Caddy continued to pick up speed. Rapidly, we were gaining on the other cars, the Olds in the left lane, and the SUV in the right.

We flashed through another intersection and were closing in fast on the Olds. Too fast! I readied myself for an impact and screamed, "Aaron, slow down, we're going to hit him!"

Bracing one hand on the dashboard, I held the phone to my ear waiting for the emergency dispatcher. With only a few feet until impact, Aaron suddenly swerved the Caddy into a break in the oncoming traffic, around the Olds, and past the SUV. His foot remained pressing the gas pedal to the floorboard as he accelerated back into the lane and ahead of the paparazzi.

When they had fallen fifty yards behind, Aaron yelled, "Brace yourself, A. J.!" then he yanked the steering wheel to the right, causing the giant Caddy to slide across the roadway, perpendicular to the oncoming paparazzi.

This, I thought, is how I die.

The acrid smell of burning tires flooded the air as we skidded sideways, sending particles of rubber into the interior of the car. My phone flew out of my hand and bounced down the street as a plume of dust and chicken shit filled the car. Then, the front tire on the passenger side blew, shooting chunks of rubber toward the oncoming cars. A shower of sparks followed as the rim carved into the asphalt, until the car slowly came to rest. The noise of our skid was immediately replaced by the screeching of the SUV and Olds fishtailing to a stop, coming to rest inches from my door as a cloud of dust, gas fumes, and burning rubber enveloped us.

"Are you fucking nuts?" I yelled at Aaron.

"Are you fucking insane?" screamed Mark as he leaned his head out of the SUV.

"Are you fucking crazy?" shrieked Justin as he leaned his head out of the Olds.

Aaron, clearly shaken, did not respond.

Pedestrians quickly surrounded our cars and it took Mark and Justin several minutes before they could back up through the crowd and pull around to continue their pursuit of the limousine, which had disappeared far into the distance. The Caddy, however, was blocking traffic on Sunset. A man wearing a camouflage jacket and a red bandana on his head stuck his head through my window.

"Hey, are you guys alright?" he asked.

"Yeah, I think so. Aaron, are you okay?" Aaron nodded, his eyes fixed on the dash.

"Think you could get some folks to help push us off the street?" I asked.

"Sure," the man yelled, and began directing people as they moved the crippled Cadillac out of traffic and onto the shoulder.

"Thanks," I waved.

I waited a few moments, letting my nerves settle before opening the door and walking back down the side of the street in search of my phone. I followed the Cadillac's deep black skid marks for a seemingly endless distance before spotting it. Running out into the road, I reached down and retrieved the phone. It was destroyed. The screen was shattered, the case flattened by traffic.

I stalked back to the car, my body vibrating with rage both for my phone and having nearly been killed by Aaron's driving. I threw open the door, ready to unleash a volley of anger, but my fury dissipated instantly when I looked at Aaron, his forehead resting against his hands, which were still gripping the steering wheel. He was sobbing with unreserved emotion.

"Aaron. Aaron, are you okay, man?"

I touched a hand to the back of his neck.

"Aaron?"

Slowly, he lifted his head toward me. His face wet with tears. "Aaron!" I pleaded, "Get it together, man. We've got to get out of here before someone calls the cops. Are you okay?"

He nodded and lifted a hand off the steering wheel and wiped his sleeve against his eyes and nose.

"Jack and spare in the trunk?"

"What?" Aaron asked.

"The front tire needs to be replaced. Are the jack and spare tire in the trunk?"

He handed me the keys and I popped the trunk and removed the spare and jack. Thankfully, when the mechanic at Potts Camp checked out the car, he had taken the time to fill the tire. Within a few minutes, I had the new wheel installed. I climbed back into the car with Aaron, who was staring through the windshield, off into the distance.

"C'mon, let's get out of here." I said with urgency, as my anger began to return. "What the hell were you trying to do, man? You almost killed us. And now she's gone! That was your chance to meet your daughter. Now, because of that little stunt of yours, we've lost her." I paused. "And look what you did to my fucking phone," I said holding up what remained of Apple's latest innovation.

Aaron looked at me, but his teary eyes focused someplace far away. He was quiet for what felt like hours before he said, his voice cracking with emotion, "I had to make a choice about my daughter, one that I hope you never face—whether to see her or to save her. I had to keep them away from my little girl. They could've killed her. I figured if I blocked the road, it would give her time to get away." Sensing my anger, he continued, "I was never around for her when she was growin' up. Wasn't there to teach her how to drive, wasn't there to walk her down the aisle or for the birth of her children, you know, all those things parents do for their children. I wasn't there to do any of it." His eyes focused on mine.

"Son, you're gonna have a little girl of your own. When you do, you'll know why I did it. Maybe you'll be a better daddy than I was. But you ain't gonna understand until that happens to you."

Slowly, my anger began to subside.

"Aaron, what do you want to do now?" I asked in a calmer voice. "We've got to get going before the cops show up. We can try to follow her route. It's a long-shot, but maybe we'll get lucky and spot her limo somewhere."

Aaron didn't respond.

"It's been a long day. Maybe we should head back to the motel?"

Nothing.

"Do you want to go somewhere else? Maybe get some food?"

Aaron remained mute, unmoving. Finally, after sitting for several moments in silence, he whispered, "I want to go to the beach."

Had I heard him correctly? Did he say 'the beach?' At 11:30 p.m.? What was going on? What was he thinking? I heard the sound of sirens rising in the distance. They snapped Aaron into motion. He turned the key and the old Caddy rumbled to life. Then he slowly turned his head, looking for oncoming traffic, and made a U-turn on Sunset. Within moments, we were headed west toward the ocean.

Thirty Four

I tried to remain quiet, wondering whether Aaron had suffered some sort of mental breakdown. Perhaps, I thought, if I just gave him some time he would snap out of it, but after driving in silence for fifteen minutes I couldn't stand it anymore.

"Hey," I asked gently, "do you know where you're going?"

Aaron didn't acknowledge my presence as he steered by reflex on roads driven long in the past. He drove as if he were alone in the car, winding us through the neighborhoods of Brentwood, Rivera, and Palisades, until we reached the Pacific Coast Highway. From there, we turned south and went a few miles further before he pulled off and parked at a place named Will Rogers State Beach.

Without saying a word, Aaron opened the door, climbed out and strode over a low dune and down toward the surf. Where was he going? I wondered. What was he going to do? He was acting like he was possessed. When Aaron was a few yards from the water, it occurred to me—he was going to drown himself! He must be so distraught over losing Lisa Marie that he was going to end it all. I launched myself out of the car and ran up the dune toward him, my feet slipping in the sand. Would I be able to reach him in time? Did I still remember CPR from that summer in high school when I was a lifeguard? How cold was that water? Shit, I bet it was really cold! A few feet from the surf, Aaron turned and walked along the water's edge. I paused to catch my breath and watched as he headed up the beach for fifty yards. There he stopped, turned his face toward the ocean, the full moon breaking above the horizon, raised both hands over his head, and began what looked like deep breathing exercises before seating himself on the sand in a cross-legged lotus pose. I gazed at Aaron for a few moments, wondering what he would do next, but he remained serenely motionless.

No doubt about it. This had been the strangest damn week of my life.

It had been a long time since I'd seen the Pacific Ocean—probably not since I was in college in Oregon—and I'd never visited the beaches of Southern California. On this beautiful evening, I finally understood why people paid such insane house prices to live on the coast. The moon that night was full, powerful, and unrelenting, providing a surreal illumination to the sand and a beautiful luminescence on the breaking waves. The moonlight, although bright, filtered out any color. The ocean was black and white, grey and silver. It reminded me of a scene from an early 1960s movie with a hypnotic soundtrack furnished by the lapping waves. As I sat down and looked out over the ocean, my thoughts returned to Mo.

Damn, I missed her.

At that moment, I would have given anything to have her pressed up against me, watching this beautiful spectacle of a night. I realized I had never been happier than when I was with her. I loved her childlike glee each time we saw the shoestring of bats fly from under the Congress Street bridge on a warm summer night, how she took pride in always being able to hold more donut holes in her mouth than any other patron at Gourdoughs, and the way she licked the BBQ sauce off her fingers between each bite of ribs at J. Mueller's. But what I loved most was just being with her. It could be something as simple as watching her grade student essays on a Sunday morning. I'd be plowing through the *Austin-Statesman* and as I'd take a sip of coffee, I'd look over at her watching the way she pushed a long strand of hair behind her ear every few seconds, the wrinkle of her nose indicating a sloppy grammatical error. How could anyone look so thoughtful and so sexy at the same time, I wondered. Once I started looking at her, it was rare that my eyes ever returned to the newspaper.

But did she have any idea how frightened I was to be a father? I was certain I would screw it up. If that happened, any chance of a life with Mo would be over. She thought I didn't want to be tied down, but the truth was I didn't know *how* to be tied down. I'd only had one long-term relationship in my life and that was with my Fender. Now, she was expecting me to dedicate myself to being a parent. What if I moved back in with Mo and we had the baby and I couldn't handle it?

I glanced over at Aaron. He remained seated and unmoving, as if locked in a trance. I thought back to what he had told me: *being a daddy is all that really matters*. Here was someone who had it all—music, money, fans—and he was willing to walk away from it. The only thing that pulled him back was the love he had for his daughter. Could I feel that love? Could I take that chance?

I don't know how long I sat there, ruminating, before I saw Aaron raise his hands and draw in a deep breath. He slowly stood up and walked in my direction. He was just a few feet away when he noticed me in the moonlight. Startled, he said, "Son, whatcha' doin' here?"

"Thought I'd enjoy the view."

Glancing back at the ocean, he agreed, "There ain't anything like it. Down the street a piece is a place called the Lake Shrine. I'd sometimes visit there to study meditation and yoga with this yogi spiritual woman, can't recall her name now. It was about the only place I could go where I wasn't treated as 'the King,' but as a person trying to find their inner self. On some nights, when I was feeling particularly troubled, I'd drive out to this beach and sit alone for hours, searching for an answer."

"Did you find it?"

"Not often. Most times I'd just fall asleep on the sand and wake up with the sunrise. That wasn't too bad either." He laughed.

"How about tonight? Did it work?'

Aaron looked at me and in the bright moonlight I could see a sliver of a smile. "Suspect it did."

I trailed behind Aaron, as he walked back to the car, waiting for him to say more, but he was quiet. Finally, as we got into the car, I asked, "Aaron, where do you want to go? Do you want to go back to the motel?"

Aaron turned to me as he shut the door.

"Don't think so. I don't need anything there and your gear is still in the car."

"Well, it's only a few hours until sunrise, I guess we could sleep here…"

"Son," he said with a long pause, "I think it's time for me to go home."

"Go home? What do you mean?"

"I mean Mississippi."

"What?" I exclaimed. "You can't be serious! Why?"

There was no reply as Aaron started the car and turned onto the Pacific Coast Highway.

"Don't you want to find a way to see your daughter?" I implored. "I thought you wanted to be reunited with Lisa Marie!"

Silence.

After several miles, I was at my limit. I felt emotionally betrayed. I had trusted this old man, drawn close to him by the music and the miles. Now, he wanted to leave me.

"Say something, damn it!"

Aaron glanced at me. "It's time for me to go home," he repeated softly.

"I don't understand! I thought you wanted to meet your daughter."

"I do. But I know now that it wouldn't be how I thought it was gonna be. You heard all the terrible things those—what did you call 'em—the paparazzi—were yellin' at her. It would only get worse. If people had just forgot about me, perhaps, I coulda found a way into her life. Ain't no way that can happen now."

"But she'd have her father back. Wouldn't that make it worthwhile?"

"Yeah, her Daddy would be back in her life, but it'd be a daddy she hasn't seen since she was a little girl, a daddy who deserted her, who wasn't there to help her through all of those tough times."

"What about performing?" I interrupted. "I'm sure there are places out here where you could get a regular gig. Remember that guy Blake in Vegas? He'd hire you!"

"Entertainin' is a drug, son. No different than any of those I used to take. With it comes a lot of dark things. Over these last few days, I've felt it startin' to get back in my veins. What's that expression my Mama used to use?" He paused, as if searching his memory. "It's like I'm a moth drawn to a flame. I know where this is headin' and I don't think it would end too well for me—or for Lisa Marie. The world's moved past. It may still remember me, but everythin's different—the people, the music, the politics. Hell, phones ain't even used for talkin' no more." He paused for a moment, before continuing with an air of resignation. "I've got to go back."

I looked out the window at the slow rolling waves breaking on the shoreline, feeling very much that I was in the middle of one of life's emotional intersections. I didn't know where they led, but there were two paths ahead of me; one was with Mo and a daughter, and the other alone. Both were frightening, but only one felt like it had the possibility of happiness.

We drove on for a few minutes before Aaron asked, "What about you?"

"What do you mean?"

"What's gonna happen to you? What are you gonna do next?"

I looked at him for a moment. Sheepishly, I asked, "Do you think you can give me a lift to Austin?"

Aaron laughed and reached over and slapped me on the back so hard it hurt. "I knew you'd figure it out!" he exclaimed.

We drove in silence for a few miles beneath the ethereal glow of the full moon. I was lost in meditation, mulling over all that Aaron had said, turning it over in my mind. I realized that he was right. Aaron interrupted my thoughts.

"Son?"

"Yeah, Aaron?"

"How do I get to Austin?"

Thirty Five

The next twenty-four hours were a blur. Our decisions gave way to momentum, and we drove the 1,200 miles from Los Angeles to Austin, trading off time behind the wheel and stopping only for gas, fast food, and bathroom breaks. The first of these stops was at Tommy's, an L.A. fixture for the high and hungover for years. We managed to get there just before it closed. Aaron insisted on trying a double chili cheeseburger, a chili cheese dog, fries, and a large Pepsi—an impressive gastronomic accomplishment at any age, but especially for a man in his seventies.

"Aaron," I asked, "do you think all that food is such a good idea? It's almost two in the morning. Don't you want to sleep?"

"Sign says this place is famous for their chili burgers n' dogs. It would be a shame if I didn't at least give 'em a try. Son, I've *only* been eatin' healthy for the last thirty years. A little fast food ain't gonna hurt me. Besides, I'll drive for a while and you can sleep."

I looked askance at the large bag of food Aaron carried to the car, but didn't argue with his desire to drive. The truth was, I was exhausted, completely drained after the week with Aaron—the miles, the gigs, and the near-crash earlier in the evening. I helped him navigate onto I-10 and then, wadding up my jacket as a pillow, leaned my head against the window and fell quickly asleep.

It was five hours later when I awoke to the piercing blue light of an early morning sky. I stretched and looked over at Aaron. The debris of his Tommy's meal littered the seat and floor.

"Hey there, I wondered when you would finally wake up."

"Mornin'," I mumbled.

"Son, I got somethin' to show you. It's a trick my daddy showed me."

"What's that?"

"Here," he said taking his right hand off the wheel and pointing it in my direction, "pull my finger."

"What?"

"Go on, pull my finger."

Reflexively, I reached over and tugged his finger. When I did, Aaron released a thunderous fart.

As he choked back his laughter Aaron said, "Didn't think I'd be able to hold that until you woke up. I built up a hell of a lot of back pressure, if you know what I mean."

Like the gap in time between the sound of thunder and the following bolt of lightning, there was a delay in the second part of Aaron's little joke. It arrived about three seconds later in the form of one of the most noxious smells I have ever encountered.

"Jesus H. Christ, Aaron!" I yelled as I began to cough and gag. "That makes the chicken shit in this car smell like perfume." We simultaneously grabbed for the window handles as he continued laughing.

"At my age," he gasped, "I probably shouldn't be eatin' chili no more." We both broke into a laughter that filled the next many miles.

That's how the rest of the day went. We'd stop for fuel or food before switching drivers. Aaron insisted on sampling every burger he could find. He tried them all: In-N-Out—where, for the record, he insisted on a "triple burger, animal style"—Carl's Jr., McDonalds, and Burger King.

At one point, I said, "Aaron, I've never seen someone eat so many burgers. You approach each fast food joint like it's the Last Supper."

He paused as he chewed the remains of a bite of burger. "Well, it's kinda like that. Back home we don't have food like this. I know it's not good for me, but damn, I do miss it. I'm gonna get as much of it as I can before I go back."

We rolled past the endless sprawl of Phoenix, the deserts of Tucson, on through to El Paso and the empty, interminable miles of West Texas. I kept asking, but Aaron didn't want to stop at a motel. Instead, he replied, "I need to keep drivin' before I change my mind."

The miles flew past as I tried to squeeze every moment for memories I'd reflect on in the years ahead. Some of the hours we'd spend singing. I'd whip out my guitar and imagine the Caddy's big interior as a soundstage for an MTV 'Unplugged' session. We'd reel through songs like *My Baby Left Me, Evil Hearted Man,* and *That's All Right* and then switch it up with a few slower numbers like *It's Now or Never.* Looking back on it, if my phone hadn't been broken, I could have made a fortune recording our impromptu mobile sound session.

During one long stretch of driving, Aaron asked me to teach him some new songs, ones that he could bring back to Virgil and the boys. The request stumped me for a bit. I hadn't thought about what the King would sing if he were still performing. Rap was clearly off the list, as was most current rock, given the over-production. Today's country music, bearing little relationship to its musical origins, was also a non-starter. I played Aaron a number of tunes from some of my favorite singer-songwriters to see if any of them were interesting.

He settled on a couple of numbers by John Hiatt, *Drive South* and *Memphis in the Meantime,* Keb Mo's *City Boy,* Sheryl Crow's *Drunk with the Thought of You,* Van Morrison's *Beauty of Days Gone By* and *Daddy's Little Pumpkin* by John Prine. It was surprising how quickly Aaron absorbed the music. I'd awkwardly sing the song once and he'd listen attentively. On the second pass, he would sing along and remember most of the words. The third time through, he'd add some flourish or additional element to make the song his own. The only exception was Mojo Nixon's *Elvis is Everywhere.* No matter how hard he concentrated, Aaron couldn't make it to the end without breaking into cackles of glee.

* * *

It was slightly after 1 a.m. when we arrived in Austin. Aaron pulled in front of the house I shared with Mo and shut off the car. The night was humid, grey halos reflecting around the streetlight above us. The only sounds were the creaking of the Caddy as it began to cool, set against a backdrop of the cicadas still enjoying their booty call.

"Well," I said, pointing at the small bungalow, "this is my place."

"Looks nice."

A silence descended between us.

"I can't tell you when I've had a stranger week."

"I'll say the same," chuckled Aaron.

"Listen, I've told you, I'm not too good with commitments. It's probably the reason I'm not too good with goodbyes, either." I paused and cleared my throat feeling surprisingly emotional. "I guess what I'm trying to say is, well, thanks. Thanks...Elvis."

I reached out my hand and he grasped it firmly, pulling me into a warm, lengthy embrace.

"Thank you, son. And, it's not Elvis—it's Aaron. Don't you know Elvis died more than thirty years ago." He grinned and patted me on the back one last time.

I gave Aaron a long look before I got out of the car, trying to commit him to mind, but I knew that his was a face that would never be far away. I grabbed my gear out of the back seat and shut the car door and walked up the wooden stairs to the front door. As I dropped my bags onto the porch and fished the key out of my duffle bag, I heard the Caddy's engine rumble to life. I put my hand on the doorknob and looked down the street to watch as the taillights of the Caddy disappeared into the mist of the warm Southern night.

Epilogue

It's been a number of years since that evening. I haven't seen Aaron since. Of course, I didn't expect that I would. He made just one request during our long drive through Texas toward Austin. "Son, I've got a favor to ask. I'm thinkin' you're gonna want to tell people about me, and all that's happened this last week. I'm not sure whether anyone would believe the story, but just the same, I'd appreciate it if you could keep it all a secret for a few years." He paused, looking out at the solitude of the West Texas desert. "Yeah, I'm thinkin' four or five years is 'bout right. By that time, I'm sure I'll be with Mama."

I've kept my word to Aaron. Although I wanted to tell people, especially Mo, about Aaron and our travels, I've held to my promise. And of course, once I returned home, reality quickly overtook any plans I might have had.

I moved back in with Mo. I wasn't sure how she would react, but when she awoke and found me lying next to her she let out a shriek of surprise and joy before beating her fists on my chest like a Taiko drummer. This cycle repeated itself every few seconds for about ten minutes before it concluded with my first sexual experience with a pregnant woman.

It's something I highly recommend.

Afterward, we held each close and I found myself telling Mo things that I had never shared. Through tears, I told her of the pain I felt growing up with a man who was a father in name only and a mother who was lost in a bottle. And I admitted my anxiety over whether I could be the partner she needed and the parent she expected and deserved. Mo listened without interruption and squeezed me tight. Then, when I was finished, she reassured me that her love was strong enough for the both of us and that it would all work out. Listening to the strength in her voice, I knew that it would.

A little over seven months later, our daughter arrived in our life. Naming her was the first test of our relationship as parents. I wanted to name her

Elvira in honor of the man who had so changed my life. Of course, I couldn't explain my attachment to the name to Mo.

"We are *not* naming our daughter Elvira. It's not going to happen. Full stop."

"Mo, be reasonable. I think it means 'truth' in Spanish. Isn't that a wonderful value to make part of her life?"

"I'll give you some truth! The only things that come to mind when people hear the name Elvira are that country song from the 80's and that goth chick Elvira, *Mistress of the Night*. No way, we are saddling our little girl with that for life."

We settled on the name Emily. And from the moment she opened her eyes and first looked into mine, I was a goner. It was over for me. To my surprise, I realized that the one thing I wanted most in life was to be a father. On reflection, I think that's what I learned most from my time with Aaron.

A little over three years later, Emily played the role of an exceptionally short and inattentive maid of honor when Mo and I were married. The word "beautiful" does not begin to convey the way Mo looked that day. Watching her wearing the same gown that her mother had worn at her wedding, with her pair of battered red, Lucchese boots poking out from below the hem of the beaded, white dress, took my breath away.

Sweet Lil played our wedding. That's one of the only certain benefits of being a musician—the wedding band is free, provided there's an open bar. We took advantage of both that night, playing and dancing until the sun came up the next morning. Through it all, I kept imagining how wonderful it would have been to have Aaron there singing for us.

I think about him often, wondering if he ever feels that he made the wrong decision, that he should have continued trying to reunite with his daughter. Was he still saddened realizing that to her he was just a memory fading in the past? I dwelled on this frequently until I saw the article in *Guitar Riff Magazine*. It was a lengthy interview with Lisa Marie at her home in Sussex, England, done after a recent tour.

GRM: I would be remiss if I didn't ask you about your father.

LMP: (Laughs) No problem. It comes with the territory.

GRM: How big an influence was he on your music?

LMP: Obviously, there is a strong physical connection, whether it be in my vocal chords or the structure of my mouth. After all, half of my chromosomes are from him. And growing up in a musical household definitely had an impact. I remember as a girl we always had musicians and entertainers visit our house. Dinner always ended with some kind of impromptu jam session with them. It was only many years later when I was a young adult that I began to understand how famous they were.

GRM: But what about the music itself? Your choice of songs, your phrasing, the musicians in your band? Do you think your father had an influence on these?

LMP: (Sipping her wine) I think everyone tries to go in that direction, but I don't see it. My songs, my singing, my band…those are influenced not by my father, but by Elvis Presley. In other words, he affected me to the same extent he touched musicians generally. Not just because I was his daughter.

GRM: Do you ever feel that being his daughter is a burden on your music?

LMP: I don't feel any differently than 99% of the musicians out there. You see, most of us on the stage are mere musical mortals. We do what we do based on what we learn from others and we advance it incrementally. That other 1%—they take the music to an entirely different place, while the rest of us watch and say 'Wait, you can do that?' Elvis was certainly one of those people, the Beatles were as well, and, of course, Dylan. Later Cobain and Nirvana did that with grunge, and the Sugar Hill Gang, with the genesis of rap. So, no, I've never felt the name Presley to be either a burden or a benefit.

GRM: Do you still feel any connection with your father? After all, you were only about nine or ten years old when he died.

LMP: (Taking another sip of her wine) We're all surrounded by Elvis. It's been more than thirty years since he passed, yet he's omnipresent. His movies, songs, likeness, he's still everywhere.

GRM: Of course he is, and part of that is the result of your family's active licensing activities. But I'm asking something more personal. Do you, as his daughter, still feel a bond toward Elvis, you father?

LMP: (She pauses and looks out the window before taking a deep drink of wine) I do. I always feel he's with me; sometimes that feeling wanes and waxes, but it's always there. A few years ago, I was playing a gig in Hollywood at the Roxy and I felt his presence. It was something almost tangible, almost real. I even changed the song list to dedicate my encore to him. I knew he was there that night…and that he loves me. Wow, this wine must be getting to me. Probably, a good place to end this.

As I read those last lines, I had difficulty keeping from crying. Somewhere, I prayed that Aaron would see them too.

These days, I still play with the band, but my other occupation is increasingly pulling me away, being what my friends call a stay-at-home dad. I've discovered that it is the most fulfilling gig I've ever had. Each morning, I get up and make breakfast for Mo and pack her a lunch before she rushes off to classes. Then I wake Emily, get her changed, and feed her breakfast. Some days we go shopping; some days she "helps" me clean house; some days we just play.

Emily loves to have me tell her the story about Aaron. She was the first person I told about that most unusual week of my life. I thought she could keep it a secret, but one night, as Mo and I were putting her to sleep, Emily said, "Daddy, tell me the story about the King."

"What story is that?" Mo asked playfully.

"Oh," I said awkwardly, "it's just a silly one I made up about a king and queen."

"Daddy, there's no queen in the story," squealed Emily. "Tell the one about Elvis the King and how you played music with him!"

Mo gave me a quizzical look and left the room, while I finished putting Emily to sleep.

Up to this point, Mo had never asked directly about what had happened, just an occasional subtle inquiry, like: "Were you always safe on your trip?" or "Did you say you were in Vegas?" That's a bit unusual for her because she tends to enjoy a full-frontal attack when it comes to extracting personal information. My guess is that she sensed that I had had an intense experience, something that I would share with her over time. Or maybe she was afraid of what I would tell her. Anyway, that time finally came later that evening when Emily was asleep.

Once she got me started with her questions, I couldn't stop. Everything about that week just spilled out. The thing is, Mo believed me. She knew that I was telling the truth, that Elvis was still alive. It was she who encouraged me to write this book. In fact, both of my girls helped me with it. Mo did the editing, and Emily, from her high chair, contributed drool, Cheerios, and Gummy Bears to the pages as I would mark up the manuscript on the kitchen table each day. I found that when Emily was napping was the best time for me to write. I'd plug away for a few hours each day, reliving those miles with Aaron. Frequently, I'd stop and try to imagine where he was now.

I don't recall when it started, but we end our day the same way each evening. It's become a Shanks family ritual. Mo, Emily and I move out to the front porch, sit on a large bench, and watch the crimson sunset give way to rose and then blush before it fades toward a new day. As it does, Emily looks up from her position snuggled between me and Mo, and says, "Daddy, play one of the King's songs."

I smile, reach over for my guitar, and begin to softly sing.

Acknowledgements

This story originated fifteen years ago while on a long drive south along California Highway 1 to visit a friend. Along the way, I noticed a number of billboards using Elvis's image and heard at least a half-dozen of his songs on the radio. A gas station where I stopped sold Elvis branded cigarette lighters and auto air-fresheners. A few weeks later, while visiting Portland, Oregon, I stumbled upon a unique museum and art gallery (now closed) known as the *24 Hour Church of Elvis*. The man's presence was everywhere despite the fact that he died decades earlier. This lead to the idea: What if he hadn't died?—and, thus, the genesis of this book.

My appreciation to Joe Buchwald for the cover art. Creativity runs through his bones.

Special thanks to Mary Sullivan Walsh and Emily Dillon. One could not have better and more patient editors.

And many thanks to my family, friends and colleagues (too many to name here) who have provided comments, corrections, criticisms, and calls for me to just finish the damn thing.

CPSIA information can be obtained
at www.ICGtesting.com
Printed in the USA
LVHW090320130120
643410LV00001B/6/P